The Woman in the Trunk
a mafia romance

—

Jessica Gadziala

Cover Designer: Jessica Gadziala
Cover image credit: Getty Images - thawornnurack / Public Commons

DEDICATION

This one goes out to my ARC team who never complain, no
matter how many questions I throw at them.
You girls are the best.
I wouldn't be where I am without all of you <3.

The Woman in the Trunk

Prologue

Lorenzo

I had a hundred years in the trunk.

Kidnapping was kidnapping.

Throw in some extortion to make shit worse.

Then when you took them across state lines, you were fucked.

When they had a bump or bruise anywhere, you nabbed yourself an aggravated federal kidnapping charge. Even if she banged her own fucking head.

Add on the gun in my jacket, the mysterious package I needed to pick up—that looked suspiciously like several bricks of cocaine—and the fact that I was a known member of the New York City Cosa Nostra, and I was looking at life in prison if I got caught.

That was why I had a soccer-mom hold on the steering wheel and a granny tap on the accelerator.

And once I got back to the city, shit would only going to get worse.

False imprisonment.

Sprinkle in some possible torture.

Maybe a murder.

But yeah, I'm getting ahead of myself.

Let's go back to see how the fuck I got myself in that situation...

Chapter One

Lorenzo

"Not now." The words growled out of me as I cocked my arm backward before swinging, my fist connecting with a jaw with a satisfying cracking noise.

I shouldn't have enjoyed it. Nor should I have felt a stirring of pleasure at the groaning and whimpering that accompanied a broken jaw. There was no denying that I did, though.

What can I say? When you grew up as the son of a mafia *Capo dei Capi*—boss of all bosses—you developed some fucked up interests. Like inflicting pain.

"You know I wouldn't interrupt if it wasn't important," Emilio, my cousin, said, closing the door behind him.

Turning toward him, I found him leaning against the door, likely wrinkling my gray suit jacket that was hanging there.

Emilio was a bucker of convention. Which meant that today, he had on slacks but no suit jacket, just a simple black shirt, tucked in. I was convinced the only reason he bothered to tuck was to show off his belt buckle collection. Today, it was a more understated silver scorpion.

Emilio didn't inherit the dark hair and eyes of my father's side of the family, taking instead after his mother which had his hair a light brown, and his eyes a dark blue.

"What is it?" I asked, reaching up to wipe sweat off my brow, only to notice the red staining my fingers and palm, then use my rolled-up sleeve to complete the task instead.

Emilio's gaze went to the man currently cuffed to a folding chair a few feet behind me, the left side of his face swelling quickly from the jaw break. His right eye was swollen shut, his nose still trickling lazily.

"You almost done here?"

Not nearly.

"Hold on," I said, turning back, cocking my arm, and landing an uppercut under his jaw. He was out before the chair teetered on two legs for a second before falling backward, colliding with the floor. "That should shut him up for a while," I said, making my way toward my cousin, letting him open the door so I didn't spread blood everywhere.

We were in the basement of a butcher shop that had been in the family since my great-great-grandfather came over from Italy about a hundred years before. I stopped to wash my hands in the utility sink in the short hall between the back room I was using to earn compliance from someone who decided it would be okay not to pay us for a couple months and the main storage area.

"Alright. What is so important?" I asked as we moved into the storage space, metal racks bending under the weight of decades-worth of crap that no one bothered to pack up and get rid of. The room was always dusty and musty, wetness seeping in through the walls. My father couldn't even come here without getting a wicked allergy attack from the mold tucked in hidden corners. Not that he ever got his hands dirty anymore.

"Just got back from seeing your father," Emilio said, sighing heavily. No one enjoyed a meeting with my father. Better him than me, though, at this point. I generally kept myself busy enough that he didn't bother to request my company. It was an arrangement that seemed to be working for us thus far.

"What is he up to now?" What I really wanted to ask was *What the fuck is he screwing up now?* But you had to be careful how you spoke to or about my father. Someone with an ego as fragile as his was, didn't take kindly to any sort of criticism.

"He's got a job."

"For you or for me?" I asked, already mentally ticking through my overly booked schedule. I could hardly fit a morning workout in these days, let alone another job.

"He doesn't want me to do it. He wants my eyes on the new puppy," Emilio said, referencing a new soldier my father had added to the crew, a sniveling little asshole who only got in because he was such a kiss-ass. During one of our many arguments, I had told my father as much. The yelling match that followed was why I hadn't been in my father's presence in several months. But, clearly, he took my concerns seriously enough to have eyes on the little bastard.

"That puppy would be better off put down," I grumbled, shaking my head. "Who did he suggest for it, then?" I asked, thankful that Emilio had unofficially started to defer all my father's orders to me. It was borderline treasonous, but if we wanted our family to stay at the top of the Five Families, we needed to make sure he wasn't being a fucking idiot about shit.

"He floated the idea of putting Brio on it."

Brio was a capo who had started as a ruthless enforcer when he was all of fifteen. Emilio and I had grown up with him, knew the depravity he was capable of enacting if he was commanded to. I'd never seen someone as capable of turning off their humanity as Brio was.

"What is the job then?" I asked, figuring it was something along the lines of intimidation, debt collection, or simply a plot of revenge.

At that, Emilio reached up, rubbing the back of his neck. Uncomfortable. Emilio had grown up like me. Hard. Exposed to the ugly of the world. Not much got to him.

"He's got to pick someone up."

"As in to take them for a drive?" I asked, meaning to some undisclosed location to put a bullet between his eyes. We'd gotten careful about how we phrased things when in enclosed spaces. The feds got good in the nineties and early two-thousands with their tech. We didn't take chances.

"As in bring them over for breakfast. And lunch. And dinner..."

So holding someone for some reason. We didn't exactly take hostages often. It was ugly business. There were a lot of ways for it to go wrong. But it had certainly happened a handful of times since I was sworn in. I was sure it was a practice that would continue when a situation called for it.

"Someone we haven't seen in a while," I assumed, meaning someone who owed us money, but had been avoiding us.

"An old friend's daughter," Emilio told me, making my spine stiffen, my heartbeat tripping into overdrive.

There weren't a lot of hard and fast rules around the mafia. Sure, back in the day, in the golden ages, there were. No drugs. No women or children. That flew out the door around the time all the old capos were catching RICO charges, leaving young and hungry and unscrupulous men in charge that had no business being at the top.

That was when my father came into power.

He didn't have a fuck of a lot going for him in terms of merit, but he'd never kidnapped someone's daughter before. Or sent fucking Brio to do it.

"And he's sending Brio?"

Now, granted, Brio wasn't a danger to society as a whole. He wasn't some out of control rage machine, some sick fucking woman-beater or rapist. But still. Sending Brio for a job that sounded like it required kid gloves, not boxing ones, seemed like overkill.

"I know," Emilio agreed, nodding. "That's why I'm here."

"Was he calling Brio about it?"

"He had a meeting with D'Onofrio," Emilio said, meaning one of the other bosses in one of the other Five Families. "But he said he would deal with it after that."

"Shit," I sighed, checking my watch—white gold, costing more than some people's new cars. I had a full day, week, and month planned. But I wasn't going to send off our rabid dog to handle some unsuspecting woman.

"Yeah."

"Alright. I will clear my schedule. I'll handle it."

"You're gonna have a house guest?" Emilio asked, brow arching up.

I didn't have time to babysit a kidnapped woman. I didn't *want* to have time to do that shit. That said, I knew I had to.

"Better me than anyone else," I said, shrugging.

When it came to level heads, my father wasn't known for one. Clearly, I got mine from my mother's side of the family. Not that I would know. She'd been missing for longer than I cared to think about. And everyone knew that people didn't just go *missing* when they were connected to the mob.

"How about I finish this," Emilio said, waving a hand toward the closed door to the other room where the chair was thumping against the cement floor as the man attached likely tried to inch his way toward the door. As if he had any chance of escaping before we were done with him.

"I'd appreciate that."

"And send me your list of shit for the next few days. I will handle that."

"You?" I asked, smirking. It was no secret that Emilio was not what anyone would call a workaholic. He did his job. He didn't volunteer to do more. Which was fine. That was why there were soldiers, and there were capos, and there were underbosses like me. Though, if I ever got into my father's shoes as *Capo dei Capi*, I would force Emilio to buck the fuck up and accept an underboss position.

"I know. It will seriously cut into my social calendar, but I will have to endure," he said, smirking.

"I appreciate it," I said, nodding, mentally trying to figure out which jobs could simply be put on hold, and which ones I would need Emilio to handle. I could cut it down, so I could handle some of it when I got back.

"Go get to your old man before he gets to Brio."

"Yep," I agreed, clamping a hand on his shoulder before going back into the room and grabbing my jacket off the hook on the door. "It's your lucky day, asshole," I told the man who let out a pathetic whimper. "I have to tap someone else in who is likely going to go easier on you. But it's still gonna fucking hurt. And if you don't have the money by next Friday, you're going to see me again. And we are going to play dentist. One by fucking one," I said, tapping my front tooth with my finger before turning and walking out.

He'd have the money.

They always did.

If they had to commit armed robbery for it. I didn't give a fuck so long as we got what was ours. Plus the interest he'd agreed to when he'd borrowed the money to begin with. No one got shit for free in this world. And no one got away with stiffing the Costa family.

I made my way up the stairs and out the back door of the butcher shop, which put me on the side street where my car was parked. At first glance, it didn't look like a money car. A simple black sedan. No bells and whistles. Nothing that would stand out in traffic. But it cost me a mortgage down payment for an affluent suburb regardless. Some of the families had learned from the mistakes of generations that had gone before them. Like how being too flashy was a surefire way to ensure a tax audit.And if you didn't have enough on the books to justify that three-hundred-grand car, shit was going to get real. And quick.

Plus, whichever fed was taxed with following your ass around on any given day was going to spot a flashy yellow Ferrari faster than my black sedan. I could shake a tail. That was more important to me than having others see how rich I was.

My father lived in a brownstone that my grandfather had bought before my father was even born. It was old and ate more money than anyone should have to put into a house, but it was part of the family legacy, and just flashy enough that my father liked the looks he got when someone saw him heading outside. New York was a city of a lot of wealth, but it was still always a bit shocking to see someone stepping out of an eight-million-dollar brownstone to grab coffee and a paper at the bodega around the corner.

I parked out front when I got there, seeing Vin D'Onofrio making his way down the street toward his waiting car, his guard a few feet behind him. He looked irritated, as anyone would after speaking to my father.

Taking a deep breath, I climbed out of my car, nodded to my father's guard on the stoop, and letting myself in the house.

The inside was what you'd expect, with a center staircase leading up, a parlor to the left, and a dining room to the right. I moved forward, knowing I would find my father in his office, across from the kitchen.

For all the money he'd put into the place, it was surprisingly dated. The wood was stained too light, too out of fashion. The floors were worn, desperate for refinishing. The cabinets and backsplash clashed, and the countertops were dull from age.

It needed someone to bring it back to its glory. That man would not be my father.

"I need another cup of—oh," my father, Arturo Costa, cut off, head jerking back at seeing me towering in the doorway instead of one of his men.

Like my level head, I got my appearance from my mother's side of the family. Where my father was the short side of average with a barrel stomach and a receding hairline, I was well over six feet, lean and fit, with a full head of dark hair.

The study, like the rest of the house, was in need of renovation. The dark wood was oppressive, the leather sofa creased with age, the carpet faded. Hell, I could smell the age of all the books on the shelves. Books I knew for a fact he never picked up to read, let alone dust.

"Father," I greeted, moving in slightly, but only enough to lean against the wall, just inside the doorway, not wanting to be closer to him than I needed to be.

"What are you doing here?" he asked, jerking his chin up as he sucked in his stomach. It was a ridiculous move, a testament to the fact that he felt insecure around me. It had to piss him the fuck off that panties dropped wherever I went, and he hadn't been able to get laid without paying for it for years.

"I ran into Emilio when I was finishing up a job. We'll have that money," I added, even though I was sure my father didn't keep up-to-date with the day-to-day debt collecting like I did. "But he said there was a new job. I wanted to volunteer for it."

"You?" he asked, brow lowering. "I thought you were too busy for anything."

"I recently had an opening." Thanks to Emilio. "I'd be happy to handle it. That way you can have Brio, if you need his... particular skill set. We all know how long and tedious house guests can be."

"True," he agreed, torn. On the one hand, he knew I was right. On the other, he didn't like knowing that. "And I already agreed to handle that shit with New Jersey," I told him, meaning a meeting I had subtly stolen out from underneath him with the boss of the New Jersey mafia, the one who ran the import docks. My father was trying to broker a deal to get the Russians to be able to bring in guns. But the New Jersey family was resisting, as they had a treaty with the local arms-dealing MC. It was delicate business. And my father was a bull in a China shop. "I can do this on the way there or back," I said, shrugging. "Why make anyone else go out of their way when I am already all over the place?"

"Alright. Yeah. I think that will work. I am going to need Brio. I just remembered." Bullshit. That was bullshit. But I had learned a long time ago to let him have his pride. He was ugly if he had that bruised.

"Where am I picking up my new guest?" I asked.

"She is usually kicking around the city," he told me, waving a hand. "But there is a vacation house down in Cape May. That's where my intel says she will be for the weekend," he said, scribbling an address on a piece of paper, holding it out.

Pushing off the wall, I walked over and took it, checking it out, tucking it into my pocket to shred when I left.

"Anything I need to know?"

"Don't know much. She's small. Five-two. Black hair. I was told that you would know her when you saw her."

"Okay, got it," I agreed, nodding. "You want me to handle the contact with her father? Our usual check-ins?" I clarified. "Take some burden off you," I added, stroking that notorious ego of his, because he never seemed to sense my subtle ways of stealing the risky jobs out from under him.

"I have a lot going on now. That should work."

"Great. I got it. I will head out tomorrow," I added, making my way out to the door. "I will tell Frank to get you more coffee on my way out."

With that, I left before he could engage me in another argument. It was important I stayed as diplomatic as possible. With my father's temper, there was no telling what he was capable of. There had been more than one capo who took out his own son in the past. I didn't want to be added to that statistic.

Sure, from the outside, the simple answer would be to take out my old man, get Biblical and shit. But if I did that, the other bosses would take me out. Because you didn't get to take out a made man in the mafia unless you got the approval of all the other bosses.

So for the time being, I had to adapt, accept, work things behind the scenes like I had been doing for years.

Back at my place, I packed a bag, had a couple drinks, tried to tell myself that it didn't bother me that I was heading out of town to fucking kidnap a woman—something that didn't go against my father's moral code, but did go against mine.

I consoled myself that this leg of the job would be easy, just a quick snatch and grab. Not too much of a hassle. No one would get hurt.

Then, hopefully, it would all be over quickly.

I had never been more wrong about anything in my life.

Chapter Two

Giana

"Gigi, you're here," Penny, the housekeeper of the Cape May house, greeted me as I made my way in the door.

"Oh, Jesus," I hissed, hand flying to my chest as I whirled around to find the woman sitting in the rocking chair my grandfather used to occupy every summer of my childhood.

"Didn't mean to startle you, dear," she said, giving me a sweet smile.

"What are you doing here?" I asked, no edge to my words. I loved Penny. Even if she was only supposed to be in the house to check the mail, make sure the air, in the summer, and the heat, in the winter, were working properly. As well as the very occasional dusting or general upkeep. If there was any sort of heavy lifting, there was no way we would have continued to employ Penny, who was somewhere in her mid-eighties, though she was spry enough to pass as a full decade or so younger.

She was a sturdy, average-height woman with a shock of long white hair and bright blue eyes that shined out of her well-lined face. As always, she had on a dress in plain white, adorned with about half a dozen necklaces and stacked bangle bracelets that went nearly to her elbow.

"Oh, I come now and again. Enjoy the silence. Let the strangers see that someone is around. I like it here. It has many fond memories."

Penny had engaged in a short and—at the time —tawdry affair with my grandfather just weeks after my grandmother passed. While my grandfather never got serious about a woman after his wife's death, Penny clearly carried a torch, even after his passing. "I would have cleared out had I known you were coming to visit."

It almost sounded like she was chastising me for visiting my family vacation home. Had I loved her any less, I would have been offended. As such, she was like a kooky great aunt that I couldn't help but adore.

"It was a spur of the moment idea. I needed to get out of the city for a little while."

"I don't know how you live there. It gets so loud and packed."

"And Cape May doesn't, in the on-season?" I clarified, putting my rolling suitcase beside the door, moving to sit down on the hideous floral armchair across from Penny.

"Yes, well, it passes," she said, waving a hand.

It wasn't passing right now. Which might have been why she was in my family home instead of her own. Penny lived in a beautiful Victorian on the corner of the main street in downtown where the shops and restaurants and nightlife were crazy all through the summer.

My family home was a small ranch-style white structure with black shutters that was a fifteen-minute walk to downtown, but only two blocks from the beach. I wasn't here for the beach. I would go, but at sunrise or sunset. I wasn't a fan of the nearly shoulder-to-shoulder crowds, of crappy music blaring from someone's portable speakers, or shrieking kids. I liked kids, but I was here to unwind, and I knew that would put me on edge.

I'd had a rough month.

I needed some space to breathe.

And since there was no extra money to get myself a hotel room somewhere quiet, I had to settle for the family vacation home. With its awful décor and the fact that it was the worst time of year to visit when you wanted to be alone.

"You look tired, Gigi," Penny said, clucking her tongue.

"I am," I admitted. I wouldn't lie, I wanted a little sympathy. I had been running myself ragged for months. It was thankless work. And I was feeling drained and needy.

"Well, you will be able to unwind here," she said, rising from her rocking chair, reaching for her oversized paisley bag. "Just let me know when you head out. I will come back to keep an eye on things. And if you need anything while you're here, you know where to find me."

"Thank you, Penny," I said, watching as she made her way to the door, inwardly wishing she would have stayed around, would have shared a cup of tea with me.

I didn't mind being alone. I was used to it. But it would have been nice to have someone with me for a little while, so I didn't wallow too much.

But if she was leaving, instead of tea, I was going to have a stiff drink.

With that in mind, I made my way into the small kitchen, dominated by truly heinous green backsplashes and mismatching wooden doors on the cabinets which almost—but not quite—distracted you from the fact that the linoleum on the floor had been only partially replaced a decade or so before, leaving half of it dingy and faded, and half of it bright and new. All of it, however, was ugly, with its faux parquet that fooled exactly nobody.

We didn't keep much in the pantry at this house, seeing as we never knew how often we would be able to visit. When I opened the door, I found a few cans of tomato soup, sugar in an airtight container, beans, and what I was after. An entire shelf of hard liquor that, luckily, never went bad.

I reached for the whiskey, twisting off the top, and drinking straight from the bottle. It was fine. I was planning on drinking every drop of it before I packed up and headed back to the city bright and early on Monday morning.

I drank a solid two fingers' worth standing right there in the center of the kitchen before making my way back out onto the front screened porch, tossing one of the musty cushions to the floor, and sitting down directly on the wicker. Propping my feet up on the coffee table,I watched the crowds of people making their way down the street toward the beach with their rainbow umbrellas and their folding beach chairs, their towels and swimmies and blow-up pools for babies who can't go in the ocean.

I was still there when they returned a half an hour shy of dinnertime, parents' shoulders drooping, faces flushed, children grumbling, babies whining, everyone probably itchy from the sand and starving and dehydrated.

I was working my way to dehydration thanks to the whiskey and the ungodly hot temperature outside.

I probably needed to eat too, I decided, screwing the cap back on the bottle, making my way inside, going for one of the cans of tomato soup, knowing that ordering in was out of the question. My budget was tight, and I wasn't looking forward to making it any tighter. So, I would make do with what was here as well as the couple things I had packed in my suitcase. Which meant a lot of protein bars and some instant oatmeal packets.

I had no business escaping the city, shirking my responsibilities, getting some time away.

Time away meant my father could sink the business even further into a hole.

But I had just hit my wall.

I couldn't take another minute of it.

I had to get away from the pressures of it all before I snapped and did or said something I would regret.

As a whole, I had my family's notorious temper, but I had always been better at controlling it. Maybe because I learned at a young age that when my father blew his top, things went sideways quickly because no one acted rationally when on an irrational tirade. But I had been controlling it for months. No, years. And from the looks of things, there seemed to be no end to the frustrations, so I would need to control myself for months or years to come.

At least, if I couldn't figure this out, if I couldn't get us out of the bottomless void my father had trapped our family in when I was a little girl.

So I needed a little distance, a little room for some calm and patience to burrow back in. Then I could go back, keep plugging away at my five-year plan to fix this situation. If I could just keep my freaking father from making it any worse in the process.

Lofty goals, with his track record, but I was going to do my best.

We had to fix it.

Or he was going to get himself killed.

And possibly me in the process.

My life might not have been worth much at this point, but it was mine. And I would be damned if I'd let my father's stupid business decisions take it away from me.

In my back pocket, my phone buzzed six times in a row. Texts. Likely frantic ones from Liane who was having a heart attack over something or another at work. I ignored it, trying to remember that I promised myself a weekend away. But on the eighth buzz, I set my soup down, reaching for it, scrolling through the texts.

Liane had been working at the family business since the beginning of time. I was pretty sure she was my grandfather's first hire when he'd opened shop. She was high-strung and prone to getting overwhelmed easily and overreacting to the most minor of problems. But she had become a sort of face of the business, always stationed at the register bright and early every morning, knowing more customers by name than I did.

Apparently, the shipment I'd ordered in earlier the week had come in. With a third of the items I had ordered missing. Liane, bless her sweet heart, was convinced there was simply some glitch, some misunderstanding as to why we were getting one-fifth the flour I knew we needed, half of the butter, nearly none of the fruit.

I, unfortunately, was just jaded enough to know the truth.

My father had gone behind me and edited the order, cutting corners that couldn't afford to be trimmed.

This was why I never left town, damnit.

On a sigh, I dialed my father, feeling my pulse pounding in my temples and throat. This man was going to give me a heart attack at the ripe old age of twenty-two.

"I'm busy right now, Gigi."

"Not too busy for this," I told him, reminding myself not to grit my teeth. "Why did you screw with the supply order? We needed everything I ordered."

"Berries are expensive. We need to cut back."

"Berries are *necessary*," I insisted, closing my eyes, willing myself not to cry out of sheer frustration. "We have that order for the wedding this week, Daddy. Remember? They ordered strawberries and blueberries and freaking goji berries. We have to have them."

"Yeah, well," he said, trying to buy time, knowing he was wrong, but not wanting to admit it. "I will send someone out to the store."

"It will cost twice as much at the store! That's why we order wholesale. Jesus Christ. This is not rocket science, Daddy. You need to stop screwing around with the orders. I know what I am doing." I had, after all, been doing it since I was sixteen years old, since he proved wholly incapable of doing it himself.

"Yeah? If you know what you're doing, why are we just barely scraping by every month?"

His voice was raised, that notorious temper rearing its ugly head.

He had the worst combination of traits. Complete ineptitude blended with too much pride to ever admit he didn't know what he was doing. And then a sprinkling of denial, a heaping tablespoon of anger, and a nice dollop of entitlement to top it all off.

If it weren't for my grandfather and his legacy, I would have walked away as soon as I was legally able to do so. But I had made my grandpa a promise on his death bed. I would take care of the bakery. I would make sure it continued on. It would be around for my children, my children's children.

Nerves frazzled, I was beyond taking a deep breath and letting his accusations go. The whiskey and the sleepless nights were wearing me too thin.

"I think we both know why we are just barely scraping by every month, Daddy. And it has nothing to do with how successful the bakery is, and everything to do with those *friends* of yours in the mafia."

"Watch your mouth, Giana," my father snapped, voice rough.

Just this once, I didn't. I didn't want to. I wanted to unload all the rage, all the frustration, all the utter helplessness I had been feeling for years *for* him, *on* him. Where it belonged. I'd been carrying the burden of his shitty decisions around for too long.

"Why should I? You know I'm right. You took a shitty deal with shady people, and then continued to let them walk all over you for decades, dragging our family further and further into debt because you didn't have the balls to stand up to them, because you were too enamored with them to even want to? Newsflash, Daddy, they don't want you in their organization. They think you are a pawn to be used, nothing else. You are embarrassing yourself by kissing their rings like you have been doing all this time."

"You know what, Gigi? Fuck you," he snapped, hanging up.

Tossing my phone onto the table, I stood there in the middle of the kitchen with shaking hands, anger an uncomfortable, bubbling sensation inside, something that couldn't be denied, something I had no outlet for.

So I gave up on dinner, reaching instead for the bottle of whiskey.

If nothing else, it would ensure I would finally get a full night of sleep for a change.

Or so I thought.

I was down the hall, curled up in the king-sized bed in the master bedroom I never got to stay in before, finding the mattress lumpy and hell on my hips and shoulders when I tried to sleep on my side, so I ended up halfway on my stomach, my leg cocked up, face buried in a pillow. My body was damp with sweat since I refused to put the air cold enough to actually cool me off, seeing as it simply cost too much to do so, and no one was typically around to have it matter anyway.

Sleep was restless, marred by dreams that had been plaguing me since I was fifteen—not dreams at all, but awful memories, ones that made me wake up gasping, panicked, unsure of my surroundings for a moment before falling back to sleep.

It was the fourth time I woke up that I realized it wasn't a bad dream that woke me.

Oh, no.

It was the harsh reality.

Where I was alone in a house.

And a man was looming in the shadows.

My heart flew upward, lodging in my throat as a choked gasp escaped me. Why I didn't scream was beyond me. Maybe because of that pesky heart-in-throat situation. I felt it bubble up but get trapped, letting only a whimpering animal sound escape me as I flew upward in the bed, whacking my head against the wooden headboard. I tried to shake off the traces of sleep, think straight enough to figure out how I could get away, what weapons might be nearby to use against him.

There were no guns here. I had one at home. We had them at the bakery. Both legal and not-so-legal thanks to the nature of my father's connection to the mafia. But I would never leave a gun in a house that was rarely occupied. And the place was sparsely decorated after my father sold off a lot of the collectibles his parents had once filled the space with.

There was nothing.

Except...

Oh, thank God for drinking yourself to sleep, I decided as I realized the clunky, thick, glass whiskey bottle was on the floor beside the bed. Likely just out of sight. If he got close, I could reach down, grab it, bash him with it, then get away.

"Don't scream," a deep, gravelly voice commanded. It shouldn't have sounded sexy given the circumstances, but it did somehow.

"Fuck you," I said with a scoff, opening my mouth to suck in some air, deciding that this was the perfect time for a horror movie scream queen impersonation. The houses were practically stacked on top of each other this close to the shore. Someone would hear me. Someone would call the cops or come running. Something.

But before I could even finish pulling in that breath, this giant of a man was across the small space, his hand grabbing my ankles, yanking me down onto the mattress, allowing his other hand to clamp down over my mouth. I'd never really had the occasion to notice the size of a man's hands before, but with one covering damn near all of my face, I was noticing his. As well as his dark eyes, and the juts of his cheekbones. And what looked like maybe a scar down his eyebrow? It was hard to see with just a glint of moonlight coming through a crack in the curtains.

"Don't make this more difficult than it has to be," he demanded, using his free hand to reach down.

I couldn't see what he was reaching to do. But it didn't seem to take a lot of thought. Men didn't break into the room of women while they were sleeping to offer them pamphlets about our Lord and Savior.

They were there to lay claim to the canvas of your body, to splash it in shades of red, to make what was once something safe and beautiful, foreign and scary and ugly.

I knew.

God, did I know.

And I would be damned if I ever knew that again.

I was small. I knew this. I got confused for a child more than once a week. I had to provide several forms of ID to get into clubs. I was short and slight and I wasn't exactly a big fan of lifting weights, so I wasn't all that strong either.

But women could lift cars off babies.

I could fight off this man to save myself from rape.

Decision made, my feet lifted as my brain scanned through memories of the self-defense videos I had watched online when I was younger, both legs widening like a butterfly's wings before ramming outward, slamming into the man's hips, catching him off-guard enough to stumble back a foot.

Only a foot.

But a foot was all I needed.

I scrambled down off the bed, hand closing around the neck of the bottle, turning it, then rising up, swinging back, and slamming it forward, cracking it more off the side of the man's neck and jaw than head seeing as I wasn't tall enough to get higher.

"Fuck," he hissed regardless, head jerking back as I shoved past him, feeling his hand grab my wrist. Hard. Hard enough to bruise, making me whirl around, hand shooting out, nails bared, to scratch across the exposed skin of his neck.

"Jesus Christ, hellcat," he snapped as I yanked my wrist free, turning, mind set on running, getting out the front door, onto the street, finding some help. This town went to sleep late in the summer. Someone would be lingering around somewhere.

It would be okay.

I would be okay.

It was only a couple yards to the front door.

Heart hammering, brain swimming, muscles feeling foreign and shaky, I barreled through the bedroom doorway and into the hall.

Smelling freedom, I made a beeline for the front door.

Only I forgot one thing.

The goddamn braided rug that was set in front of the door. The same braided rug that had been there my entire life. The same braided rug that had always been a safety hazard, since no one ever bothered to put a pad beneath it to prevent movement.

I realized my mistake the second my front foot landed on the oval rug, and my forward-moving momentum made it slip backward even as my body kept moving forward, sending me flying.

I knew the second it happened that I wasn't going to go down, hit the floor, maybe be quick enough to brace myself on my forearms—not my hands, never the hands. No. There wasn't enough floor space left.

Nope.

I was flying forward.

And I was going to collide with the doorjamb.

Then, just a second later, that was exactly what happened.

There was the surge of fear, the crack of pain, and then... nothing.

Absolutely nothing.

Chapter Three

I hadn't taken a vacation since I was some asshole teenager on spring break, taking one of my father's cars, packing it full of friends, and driving it down to Mexico.

Without the protection of my father, I was just some schmuck in a car worth a hundred grand with a suitcase full of cash.

Within a week, the car was stripped for parts, and my cash had been taken after I got my ass fucking handed to me, leaving me bleeding on some side street.

You'd think as I crawled out of that alley drinking my own damn blood that I would have called my old man, had him come down there, throw his power and money around, get revenge for me.

But it had been the most freeing night of my life, and a hell of a learning experience.

The family was a nice security blanket. I had layers of protection. But when push came to shove, and it was just two men in an alley, I'd been a skinny, useless kid with no way to win a fight.

I got back to the city, took my ass-kicking from my father, who'd been pissed about the car more than anything, then I found myself a teacher who made sure I would never be that useless again in a fight.

It was around that same time that I had started taking on more family obligations, which meant things like vacations were part of my past.

Hell, the year before, I'd worked every weekend, every major holiday. This year looked to be a repeat of the same thing.

Maybe the man at the top got to take it easy, but those closest to him had to bust ass to keep things running smoothly, to keep him in the lap of luxury. That was especially true when your job involved dozens—if not hundreds—of people who would gladly see every member of your family with slit throats, bleeding out on the doorstep as they moved into your house, your position of power.

But as I was driving into Cape May, an area that was overwhelmingly a vacation spot, I could feel the itch to get away, to take a day, to sit down on my own couch for more than five minutes; to hop a plane and say "fuck it all" to everything back home for a week or two.

I couldn't imagine how I would fill that time.

Maybe get some sleep for a change.

But that wasn't in the cards, I reminded myself, turning off the main drag by the shore to do a drive past the house, wanting to learn the layout, to be able to get in and out easier when the sun went down and the town quieted.

I didn't anticipate how late things would stay lively, leaving me twiddling my fucking thumbs until after three in the morning, which gave me a very small window before sun up to get the girl out and leave town unseen.

The ranch-style home didn't have any yard to speak of, but boasted an enviable side driveway, one of only three houses on the entire street that had one.

Cutting the lights, I backed in, so the neighbor didn't see me, coming to a stop with my trunk right near the side door. Climbing out, I popped the trunk, grabbed a lock-pick set, and worked on the kitchen door.

Why Leon Lastra kept a vacation home and didn't bother to protect it from even the most novice of petty thieves was beyond me as I opened the lock and moved inside. Who didn't at least have a deadbolt on a house where they only spent a couple days every year?

Though, that said, Leon Lastra was, by all accounts, a fucking moron, so nothing he did—or didn't do—should have surprised me.

The house itself was dated, in desperate need of a renovation. And a part of me was a bit pissed off that he hadn't put the work in, then used the house as a rental to help bring in the money he owed us. It didn't take rocket science to think of the idea. But Leon was never much of a thinker. People who had a good head on their shoulders didn't typically end up indebted to the mob.

We could have taken the house, instead of some convoluted plan to kidnap the bastard's poor daughter. But my father wasn't a fan of hearing my ideas.

Reaching into my jacket, I drew out my gun, hoping I wouldn't have to use it, that Leon would be smart enough not to charge at me.

A quick search said all the rooms were empty. But the car outside said someone was around.

Which meant that the girl or her father, or both, were in the master.

When I got in, though, all I found was a woman on the bed in a pair of short shorts and a tank, her leg cocked up, her long, dark hair fanned out over her back and shoulders.

Alone.

I moved into a corner, getting into the shadows, waiting to make sure Leon hadn't just walked around the corner to pick something up from the store or something.

I felt very much like a creep as I stood there, gaze moving over the sleeping girl's body, taking in the soft jut of hip, the round ass just begging for a slap, those fit but thick thighs, giving me ideas about getting leg-locked with my face buried between—all causing an inappropriate and distracting hard-on build.

Half an hour passed of nothing but the restless dreams of the girl in the bed, likely brought on by the fact that the room was hot as fucking hell, and the ceiling fan and the fan propped in the window weren't doing a damn thing but blowing around stagnant, hot air.

Finally, one of the dreams, or maybe some sixth sense finally realizing I was creeping in the corner, woke her up.

What happened next was a bit of a blur.

I expected to be on her and have her bound, gagged, and duct-taped in a matter of seconds.

But she had more spirit in her than I expected, more strength in her small body than seemed possible.

And I'd somehow missed the fucking whiskey bottle until it was whacking into my jaw and ear.

I was right on her heels when she raced through the house. It wasn't hard to keep up with someone who was about a full foot shorter than you. Each two of her strides was one of my own.

I saw the rug slide underneath her foot, felt the dread tighten my stomach muscles as my body seemed to brace for her inevitable collision with the doorframe.

"Shit," I hissed when she collapsed down to the floor, out cold.

On the one hand, it would make the binding and dragging part a lot easier.

On the other, if shit went down and the law came after me, I would get blamed for the damage.

But what was done was done.

On a sigh, I moved forward, grabbing her shoulder, rolling her onto her back as I flicked on the small entryway light so I could see what I was doing.

"Fuck," I hissed when my gaze fell on her face, really seeing it for the first time. "God fucking damn it," I growled, raking a hand through my hair.

My father had conveniently left out the fact that she was a fucking *kid*. Close to adulthood, sure, there was no mistaking that. But her face was young, plump in the cheeks. I bet she had dimples when she smiled.

Kidnapping someone was never good business. Kidnapping a child?

I just reserved my first-class ticket right to the centermost ring of hell.

Pissed, but resigned, I kneeled down, probing the cut on her head for a second to make sure no real damage was done. I'd knocked my head around enough to know something superficial from something serious. She would wake up with a throbbing headache, maybe a little nausea, but she would be fine.

I put the gag in her mouth, and a layer of duct tape over that for added security, then cuffed her arms in the front. Behind the back was always preferable, but I was feeling fucking guilty about the whole thing, and I figured it would hurt like a bitch to roll around on your arms and shoulders in the back of a trunk for hours.

That handled, I hefted her up into my arms, walked through the house, tucked her into the trunk, closed it, got into the front, and drove off.

Really, I should have known the little hellcat wouldn't be a model kidnapping victim.

I wasn't more than a half an hour into the ride when the back of the car started knocking around. I shrugged it off. Any rational person would start rolling around and trying to break free when they woke up in a trunk.

I would learn, eventually, not to underestimate this kid.

But at the moment, I was just driving along the fucking parkway, doing the speed limit, using my blinkers, making sure no one would peg my car as suspicious. I drove in the slow lane, for fuck's sake.

Then the back seat slammed forward, and a girl was worming her way out of the trunk.

"Jesus fucking Christ," I snapped, surprised, jerking the wheel, swerving toward the car in front of me, then over-correcting to avoid clipping his tail. I straightened the car, then pulled over to the shoulder.

"Mother fucker," I growled when the tire caught some sort of debris there, blowing out, making me brake hard before I did any damage to the rims.

Anxiety gripped my system, knowing we were in the broad goddamn daylight now, that cars were whizzing by, and anyone might stop and try to be a Good Samaritan. Or the cops might happen by.

And I had a girl trying to free herself through the backseat.

"Fuck," I snapped again, whipping off my belt, flying out of my side, opening the back, grabbing the girl's shoulders, shoving her back into the hole she'd wiggled out of, then slamming the seat back into place. Inwardly chastising myself for not thinking of that safety feature, I took a seat in the back, legs braced against the front seat so I could apply pressure to the back one as the girl slammed up against it.

Reaching for my phone, I dialed up the only person I knew I could trust with this.

"Having problems already?" Emilio asked, snickering.

"You have no fucking idea. This girl just burst out of the back seat from the trunk on the parkway. I flew off the road. Tire is shredded. I obviously can't get out to deal with it. Or call Triple A. I need you to come, trade cars with me, and handle this shit."

"Sounds like an awful lot of trouble," Emilio said, and I could hear the smirk in his voice. "And you know me, not a responsible bone in my body."

"Milo, come the fuck on. I don't have time for your fucking around."

"I'm on my way. I'm just saying, you're losing your touch with the ladies, man."

"Yeah, and if you were here, she'd come with you willingly," I scoffed, wincing at the muffled scream coming from the trunk.

"Well, I am much better looking than you. Not to mention charming," Emilio said, chuckling. "Give me a mile marker. I will be there as fast as I can."

With that, I sat and waited, leaving my station only for a moment, to reach for the stereo, turning it up in case someone did try to stop and be a decent human being.

Thankfully, though, no one wanted to be decent this day in particular. Which was good. I liked assholes. That was why I enjoyed where I lived. Everyone minded their own goddamn business.

"Yeah?" I barked into my phone seeing my father's right-hand-man, Terry's, name on the screen.

"Need you to pick up a package," he said, cutting to the chase.

"I am already dealing with a package," I reminded him.

"Yeah, well, make room for another."

"Not another houseguest," I said, stomach dropping.

"No. Just a care package," Terry said in that nasally voice of his, thanks to one too many nose-breakings when he was my age. Likely due to the fact that he always thought he was more important than he was.

"Terry, I'm fucking busy here."

"You want me to tell your old man that? You're too busy for orders?"

That was a challenge, a threat. Because Terry had been vying for the underboss position for years. And he was resentful that I had gotten it, albeit begrudgingly. Kissing ass would get you all sorts of places, as he would know, but it was no substitute for hard work, and aptitude.

"Where is the package?"

"P.A."

"P.A.? There is no one closer than me without a houseguest in the car with him?"

"No one your father wants handling it."

To be perfectly honest, my father likely forgot that I was doing this pick-up today. He wasn't exactly great about keeping shit straight. But Terry was right; I couldn't say no. I had to do what I was told to do, or I risked losing my place. Which likely meant losing my life. And I'd be fucking damned if brown-nosing Terry got my position in this family.

"I'll handle it. Give me an address," I said, figuring I could pawn the girl off on Emilio if I had to, deal with the car and the package myself and let him bring her back to the city, deposit her in my apartment, get a guard or two on her. Or fucking five, with the spirit she had.

Even more frustrated than I had been five minutes before, I plugged the address into my phone, checking the route, seeing I would be going a solid five hours out of my way before circling back. I would just barely be able to squeeze in the meeting with the New Jersey family before getting back to the city finally.

It would be a tight timeframe, but I could manage. Once I got rid of the girl.

"No can do," Emilio said when he arrived, standing in the open door, smirking at the jostling trunk.

"What do you mean 'no can do'?" I asked, watching the traffic flying by, wondering how the fuck we were going to transfer an actual human being from one trunk to the other without being seen and reported.

"I have that meeting I am covering for you with the D'Onofrios," he reminded me. Apparently, Vin hadn't been happy with the way things had gone with my father. He wanted to have a talk with me. And since I was busy, I had told him I would send Emilio. I couldn't exactly call him again and say that, on second thought, I was going to send someone else. Emilio had to go. Which meant I was stuck with a girl in the goddamn trunk across more state lines, for likely a full twenty-four hours, then all during my meeting in New Jersey, before I could finally get us back to the city.

"We are going to need to stop somewhere," I realized, knowing I could go a long while without sleep, but we would need a bathroom, and food. Privacy for all of that. I couldn't exactly pull up to the local gas station with her, now, could I?

"Where's the pickup?" he asked, knowing the area better than I did, having extended family scattered all through Pennsylvania. Rattling off the address, he thought it out. "There's a motel off that way. Nothing fancy. Your average sleep and fuck type place. By the hour or the night or the week. Can't guarantee you won't get bed bugs, but can guarantee everyone will mind their own fucking business. I can call ahead. Make some arrangements to have a room open for you. You can just go right in then."

"I'd appreciate that," I decided, knowing stopping anywhere wasn't going to be ideal, but there was no way around it, not if I wanted to make the pick-up on time, get to the meeting on time.

"Not a problem. Oh, here he is," Emilio said, jerking his chin toward the massive pick-up that was moving in behind his car, making a bit of a metal wall.

"You brought your little brother into this?" I asked, shaking my head. Anthony was all of eighteen, a late-life baby who was desperate to be an official part of the *family* by more than blood.

"He's going to get the donut on, so I can drive this thing back to the city. And I figured we could use more of a shield from curious eyes," he added, waving a hand toward the cars whizzing past.

"Alright. Good thinking. Pop your trunk," I demanded, taking a deep breath, knowing we would only have a few seconds to get this right. "Anthony," I greeted the younger, more serious version of Emilio. He was wider, more strongly built than his older brother, someone who'd played football all through high school, and it showed. "I am going to need you to help me move her," I told him, tone serious, getting a nod from him.

If there was anyone in the world who wasn't a made member of our family that I could trust, it was someone as hungry to get there as Anthony.

With that, I shot out of my seat, hitting the trunk button then rounding the car and flipping open the trunk to find the girl staring up at us, eyes wide and unseeing for a moment, accustomed to the dark, before they landed on me, seeming to register something.

And I was pretty sure I wasn't imagining the pure, undiluted hatred there in her gray eyes as she looked at me.

"Ready?" I asked, snapping out of my curiosity, figuring I had plenty of time to work out that look later as I grabbed her shoulders and Anthony wordlessly grabbed her feet.

Short, slight, she weighed next to nothing, but damn if she didn't make it as difficult as possible to move her, wiggling her body every which way, trying to yank her feet out of Anthony's grasp, arching upward, shrugging her shoulders.

But with minimal effort, we had her out of my trunk and into Emilio's.

Slamming the lid, I faced Emilio, whose brows were raised.

"She's young."

"I know," I agreed, feeling the same unease in my gut that I saw on his face.

"If the order comes down..." he said, and he didn't need to say it. The order to take her out if Leon didn't pay, didn't comply.

"That order can't come down," I told him, knowing down to my twisted, corrupt soul that while I could kill without blinking, while I had done so many times in the past, I couldn't kill some kid. That was not going to happen. Not even if family demanded it of me. It was damn near treason to even think that, but there was no denying it was the truth.

"When you need me, let me know," Emilio said, and, again, I knew what he was saying. If Leon wasn't complying, we could work together to make it happen so that order never came down, so we never had to carry it through, or defy it.

"Will do. Anthony, thank you for coming out. I'll remember this when the books are open," I told him, getting a grateful nod from him. "For now, this is between us. We don't need the other families hearing this shit, *capisce*?"

"*Capisco*," he agreed, going back to the truck, grabbing some tools, and making his way back to my car.

"Here. Get going. You got a stressful couple days ahead of you," Emilio said, handing me his key fob. "I'll handle the arrangements and send your details."

"I appreciate it," I said, sighing heavily.

"Oh, and my seats don't fold down," Emilio added, smirking.

"Thank fuck," I grumbled, climbing into the driver's seat.

The ride to Pennsylvania was uneventful even as the sleepless hours started to catch up on me.

By the time we made it to the hotel, it was just about dinner time. My stomach was grumbling. My eyes were scratchy. And I was sick of driving.

The motel was every bit as rundown and seedy as Emilio had warned—a simple L-shaped structure that had a total of ten rooms, all of which had their own parking spaces right out front of the doors.

I pulled up to the one at the corner of the L, thankful for the shadows the placement allowed as I hopped out to make sure the door was open first, grabbing the comforter off the bed, going back to the trunk, tossing it over the girl, then hefting her into my arms and rushing inside, kicking the door closed.

"Alright," I started when we were inside, placing the girl on the end of the bed. "Let's talk about this," I said, squatting down in front of her, working to undo her ankles. "I'm not going to hurt you," I told her, wincing at the black eye she had forming from her collision with the wall. "My job is to pick you up, bring you with me, and hold onto you. Not to abuse you in anyway. So this whole thing is going to be a lot easier if you stop trying to claw at me."

To that, I got a pretty impressive eye roll, given the situation.

"Yeah, can't imagine that sounds all that assuring, kid," I agreed, sighing, grabbing the folding chair from the other side of the room, dragging it between her position and the door, then dropping down on it. "Obviously, this has nothing to do with you. Your father fucked up. And, unfortunately, you got caught in the middle. All we can both hope for right now is that your father steps up, so we can get you back to your life. Hopefully back to your school before the new semester starts."

To that, her brows drew together slightly, like something I said didn't make much sense. "I know, that's a few weeks away still. And it would not be something either of us wants, to have it last that long. But this all comes down to your dad. Now, we won't be staying here long. We needed a place to stop, use the bathroom, get some food. And then we will be back on the road. Once we get where we're going, I'm hoping I won't need to keep you bound and gagged anymore. So there is that to look forward to. Now, do you need to use the bathroom?" I asked, jerking my chin toward the space that was nothing more than awful dark blue tile and grout that looked like it hadn't seen a scrubbing since the eighties.

To that, I got a nod.

"Alright," I agreed, getting up, glancing inside, seeing a window too small to climb out of. "I'm not taking your cuffs off," I told her, shrugging. "You're just going to need to figure it out," I added, waving an arm toward the door.

Obediently, she stood, making her way toward the bathroom, giving me small eyes before moving inside, closing the door with her foot.

I waited, hearing the flush, the water in the sink. I wasn't trying to invade some sixteen or seventeen-year-old girl's privacy.

But then she did it.

Pulled the tape off.

Found a way to get the scarf untied.

Sucked in a breath.

And screamed.

"Goddamnit," I growled, finding the door locked, needing to kick it in, rushing inside, clamping my hand over her mouth. "Seriously?" I asked as she shot daggers up at me. "I get it's your job to make this difficult for me. But now it's my job to make that harder for you," I told her, dragging her back into the main area, grabbing more duct tape with my free hand, cutting a piece off with my teeth, then releasing her mouth just long enough to slap it on. "Now you are going to have sore shoulders," I told her, uncuffing her bound wrists, dragging each arm behind her back, securing them there instead. Satisfied with that, I grabbed her ankles, tying them to the slats under the mattress, then made my way to the bathroom for a break.

When I came back out, she was heaving hard, clearly having spent the couple moments testing the strength of the bed frame. For such a shitty place, the construction proved solid.

With that, I went to my phone, ordering delivery, going outside to wait for it.

When I came back in and set the cardboard box on the dresser, the girl's eyes followed my every move as I took out containers, pulled off tops, filled the room with the scents of baked macaroni and eggplant parm.

"What do you say, hellcat? Want to call a truce for long enough to eat a meal? I can take that tape off if you agree not to scream."

Her gaze went to me, then the box, then me again, giving me a defeated little nod. "One peep and the goddamn thing goes back on, and won't come off again, got it? I don't care if you're hungry."

To that, I got another nod.

And, it seemed, we had a momentary truce.

Of course, it wouldn't last.

The girl lived up to the nickname I'd given her.

She was pure fucking evil.

And determined to scratch and hiss every step of the way.

And me?

Well, I had to respect that, didn't I?

Chapter Four

Giana

He thought I was a kid still.

And, I guess, that worked in my favor.

Even if it didn't stop me from rolling around in a trunk for hours, every part of me getting bumped and bruised. The skin under the duct tape was sore. And I had needed to pee for hours.

Mix that with the fear of rape or other bodily harm, and I was ready to claw his eyes out when he dropped me on the bed in the motel room.

In the daylight, I was annoyed to find him ridiculously good looking. Bad guys, in real life, were supposed to be balding and pockmarked with hangover waistlines and beady eyes.

This man was nearly six-and-a-half feet of well-built handsomeness from his fit body to his sharp bone structure to his deep green eyes.

The scar was maybe the only thing that gave him away as a bad guy. Not many normal people walked around sporting a scar that ran through their dark eyebrow, upper eyelid, and then about an inch under their eye. I couldn't think of an accidental way someone might get a scar like that.

It made him serious and menacing.

And, somehow, even more attractive.

It took me an almost embarrassingly long time to put the pieces together. The nice car. The designer suit, the expensive watch. The New York accent.

In fact, I hadn't even started to put the pieces together until he started talking about who he was.

Then it finally clicked.

He was a member of the Costa family.

And knowing what I knew about the mafia in New York City—which was a lot given that my idiot father was wrapped up with them—the Costa was the top family. Arturo Costa was the *Capo dei Capi*—the boss of all bosses.

There were five New York City crime families. There had been for nearly a century.

Each family had its own structure.

Associates, soldiers, capos, underboss, and boss. Each family did their own hustles.

But one always had slightly more power than the others.

That family was the Costas.

And had been since Arturo violently stole power as a young man.

I wasn't sure if I should have been relieved that this wasn't some random rapist-murderer, or pee-myself scared that the Costa family was holding me hostage to get something out of my father.

But, as the food arrived, I decided that making sure I was fed was going to help me keep my wits about me, which might help save my life.

So I agreed to a truce with the devil.

In doing so, he moved over toward me, freeing my sore wrists, making my shoulders cry in relief. He even reached up and carefully peeled away the duct tape.

"Do you have a name?" he asked, offering me the folding chair, taking one of the containers with him to sit off the edge of the bed.

"Gigi. Giana," I corrected immediately, not sure I wanted this stranger to use my nickname, to be allowed to have that kind of intimacy with me. "You?" I asked, taking a set of the plastic utensils and cutting into the eggplant parmigiana.

"Lorenzo," he offered, surprising me.

Lorenzo.

I knew of a Lorenzo thanks to all the mafia research I had done.

"Lorenzo Costa?" I asked. The son of the most violent mafia boss since the seventies.

"Yes. And you're Leon's daughter."

I just barely held myself back from saying "unfortunately."

"Why wasn't he in the beach house with you? Who leaves their kid in a house all alone all night?"

"I'm not a kid," I objected before catching myself. It was a knee-jerk reaction from having people confuse me as younger for so long.

"Yeah okay," he agreed, rolling his eyes. "Where is Leon?"

"At the bakery right now, I imagine."

"Hopefully earning the money he needs to get you back."

That was unlikely, but I kept my mouth shut about it.

"This is the part where I'm supposed to beg for my life, right?"

"I imagine so. I don't exactly kidnap kids on the regular, so I'm not sure how all this plays out. You can roll your eyes all you want, Gigi, but the mafia usually doesn't deal in children."

"Gee, lucky me, then," I mumbled, lip curling as I took a bite of the eggplant parm that had clearly come from a frozen patty.

"I know. Not great," Lorenzo agreed. "One positive to getting back to where we need to go is the food will be good. And the bed will be less dubious under a blue light."

I felt a chuckle build, but forced it back down, refusing to find my kidnapper a little charming.

"How's your head? I can probably scrounge up some aspirin."

I hadn't given my head much thought. The constant, skull-piercing throbs had long since become tolerable. I imagined if I could get some sleep, it would be almost normal again. I'd gotten a look in the grimy bathroom mirror, seeing the black eye there, testament to my own idiocy.

"It's tolerable," I said, shrugging. "What?" I asked when his brow furrowed. It took a second to think that maybe I wasn't speaking like he expected. Maybe if I was seventeen, I would have said 'it's fine' or something like that, not that it was tolerable. I needed to be careful with that. Being seen as underage seemed like it was going to work in my favor with this family. Or, at least, with this man in particular. "Kinda hurts still," I added, going ahead and doing a pout as well.

"You went down so fast. I couldn't grab you in time."

I couldn't trust myself not to sass him about wanting me unconscious, pliant, so I focused on choking down the crappy food, washing it down with one of the bottles of Coke he'd had them add on the order.

"After we eat, we need to catch some sleep before we're off again."

"Are you going to stick me in a trunk again?" I asked, glancing at him sideways.

"I dunno. Probably. Maybe. Depends."

"On if I am a good little victim or not?" I asked, chin jerking up, something that got a lip twitch from Lorenzo.

"Something like that. Little bird is telling me your ass is going to be rolling around in the trunk again," he added, smirking.

Knowing me, I probably would.

But I was going to try to be quieter, bite my tongue, play my part. The less I fought, the more he would trust me. The more he trusted me, the more likely I was to catch him off guard and get away.

I will admit that my chances weren't great. And even if I did get away, where the hell would I even go? My father couldn't—and possibly *wouldn't*—protect me. And what was my other option? To go to the cops? That was a surefire way of getting a bullet in the back of my head.

I had no idea what the best play was. But I knew I couldn't just sit idly by and be an obedient victim until my father possibly saved me.

I knew better than anyone else that Leon Lastra was not exactly the savior type. I'd been saving his ass since I was still a kid.

So, this time, I would just have to save myself.

However I had to do that.

"I can see those gears turning," Lorenzo said, cutting into my swirling thoughts. "Don't get any ideas. You're not going to get away from me when I'm asleep," he said, and I hadn't even thought about that.

One bed.

Two people.

My stomach twisted, a knee-jerk, involuntary reaction.

"Relax," he said, voice softer. Well, as soft as someone with a deep, rough voice like his could be anyway. "I told you I'm not going to hurt you. I meant that. I don't put my hands on women if they don't want it. And I never fucking touch kids. So don't look at me like I'm a wolf about to rip out your throat."

Nope.

Just a guy who was going to hold me hostage until my father paid up. And who knew what would happen to me if my father didn't.

After dinner, I was un-cuffed long enough to be able to go into the bathroom, splash some water on my face, roll my sore muscles.

I was cuffed to the bed again while Lorenzo took a turn, then came back out, pulling off his rumpled suit jacket, hanging it over the chair, then staring dubiously at the bed.

"What are the chances this place has bed bugs?" he asked, looking a bit sick to his stomach at the prospect.

"Lift the mattress and check," I suggested, standing there while he did it.

"Don't see anything," he said, shoulders relaxing.

A big, bad mafia underboss was scared of little bugs? It was so ridiculous that it was almost funny.

But there was nothing to laugh about when, a moment later, he un-cuffed the bracelet from the bed frame and lifted it up, clamping it around his own wrist instead.

"Sorry, hellcat, can't have you trying to get away while I try to sleep," he said, shrugging, reaching up with his free hand to undo two buttons before giving my arm a little shake as he sat down on the edge of the bed, then started to inch up, bringing me with him, willing or not.

Lorenzo settled, then sighed out his breath.

"What?"

"Are you going to behave or do we need to get up so I can duct tape you and bind your other arm to the headboard?" he asked, not sounding too thrilled at the prospect.

Sleeping with my arm forced over my head and something over my mouth sounded miserable. Besides, this kind of place didn't seem like the kind of place that cared about screaming. After all, no one had come when I had cried out earlier.

"I won't scream," I offered as he reached out toward the nightstand with his free hand, turning on the TV, turning it up almost painfully loud, some old sitcom from the nineties playing.

"Good." He sighed again, something clearly weighing on him. And I wasn't generous enough of spirit to feel bad for my kidnapper, so I forced my lips shut, watching the characters that were vaguely familiar to me move across the screen. "Get some sleep, Gigi," he suggested what felt like a lifetime later, so long that I figured he'd already fallen asleep.

Eventually, with no other choice, I did.

—

I woke up to a very serious, very loud voice in my ear.

"You need to get off of me, Giana," Lorenzo's voice called, sounding sleep-rough, which was an entirely too good sound. And I was just barely conscious enough to appreciate that. "Giana, get off of me," he demanded again, voice more forceful.

That seemed to penetrate the curtain of sleep.

Get off of him?

As soon as the words sank in, started to make sense, it all came to me at once.

His breath on the top of my head.

His hard body underneath mine, stiff as a board.

His chest rising and falling under my cheek.

Oh, God.

God.

I'd crawled up on him in my sleep.

That was, well, completely humiliating.

I threw my body backward like he'd suddenly caught flame, feeling the cold of my side of the bed, realizing I must have been passed out on him for a while before either of us woke up to notice it.

"I... I never sleep on my back," I told him, embarrassed, needing to explain. "I'm a side sleeper. I... I'm not used to having someone next to me."

"I'd hope not," he agreed, voice tight, reminding me of my role. Sweet, innocent, high school senior.

"You don't have to be all pissy. I didn't mean to do it," I said, giving him the kind of sass I had been known for in my teens.

"I'm not pissy. It's just... never mind," he grumbled, folding upward, reaching into the nightstand to produce the handcuff key, freeing his wrist.

With that, he dragged me across the bed by my arm, cuffing me to his side of the bed, taking the key with him, and disappearing into the bathroom.

I couldn't be sure, but I was almost positive I heard him hiss out "fuck" as soon as he closed the door.

When he came out a couple minutes later, though, he was collected again, though he completely avoided looking at me, even when he un-cuffed me and told me to take my turn, that we were leaving.

He was all no-nonsense that morning, tossing all the food into the garbage, looking out the window, binding me, duct taping me again, checking outside one more time then dragging me outside and throwing me inside the trunk.

It was the only time I would say he was truly rough with me, my head whacking a bit off the outside of the trunk as I was pushed inside, hands shoving me into the depths, then nearly catching my foot in the door as he slammed it.

From there, it was just a lot of rolling around, trying to kick out my legs in such a way as to prevent me from slamming into the carpet-covered hard edges.

Time stood still.

It could have been minutes or hours.

My best bet was on hours.

The car stopped twice.

Once, it seemed, to get gas.

Another, I wasn't sure, but the car idled and Lorenzo cranked the music higher before the door slammed, seemingly leaving me for a few moments.

But with my arms bound behind my back, I was effectively useless.

Lorenzo got back in the car, the music turned lower, and we were moving one again.

Again, I lost track of time, but was pretty sure hours were passing before we idled again, before the music went deafening, before the door slammed and I was sure Lorenzo was leaving me on my own.

This time, I wiggled, hoping that I could get the car moving, could draw attention to me. I couldn't seem to get the position myself right to kick out the taillights, and even if I could, I didn't think I could get my hand out the opening, so the best bet was to make the car move enough that no one would confuse it for the bass in the music.

All I seemed to accomplish was tiring myself out, because before too long, the door was slamming and the car was peeling away again.

At some point, I was pretty sure I started dozing off, the soft rumble of the car on a road without many stops seemed to soothe me like it was known to do for small babies.

But then we were stopping once more.

For the final time.

I knew it because the engine actually cut, then the trunk popped and I was face-to-face with Lorenzo again for what felt like the first time in days.

"Long day," he agreed, seeming to read the exhaustion on my face as he reached in the trunk, gently grabbing my arm, helping pull me out.

We were in some kind of underground parking, but any hopes of being seen were immediately dashed.

We were alone.

Once I was out, Lorenzo shrugged out of his suit jacket, wrapping it around my shoulders. I thought it was an almost sweet gesture at first until I saw him buttoning it up, caching me—and my bound wrists—inside.

Then he was swooping low, scooping me up, and tucking my face into his chest, holding it there a bit awkwardly with the arm that was around my back and shoulder, blocking the fact that I was duct taped from view as he carried me in through a back door, then toward an elevator, not releasing me until the doors slid closed.

Then, surprisingly, he put me down, taking off the jacket, taking off the cuffs, and peeling off the duct tape.

"Private elevator," he told me, smirking a little at my scrunched brows. "This is it. The bound and gagged shit is over.

You can get a pretty free run from here on out. Except maybe I will make sure all the knives and heavy items are stashed away," he said, reaching up to touch the side of his jaw and ear where I'd struck him with the whiskey bottle.

"So, what? I'm a house guest?" I asked, watching as he held back a smile. "What?"

"Nothing, kid. Just an interesting choice of words, is all. Yeah, go ahead and think of yourself as a house guest."

"One who can't leave," I specified.

"Obviously. And there will always be someone around to make sure that can't happen. But other than that, no more locking you up or taping your mouth shut."

"To what end?" I asked, shaking my head.

"Until your father pays what he owes," Lorenzo said, shrugging, stepping out onto the floor as the doors dinged and opened.

Because, of course, private elevators always led to penthouse residences.

There would be no hallway.

No prying eyes.

No way out.

It was a beautiful prison, though, I admitted to myself as I stepped into the open concept living space.

There were floor-to-ceiling windows spanning two whole sides of the apartment, showing breathtaking views of the city below, the light already mostly gone for the day, making me realize I had lost something like twelve hours in that trunk. No wonder everything hurt and my bladder was screaming and my stomach was grumbling.

To the right of the space was a kitchen with dark wood cabinets, stainless steel appliances, and white countertops. Directly forward was a long L-shaped sectional in a deep gray with an oversize gray and white striped ottoman, everything facing the massive TV attached to the wall, floating above a wooden console table that matched the kitchen cabinetry.

Off to the side of the TV wall was a hallway that led back. To the bed and bathrooms, I figured.

Even just the main area was a massive space. I could fit my entire apartment into the kitchen.

A part of me was impressed.

The other part was angry that I felt that way for a moment because I knew where the money for this apartment came from.

From people like my father, like me, who were indebted to them, who struggled to pay their bills each month, while they lived in the lap of luxury.

"All this seems self-explanatory," Lorenzo said, waving an arm out at the space. "Feel free to help yourself to everything in the kitchen. Save for the aforementioned knives and heavy instruments," he added, giving me a boyish smile as he moved over toward the hall. "And down here," he said, waiting for me to follow behind. And, with little other choice, I did. "We have the half bath, then the guest room. Your room," he clarified, opening the door, revealing a sleek, understated space with more dark woods, and crisp white bedding. I glanced hopefully at the window above the bed, but felt my spirits plummet when I saw that it, like all the windows in the main area, was solid. There was no exit. "You have your own full bath. Don't get too excited," he said, making me turn back and see the wicked smirk he was giving me. "There is no exit from there either."

There had to be an exit somewhere.

It was basic building code fire safety.

There had to be at least two exits.

The elevator barely counted since you couldn't use that in an emergency.

"I am across the hall," he went on, moving back into said hall, extending an arm toward his door. "And then there is the gym," he said, leading me to the end of the hall and into a space slightly larger than my bedroom, stocked with all the basic essentials: treadmill, stationary bike, a stair climber, a weight bench, and about every size free weight known to mankind. "Yeah, might have to do something with those too, huh?" he asked, and when I glanced over, his hand was rubbing across the back of his neck. "I could just lock you out of here, but I figure this situation sucks enough for you. I can't deny you a little activity now and again. Alright. Why don't you settle in? I'd offer you something to wear, but I think you'd look like an infant wearing their father's clothes if I tried to give you any pants. I can give you a shirt though. I will have things picked up for you. But I imagine you are going to want to clean up now."

"I, ah, yeah." I needed to find a way out. Or find a way to incapacitate him, so I could take the elevator down and run. It wasn't hard to get lost in the city. And once I did that, I could figure out my next move. But no one said I couldn't clean up first. I felt gross and sticky from the car ride. I needed to brush my teeth.

"Alright, come on," he said, walking into the hall, waiting for me to follow him into his room.

His bedroom was unnecessarily massive, dominated by a California king-size bed with black bedding, heavy black drapes, and doors open to a bathroom and a walk-in closet that made me want to weep.

"Would you rather a tee or something heavier?"

"Since you keep the air set to arctic, I think I will take something heavier," I told him as he ducked into the closet, coming back with a red sweatshirt that likely fit him normally, but was going to be a dress on me. Which was good. I wanted to be as covered as possible. Being in booty shorts and a tank around a strange man whose intentions weren't guaranteed, it would be nice not to feel so on display.

"Your bathrooms should have everything you need. Toothbrush, paste, soap. Anything else you need, let me know. What do you want to eat?"

"Something that didn't start as a frozen patty," I said, still having a bit of heartburn from that awful meal.

"Think I can handle that," he agreed, giving me a tired, forced smile.

With that, I went back into the hall, into my temporary room, closing and locking the door.

The shower was calling my name, but I didn't immediately move in that direction. I stood just inside the door, pressing my ear to the crack, listening as Lorenzo walked into the main area.

He seemed to immediately reach for his phone.

"Yeah, it's done. I need you to pick it up from me. Yeah. That would be good. Tomorrow. For a few hours, so I can get some shit done. Okay yeah. Thanks."

It sounded like he was leaving the next day for a few hours. Maybe that would be a good time to explore things, find the second way out. Or maybe distract the guard for long enough to take the elevator down.

After that, he made a call to some restaurant, seeming to walk closer to the kitchen as he did so, making his words difficult to make out. Not that it mattered. I wasn't picky. And I was starving.

With that, I made my way into the bathroom, finding all white subway tiles in the shower stall with an assortment of small shampoos, conditioners, and soaps.

Locking the door, I stripped out of my old clothes, jumping in the water, keeping my eyes on the door the entire time, paranoia a skittering sensation inside as I rushed through my shower, quickly tried off, and slipped into the massive sweatshirt that swallowed me up entirely, coming down to my knees, obscuring anything beneath even resembling a body.

When I finally emerged from the room, Lorenzo was no longer alone, but accompanied in the main space by another man around his age, but a little shorter, a little less handsome, at least for my taste.

"Giana, this is Christopher. Christopher, Gigi. He is going to be one of the guards you will see stationed here."

"Even when you're here?" I asked, feeling the window to escape getting smaller and smaller, possibly too small to squeeze through no matter how small I might try to make myself.

"I'm going to need to sleep sometimes. And I can't have you walking around, looking for things to bash people over the head with," Lorenzo said, smirking. "Alright. Introductions made. Gigi, you're as safe with Christopher as you are with me. I am going to go catch a shower, too. By then, the food should be here."

And, what? We were going to eat together like some warped house guest fantasy?

I bit my tongue on those words, though, figuring I would get much further if he thought I was accepting of my fate, that I was calm about it. Then he might look away for a moment. Possibly even long enough for me to escape.

"You'll be fine, kid," Lorenzo assured me before turning and walking into his room.

With the door left open, I could see the breadth of his strong back as he pulled off his shirt on his way to his bathroom.

Embarrassed that I looked, that I maybe even ogled a bit, I turned back to face Christopher, finding him stationed in front of the elevator, gaze averted.

"It doesn't bother you, to have to play babysitter?" I prodded him, making my way toward the kitchen, going to the fridge. I'd used my hands to cup handfulls of water to my lips in the bathroom, but I was still dying of thirst. And if Lorenzo wanted me to play houseguest, I was going to make myself at home.

"Nope," Christopher said, still not looking at me as I went into the fridge, finding a couple coffee-flavored energy drinks and individual orange juices. Taking the latter, I leaned back against the counter, twisting off the cap.

"Really? Seems beneath you. You know, for a big, bad mafia guy."

"I do what I'm told."

I was going to get nowhere with this one, I realized. He was too determined to do a good job, to impress Lorenzo. I wasn't going to provoke him into proving he could think for himself, or sweet talk him enough to help me. Which was maybe for the best. I'd never been much of a sweet talker.

Out of ideas for the moment, I moved back toward the living space, dropping down on the couch, careful to tuck my legs just so, very aware that the only panties I had were washed out with hand soap in the bathroom and hanging to dry over the shower door.

Reaching for the remote on the ottoman, I turned on the television, flicking through the channels, pretending not to feel like my world was spinning around and I was desperately trying to hold on.

I had a lot of practice acting calm when everything was falling apart.

A couple moments later, Lorenzo walked back out of his room, no longer dressed in a suit that seemed tailored to fit him, but a pair of black lightweight cotton pajama pants and a plain white tee. Don't ask me how, but he somehow managed to still look intimidating in something so casual.

"Chris, you want to go down and wait for the food? I ordered enough for you," Lorenzo added, moving toward the kitchen. But instead of going into the fridge, he went into a cabinet, grabbing a bottle of whiskey.

And two glasses.

I watched as he poured two generous servings before making his way toward me, holding one of the glasses out like some sort of peace offering.

"I already know your poison," he reminded me as I reached to take it. "And I figure we could both use a drink. Even if I shouldn't be serving someone your age," he added, dropping down at the far end of the sectional, catty-corner to me, and I could feel his gaze on me as I took a sip.

"Yeah," I said after the burn subsided. "It must have been a really rough couple of days for you," I drawled, rolling my eyes. I was a big eye-roller when I was a teenager. And always had something smartass to say. I had to keep remembering to play my part.

"I didn't want to do this job, kid. This is not what I do. But let's just say... it was me, or it was someone a lot worse. So I stepped in."

"So, what? I'm supposed to be thankful that you kidnapped me?"

"I'm saying the devil you know is better than the one you don't. Especially in this situation."

"But it is still a devil," I shot back, watching him over the rim of my glass as I took another sip.

"Let's just hope your father works things out quickly."

My father did nothing quickly. Except blow money he didn't have.

"Can't fucking figure out why he isn't looking for you yet."

"He wouldn't know I was missing until I didn't show up to work on Monday."

"So, what, you don't go home at night?"

This was where I needed to be careful.

"I go home. Sometimes he notices, sometimes he doesn't," I told him. I didn't have to say I went back to his home, my childhood home.

"So you can sneak down to Cape May, and drink a bottle of whiskey, and he is none the wiser, huh?"

"Pretty much."

"Don't know if I should say you're lucky, or I'm sorry you've got such a shitty dad."

"Would be silly coming from someone with an asshole for a father too," I told him.

"Careful with that, hellcat," he warned, but he didn't disagree with me. Interesting.

"Well, only shitty people demand kidnappings, right?"

"And only shitty ones carry them out?" he added, brow raising.

"You said it, not me."

"I'll let that slide. Because you're a kid. And you're pissed. But let me offer you a word of warning here, Gigi," he said, leaning forward, resting his forearms on his thighs. Even hunched forward, he was massive. "You don't say shit like that about the men I associate with. Not if you want to keep your tongue."

"Are you... threatening me?"

"I'm warning you," he corrected. "That some of these men won't bother to warn you. So, for your own sake, be careful with all that sass. I might be able to brush it off as idiotic adolescence. Others won't be so understanding. Don't be stupid, Gigi."

Don't be stupid, Gigi.

I had a feeling that would be a good motto.

It seemed like fair advice.

You know, if only I would have followed it...

Chapter Five

Lorenzo

She wasn't fooling me.

Those eyes of hers, they were always looking for an exit, a way out.

Whether that was a dumbbell to the dome and a fire escape to run down, or a man to schmooze her way to freedom, she was not just sitting pretty like she wanted me to believe.

Not even after three days of finding no escape.

There was one, of course. You didn't get a pass for building codes just because your family took back control of most of the construction unions a decade before. There had to be several exits from the building, and each apartment in it.

My place was no exception.

But just because they existed didn't mean they were common knowledge, or that you could find them without knowing where to look.

Call it a safety measure.

Call me paranoid, even.

But the fire escape was behind a false storage case in my master closet. You reached in, grabbed a handle in the back, and the whole thing popped open. Then you pulled up the blackout shade, and there the window was. And right outside was the fire escape that went both up and down.

It didn't matter how much sneaking around she did—and I slept lightly enough to know she did her fair amount—she was never going to find it. She would give up and decide I had greased the right palms in the city to avoid having another entrance to my apartment. And because she'd never seen the outside of the building, she had no reason to doubt that.

Aside from the sneaking around, she hadn't been as much of an inconvenience as I had worried. She kicked around in the living room in the mornings, eating whatever I ordered, or one of the guards brought up. She watched TV. Or, rather, she put the TV on, then stared blankly out the window. When I had to run out, the guards said she went back into her room, locking the door. They had no idea what she did in there.

And she only seemed to come back out when she heard me return.

I didn't know if she distrusted my men, or trusted me. And I shouldn't have been pleased at the prospect of the latter.

When I got back, she came out dressed in one of the new outfits I'd had the men pick up for her, asked what we were ordering for dinner, then immediately told me what a shitty choice I'd made before suggesting something else.

When the food came, we tended to fall into some conversation while we ate.

Usually with her going off on a diatribe about the family, the mafia in general, and people stepping on the little guy; always managing to circle back to how kidnapping and false imprisonment were wrong.

She did all of this with a lifted chin and unnerving eye contact. Apparently, like her father, she had a temper on her, one that flared up unexpectedly and with vengeance. But she also seemed capable of dousing the flames without batting an eye, turning the conversation back to something more generic. About life. About the city. About the bakery she'd been working in since she was even younger.

It was in those moments that the reality seemed to slip away. She wasn't just some victim. I wasn't just her attacker.

And it was in those moments, too, that it got easier to forget that she was a kid. There were just ways she said things, observations about life, that she made that made her seem older, more mature.

And then, of course, I had to berate myself for thinking that shit because it was fucked. I refused to be that dickhead pedo who claimed "she was mature for her age." Or some other bullshit like that.

"Isn't Pearl Jam a little before your time?" I asked on the fourth night over Chinese that we were eating right out of the containers.

"And Frank Sinatra isn't before yours?" she shot back, referencing my knee-jerk response to the typical favorite singer question.

"Fair enough," I agreed. "Little emo of you too, no?"

"Please. Like Sinatra isn't the biggest cliché ever. Especially being who you are."

"And what am I, kid?" I shot back, daring her to say it. But she was too quick for her own good, refusing to be baited. When she wanted to dress me down with an observation about my lifestyle, she did so on her own, not because I goaded her to do it.

"Italian," she decided, giving me a saucy brow raise.

"Nice recovery."

"I do my best," she agreed, waving her chopsticks in the air. "So am I going to have to suffer through another of your awful movie choices, or can I pick this time?" she asked.

I hadn't been one for TV for a long time. In fact, I'd spent more time in my own apartment since she'd shown up than I had in months.

Before Gigi, I didn't remember the last time I watched a single movie, let alone one every single night.

She was right, though.

I had always been the kind to control the remote. And she'd sat valiantly through several lengthy action and war dramas that she clearly didn't enjoy.

"It better not be some fucking rom-com, kid," I warned her, tossing the remote in her direction.

"Don't insult me," she said, clicking through the options. "Okay this one. This was my favorite when I was in... when I first saw it," she said, and I didn't miss the slip, but couldn't figure out what—if anything—it meant.

"*Arrival*," I read before she clicked play. "What's it about?"

"First encounters with aliens."

"Seriously?" I asked, smirking. "You're a nerd, huh?"

"I just think that movies should be an escape. Watching sad war movies based on real events is depressing. I'd rather watch a bunch of people try to figure out how to speak to aliens."

"Or watch people fight with lightsabers? Or go on a quest for a special ring?"

"Careful," she said, pointing her chopsticks at me. "You might have taken all the knives away, but I'm pretty sure one of these bad boys can go straight through the eye and into the brain." The way she said it made me think she'd given the action some thought, before ultimately deciding she wasn't capable of that.

I shouldn't have found the idea of a—at the very least—chopstick lobotomy charming. But there was no denying the smile that tugged at my lips.

I liked her spirit.

It would have been easy, I imagined, to fall into the hopelessness of this situation. As the days passed and her father didn't seem to be worried about her or looking for her—turning up every rock in the city to find her.

But aside from the occasional rants, she had just settled in.

Almost like she didn't expect her father to look for her at all. Or to pay up even if he did know where she was and why she was taken.

That thought kept me awake at night, staring up at my ceiling, realizing that even my asshole father would have noticed me missing, and immediately moved heaven and earth to find me. If for no other reason, than his pride.

It said a lot about Leon that he wasn't missing his little girl.

It said more about her that she knew exactly what to expect from her father. And didn't even seem worked up about it.

I hated to think what my father would do—or order me to do—if Leon didn't end up giving a fuck about his daughter. Well, I knew I'd be tasked with killing Leon. But what would happen to Giana, this woman who had been kidnapped, so she couldn't exactly be set free?

"Hey, no," she snapped a couple moments later, shooting forward in her seat to smack my hand as I reached for a piece of sweet & sour chicken. "You're a sauce hog," she informed me.

"There's a whole pint of sauce," I reminded her.

"And you will somehow manage to use a third of that on one piece of chicken."

"You believe this shit?" I asked, looking at Christopher at the door. "I'm being rationed in my own fucking home."

"Don't talk to him. I'm this close to getting him on my side," Gigi claimed, squeezing her chopsticks close together.

Chris and I shared a look, both of us knowing it was family over everything. Always has been, always will be. But it was cute that she thought there was any way around that.

While she was distracted, I reached for the chicken, going to dip it, and dropping the whole fucking thing in the sauce.

When I glanced up, she was sending me the most *I told you so* look I'd ever seen in my life.

It was fucked up, but it was nice to have someone around. Sure, there were women in and out of my life. Always more out than in, usually not even coming into my space. The fewer people you invited into your personal space when you did the kind of shit I did for a living, the better. Your chances of trusting the wrong person, walking away, and having them plant a bug while you were in the bathroom were nil if you always went to their place to fuck. So, I hadn't really known what it was like to share a space with a person since I lived at home.

It was surprisingly nice not to be alone when you came home. And ate dinner. And watched TV.

And I was finding I was delegating work more and more to spend time in my apartment. I tried to justify it as "needing to keep an eye on Gigi," even if I knew damn well that was bullshit.

A couple hours later, I was forced to admit she had solid movie choices, that I was a sauce hog, and that the dessert I ordered was, apparently, "shit."

"Really, it's not your fault. You only thought it was good because you've never had a decent Tartufo."

"And you can make a better one?" I challenged.

"Yes. I've been making them for the bakery since I was fourteen."

"So, what, three years makes you an expert? What?" I asked when her eyes went round, like I'd said something wrong.

"Nothing. It's nothing. Look, you don't want to believe me, fine. If you want to believe me, go down to the bakery and get some for yourself."

"That wouldn't prove anything, if you weren't there to make them."

"Yes, well, I can't be there right now, can I?" she shot back, tone going cool. "Will I ever be able to go back?" she asked, point-blank.

"We are doing everything in our power to make that happen."

"No, actually, you're not. If you were doing everything in your power, you would call off your guard, and let me walk out of here. You are doing everything in your power to *keep* me here. You can't play the victim when you're the fucking bad guy," she spat at me.

"Look I—"

"He's here," Christopher said, cutting off my response, a response that was likely only going to lead to a bigger blow up.

I wasn't supposed to linger with Gigi eating dinner and watching movies and bullshitting. I was supposed to grab a quick bite, shoo her into her room, then have Gio Morelli over to talk about some deal his family—another of the Five Families—were making with the local cartel, that my father thought might piss on his deal with the Russians. It was always something. And usually blown out of proportion.

"Christopher, bring Gio up," I demanded, reaching for a couple of the cartons of food. "Go to your room," I demanded as I carried cartons to the fridge, tucking them inside.

I don't know why she grabbed for the rest of the cartons, if it was some knee-jerk reaction from being told to help clear the table in childhood. She actually looked pissed when she handed them to me.

"Why?" she asked, snatching her hand back when my fingers brushed her, like touching me made her feel slimy. Which, I guess, was fair, given the situation. "I've seen you and a bunch of your minions already."

Minions.

"Just go to your fucking room, Gigi," I demanded, no heat in my words, but she didn't like them anyway, her chin angling up, her jaw getting tight, her arms crossing over her chest.

"You're going to have to make me," she told me, daring me to do it, wanting more reasons to dislike me.

I was turning back from the fridge to do just that when the doors chimed as they slid open, bringing my guest in.

Gio was a couple years younger than me, tall, a bit more solidly built thanks to his borderline obsession with the gym. Dark brown hair, brown eyes. He had a pretty boy look about him—dimples and all—that women tended to find charming. Gio knew this. And enjoyed the benefits as much as any man would in his position.

"Lorenzo, I didn't know you had a girl," he observed, eyes moving over Giana.

"Girl being the operative word, Gio," I snapped. "She's a kid. Stop eye-fucking her," I demanded, watching as his brows furrowed as he glanced back at Giana again before looking at me.

"If you say so, Enz. What's your name, sweetheart?"

"Gigi," Giana supplied easily, seemingly taken aback by his smile.

"Gigi, I'm Gio. Giovani Morelli," he supplied. Gio was never the sort to lie low, or downplay his position in one of the Five Families. He liked when people knew who he was, and how he was connected.

"Gio," she repeated, giving him a small smile. "And what do you do, Gio?"

"Me? I'm a brick layer," he supplied, making me roll my eyes.

"What? Like... construction?" Gigi asked innocently.

"Something like that," Gio agreed, nodding, dimples out.

It was *nothing* like that.

Gio laid bricks, alright.

Of the cocaine variety.

To stock brokers and white-collar businessmen of all sorts. Federal judges. The goddamn chief of police.

"Gigi, you'll excuse us for a minute," I told her, leading Gio away, down the hall into the gym.

"Don't worry. I'm not asking," he said, shaking his head, waving an arm out toward the main area.

"Good. Because I wasn't going to tell you anyway," I told him, getting a chuckle out of him because we both knew how it worked. As a whole, the Costas minded their own business, as did the Morellis, even the D'Onofrios to an extent. It was the Espositos and Lombardis that were always trying to figure out the angles of the other families.

"Your old man, all due respect, you know I got love for your family, but he needs to calm the fuck down with the accusations already. Like we are going around trying to fuck with his business. We needed to make a deal with the cartels to get the shit shipped in. Has nothing to do with the fucking Russians or the Russians importing. They are coming in from a completely different direction with a completely different product. I don't see the issue. I know I'm being a little frank with you, but if we let our old men hash this out with veiled threats and subtlety, shit would go on for a year or two. You and me, we can handle this shit like adults in ten minutes, yeah?"

And that was why I liked Gio, why I called him instead of his father to talk about the deal with the cartel and the issue—that was no issue at all—with the Russians. Gio Sr. would have taken offense, would have made a big deal about it. The next thing we'd know, all the families would be involved, and something that could have been handled in ten minutes—as he said—would take months or years. All the while, tensions flared and money was lost. No one wanted that. Gio Jr. and I understood that.

"You tell me the supply chain, leaving out a couple vital details because I respect your right to keep that to yourself, and I will convince my father that there is no conflict of interest," I agreed, nodding.

Five minutes later, we emerged from the gym, making our way into the living space where Giana was brewing a pot of coffee.

"Oh, Gio, hold up. I have a package for you," I told him.

"Yeah, yeah. Take your time. I will be over here saying goodbye to Little Gigi. Maybe trying to convince her to hook me up with some of that coffee to go."

I was gone all of two minutes.

But when I walked back out, the air in the living space felt thick, tense. My gaze went immediately to Giana, finding her shoulders tight, back straight, eyes wide and flighty.

Beside her, Gio seemed calm as ever, holding a mug of coffee in his hands.

Not wanting to start shit with Gio if there was no shit to start, I handed off the package, watched him leave, then turned back to Giana.

"What happened?"

"What? Nothing." She said it too fast. Her words were too choked. Something happened in those two minutes. And I needed to know what.

"Bullshit, Gigi," I told her, moving into the kitchen space, grabbing one of the mugs she had set out, pouring a cup. "What did he say to you?"

"Nothing of consequence," she insisted, looking away, busying herself by wiping down the counter.

Nothing of consequence.

There it was again.

A turn of phrase I didn't expect out of someone her age.

I shook off that thought, though, knowing I needed to focus on whatever Gio had said to make her so uncomfortable. Especially because I didn't typically think of Gio as someone who made women—or girls—feel that way.

"Giana, I walked away and you were calm. I came back, you were pale and stiff. He said something. What was it?"

"It doesn't matter what he said. Or didn't say."

"It matters to me."

"I can't imagine why. I'm a prisoner here, remember?" she snapped.

"If for no other reason than this is my home. And if someone is made to feel uncomfortable inside it, that is disrespectful to me."

"Right. Only you get to do that," she told me, brows lifting. "And heaven forbid anyone dares disrespect the Great Lorenzo Costa," she mocked, moving out of the kitchen.

"Giana," I snapped, reaching out, grabbing her arm, turning her back, watching as her eyes flared.

"Oh, right," she said, recovering, ice slipping into her tone. "I am just a lowly inmate here. May I please go back to my cell now, warden?" she asked, actually fluttering her lashes at me while the venom slipped from between her lips. "Or are you not done manhandling me yet?" she added, making my hand drop her arm like it'd caught fire, not liking that insinuation. That I would hurt her.

With that, she glared at me for another second, then stormed off, slamming her door as she went.

My gaze shifted to Chris who had moved back into his position in front of the elevator.

"The fuck did I do?" I asked, shaking my head, at a loss.

To that, he shrugged.

"Kids," he said, shaking his head.

Yeah, maybe that was it.

She was just acting her age.

Chapter Six

Giana

"What's your game, sweetheart?" Gio asked as soon as Lorenzo disappeared down the hall, moving in closer, so we could speak privately.

"I don't know what you're talking about," I insisted, but felt my stomach tightening. Because something about this man said he could see right through me.

"You can flutter your eyes and you can play the innocent card. But you and I know you're no kid, Gigi. You're twenty if you're a day. And I just can't figure out why you would play that hand."

On the one hand, I felt like there wasn't a single person in this world I could trust. On the other, something inside me said that this man would only make things worse for me if I lied to him.

So I gave him the most comfortable truth I could.

"I am trying to make it so they won't kill me," I admitted, expecting those words to have some sort of impact on Gio. But nothing crossed his face at them.

"Alright," he said, nodding.

"Alright?" I repeated, spine straightening.

"Your business is your business, sweetheart. I dunno what you did. I don't need to know. Way I see it, you've got a right to use whatever you got to plead for your life. But can I give you a little tip?"

"Sure."

"If that kid card fails, the woman card might get you even further. You're just Lorenzo's type."

"I'm not going to whore myself out to live," I shot back, voice raising.

"Just saying, sweetheart. You got options."

"Are you going to tell Lorenzo?"

"Not if you don't make me."

"How would I make you?"

"Don't know yet."

"That's not exactly helpful."

"Tough shit, *kid*," he said, smirking, smile just big enough to make his dimple peak through. "Don't like the uncertainty, I recommend not getting yourself involved with the family," he told me.

"I didn't get myself involved in anything. My father did."

"Little tip, babe," he said, giving me a hard look. "Stop being a victim in your own life."

Before I could snap at him that I wasn't a victim, that he didn't know what he was talking about, that Lorenzo and this family were who had turned me into a victim of kidnapping and imprisonment, Lorenzo was moving back into the main space, gaze flicking between the two of us, little vertical lines forming between his brows, making it clear my surprise and uncertainty and indignation must have been clear on my face.

And I maybe took that out on Lorenzo.

I tried to remind myself as I paced my room that it wasn't exactly misplaced, though, since I wouldn't have been put in this position if Lorenzo hadn't taken me, that I wouldn't have been annoyed with Gio, and snapped at Lorenzo. That I wouldn't be having some grandiose existential crisis as Gio's words kept playing across my mind no matter how many times I tried to fight them.

Maybe I had been so pissed because there was a sliver of truth in his words.

I had chosen this life. I had chosen to stand beside my father through all of his screw-ups. And when I was younger, of course, I had no choice. My mother was gone. My father was all I had in the world. And his immediate financial security impacted my life as well. If he didn't keep the bakery running, we would lose it. And the house. And any form of safety I had known.

But as I got older, after I was of-age, especially, staying and dealing with the constant stress, being shit on by a man who didn't appreciate all the work I was putting in to keep his family business running, to keep his head above water, did sort of make me a part of my own victimhood, didn't it?

I chose to go there every day, to be scolded, to have my decisions constantly undermined. I took on the stress that he created.

Those were all conscious decisions I made.

So, yes, I had been a victim in some respects.

And I had made myself that.

The family business was important to me. I had spent so much of my childhood there in that little bakery, learning my fractions as I stood on a stool beside my grandmother who explained it to me with measuring spoons and cups. I was taught patience watching each attempt at chocolate soufflé either burn or refuse to rise before I finally got it right. I learned about community in the connections made with repeat customers. I found pride in working with my hands, in keeping the morale up in the shop even in the worst of times.

And my grandfather wanted me to keep it in the family.

I felt like there wasn't a choice.

But there was.

Even if it was a bitter pill to swallow to admit that I had chosen my own miseries in life. Yes, even up to and including parts of this kidnapping. After all, had I moved across the country when there had been an urge to do so the day I turned eighteen, no one in the New York mafia would have been able to find and kidnap me to use against my father in the first place.

Though the actual kidnapping and imprisonment? I refused to own that. It wasn't my fault that these men thought women could be used as pawns in a power struggle or monetary negotiations.

That said, as the days were going on, I was starting to worry that maybe there would be no terms agreed to. What then? If my father didn't—couldn't—pay?

He would be killed, surely.

I was under no delusions about these men. As kind as Lorenzo had been to me, as a whole, he was absolutely capable of murdering my father in cold blood.

But if he was killed, what would happen to me? Would they let me go, only to strap me with the same shitty deal they had given my father? Always wanting more? Never letting me breathe easy?

Or would they cut their losses, make an example of me as well to anyone else who had daughters that could be used against their fathers?

I wasn't sure.

And, quite frankly, neither option sounded like something I wanted.

Sure, life was always better than death. But in this case, only very slightly. A lifetime personally indebted to the mafia sounded like hell on earth. It would no longer be something that affected me, but from a distance. It would be there right up in my face every time. And the threats I knew my father faced would be directed to me instead. Maybe even by this man who had been kind to me while he imprisoned me in his home.

For a couple days there, I had somehow started to view this entire situation like some sort of retreat, some vacation from my normal life.

I was in a penthouse apartment with every luxury afforded to me. Clothes were bought for me. Food was brought to me. And none of it cost me anything. The sheets were buttery against my skin. The products in the bathroom were more than I could ever afford, no matter how much I tried to trim my already thin budget.

And, to be honest, it was unexpectedly nice to share some time with another person.

Sure, I spent all my days with people: bakers and customers and Liane and even my father.

But my nights were quiet. And, if I would let myself admit it, lonely. I didn't remember the last time I shared a meal with someone. Watched a movie with someone. Made coffee for someone.

It had been nice, in a twisted way, to play house. To let myself forget that I was supposed to be railing against this, not settling into it.

I had to get myself the hell out of this situation.

And if my father didn't make it, I had to find a way to deal with this damn family too. I wasn't going to spend my whole life under their thumb, having them squeeze more money out of me every year for the rest of my life.

I was going to get out of this.

One way or another.

"Oh, hey there, sweetheart," a new guard called to me the following morning, sitting on the couch with a newspaper instead of standing guard at the elevator like I knew he was supposed to be. "I was told you would be done sulking eventually."

"Sulking?" I hissed, teeth clenching. "He said I was sulking?"

"That was the word he used," the guard agreed, giving me a nod.

I recognized him.

He was one of the guys standing around when I'd been moved from one trunk to the other. Not Anthony, the other one. I don't think I caught his name. But I remembered he'd been wearing a giant belt buckle in the shape of a lion. This morning, the lion was replaced with a vintage ship and hula girls.

"Well, he's an asshole," I declared, moving off into the kitchen, going for the coffee pot.

"He sure is. A lovely young lady like you would never sulk, right?" the guard asked, sarcasm heavy in his voice.

"Lovely young ladies like me don't typically find themselves kidnapped and held for ransom, so whatever reactions we have to said situation, we are justified. Who are you? Where is Christopher?"

"Chris has other jobs some days. So you're stuck with me. Emilio," he clarified when I raised a brow.

"Emilio. So, are you an asshole like your boss too?"

"Depends. I was the one who sent him to pick you up in the first place."

"So that is a yes."

"But I went to Lorenzo because the man who was initially supposed to pick you up is the most vicious bastard I've ever met in my life. And I don't think I need to tell you this, but I have known a lot of vicious bastards in my line of work."

"So, what, I'm supposed to thank you? Gee, thanks so much for sending the slightly better of two evils to rip me out of bed, throw me in a trunk, and hold me captive."

To that, I got a small chuckle, like this guy didn't let much get to him. "You know, Lorenzo didn't say you had such a mouth on you."

"No? Because he calls me hellcat. To my face."

"And you didn't do anything to deserve that name, huh?"

"Oh, I deserved it alright. And he has no idea how much worse I can be."

"But now you're all pissy at him, so he's about to find out, right? I know the deal. I have sisters."

"And they condone you being a part of kidnapping other girls?"

"Let's just say this is an isolated incident. We don't snatch women or girls off the streets in this family."

"Just me then. What did I ever do to be so lucky?"

"Look, we finally heard from your old man today. Hopefully, everyone can come to an understanding. And then you can go back to your life."

This was the first time they'd heard from my dad?

That was, well, unsettling. At best. He hadn't noticed I wasn't around? He hadn't thought to look for me? To go down to Cape May to check the house? Notice that all my stuff was still there, but I wasn't?

It was sobering to realize how unimportant you were in your only surviving parent's life.

"I don't know if I believe I will be allowed to go back."

"If your father complies, you will go back. It's not exactly good for our PR if we start murdering random girls for the sins of their fathers."

"Right. Just roughing up and kidnapping and holding them against their will then."

"The way I heard it, you hit your own head," Emilio said, smirking at the mental image Lorenzo must have put there.

"I think it says a lot about you that you find it funny that I was so terrified that I was going to be raped and murdered, I hurt myself while I tried to escape that fate."

"I guess Lorenzo was wrong," Emilio said, letting the sentence hang, waiting for me to take the bait.

And, damn it, I did. "About what?"

"You getting out of that pissy mood," he said, smiling as he brushed past me to make coffee.

"I know you think you are so—" I started, tailing off when I heard the familiar whoosh of the elevator.

My gaze immediately went there. And, damn it, there was something dangerously close to anticipation fluttering through my stomach.

And not the bad sort of anticipation either. Though, as the doors slid open, and Lorenzo stepped out—shoulders tense, jaw so tight that a muscle ticked there, eyes blazing—I realized maybe it should have been the bad sort of anticipation working its way through my body.

My pulse quickened as his gaze turned to me, that anger lapping higher and higher.

"Fuck off, Emilio," he growled, voice even lower than it usually was.

It shouldn't have sounded sexy, not when he was so pissed off, but there was no mistaking it was. It shivered across my nerve endings, making my stomach feel a little wobbly as those green eyes pinned me.

"You fucking lied to me," he growled, the sound barely able to make its way out from between his clenched teeth.

"And I'm out," Emilio said, nearly breaking his mug he set it down so fast on his way out of the kitchen, then down the elevator.

I should have been worried as the doors slid closed, taking Emilio away, leaving me alone with a livid Lorenzo.

"I haven't lied to you," I told him, arching my chin up.

"You fucking lied right to my face," he snapped, fist slamming down on the counter, making my body jolt, the coffee sloshing out of the cup and onto my hands, making me nearly drop the mug on the floor.

Carefully, I placed it on the counter instead, wiping my hands on my pants.

"What did I lie to you about?" I asked, proud of how even my voice sounded even though my lower lip felt like it was trembling.

I'd known fear in my life.

I'd known fear at the hands of men.

And the cold, slithering sensation in my stomach made my throat feel tight, made my palms feel sweaty, made the muscles in my legs start to quiver.

"You let me think you were a fucking *teenager*," he growled, forcing his hands out of fists, pressing his palms against the counter, making his shoulders hunch forward.

"I didn't lie to you. You assumed," I reminded him, shrugging, trying to act a lot more casual than I felt while two clashing emotions—fear and desire —fought for dominance in my system.

The fear, I understood.

The desire, not so much.

Maybe it was some cavewoman instinct rearing its misogynistic head. My genes wanted the alpha male of the pack. And, let's face it, when a powerful man like Lorenzo Costa was angry, he was about as alpha as a man could get without bashing someone over the head with a club.

"A lie of omission is still a fucking lie, Giana."

"What the hell does it matter how old I am anyway?" I snapped, my own temper flaring.

"What does it matter?" he asked, tone deceptively calm. "Because you've been walking your ass around my place, throwing around all that sass and all that sweet, and you have made me feel like a fucking creep for noticing it."

"You're a creep for noticing I'm here?"

"I was a creep for fucking liking it," he snapped, straightening, moving around the counter.

"You're not making any sense, Lorenzo," I told him shrugging, even as he moved into my space, toes practically touching mine.

"You want me to make it more fucking clear for you?"

"That would be nice," I agreed.

I wouldn't have agreed had I known what was to come.

Or, at least, that was what I tried to tell myself. Because anything else would have been insane. Ridiculous.

One second, there was a couple feet of space between us.

The next, his chest was crushed to mine, his hand raised, grabbing the side of my neck, pulling me in as his lips crashed down on mine.

He kissed like he lived.

Dominant.

Demanding.

Hard.

My initial shocked gasp turned into a ragged moan as his hand slid from my neck and up into my hair, curling, pulling, the pain and pleasure combination spreading from my scalp and lower. Much lower.

But before my hands could raise from their shocked position against his chest—because, surely, I was *going* to push him away, right?—he pulled away as quickly as he had moved in, leaving my body buzzing, my mind swirling.

My eyelids fluttered open, finding him staring down at me, gaze intense.

"That fucking clear enough?" he growled, turning suddenly, and storming away.

I stood there for what can only be called an embarrassingly long time, my legs shaking, but this time for a reason that had nothing to do with fear.

Unless the growing concern about why there was this oppressive pressure on my lower stomach, this clawing need inside, counted.

But, with a couple deep breaths, I managed to get my brain to think through the fog of desire.

When it did, though, I realized two things.

Lorenzo was in his room, if the door slam was anything to go by.

And there was no guard at the elevator.

As soon as the thoughts sank in, I was across the floor, pressing my finger desperately into the call button, holding my breath as I heard the swish of the car moving up, cringing when the doors opened, and the familiar ding sounded.

I threw myself into the elevator, jabbing my finger into the button, waiting for the doors to slide closed.

They did.

Just as I heard Lorenzo's voice.

"Fuck."

But it was too late.

The doors were closed.

I was part of the way to freedom.

I took a couple slow, deep breaths as the elevator moved downward, preparing myself to run.

I was not, by anyone's standards, an athlete. The idea of running if some part of me wasn't on fire, or I wasn't being chased by an angry flock of geese, sounded downright idiotic.

That said, running to escape a chasing made member of the New York mafia—and maybe the weird desire I felt toward him—seemed like a great effing idea.

The car jolted, making my stomach drop. Then the doors were opening, and I was flying.

I had ridiculously short legs, but they were working for me as I darted across the lobby, as I charged through the front door, making the doorman hiss and jump back as I made my way out onto the street.

I didn't pause to try to look around, to take in my location. I just ran blindly, knowing that I could get lost just about anywhere in a city as populated as this as long as I could get as far away as fast as possible.

I had no direction.

No money.

No ID.

No *shoes*.

And the latter realization made my stomach drop as I threw myself around a corner, running up the next block, considering all of the various bodily fluids—as well as other liquids—my poor soles were likely soaking up with each passing step.

I had nowhere to go, not really, but anywhere was better than at the mercy of the mafia. And my father's whims.

I rushed down another side street, trying to lower the chances of him finding my path.

My thighs screamed. My lungs ached. Sweat reminded me that while yoga pants and a lightweight sweatshirt were perfectly acceptable for living inside a penthouse apartment with the air conditioning set to glacier, it was not great for summer in a city where the tall buildings blocked anything even resembling a breeze.

I made it up another block before I slowed my pace, knowing that I would be less noticeable if I was moving with the pace of the foot traffic. I carefully grabbed a pair of flip-flops from a street vender when he turned his back, rushing off before anyone suspected a thing, trying not to let guilt overwhelm me. Sometimes you had to do what you had to do to survive. Even steal shoes, so your feet didn't get bloodied and blistered from walking barefoot through the city.

On a whim, I waited at the street for the light to change, reaching down to pull up my sweatshirt, deciding the tank top underneath would have to do, wrapping my sweatshirt around my waist as my gaze flicked around, trying to spot an exceptionally tall and stupidly handsome man rushing down the streets looking for me. Or his car with its very familiar trunk. I imagined by now, he had his original one back.

My stomach was in knots as I moved forward with the crowd, sure hands were going to reach out and grab me from behind, carry me kicking and screaming back to the penthouse. Or maybe I would be moved, transferred to some basement somewhere with a bucket as a bathroom and someone much worse than Lorenzo looking after me. Maybe even that guy that Emilio casually mentioned.

No.

That couldn't happen.

I was free.

Getting free was the hard part.

Staying free would be the easy part.

At least that was the theory.

The further I got away, the more I realized I had very little chance of staying away without, at least, some money.

I wasn't stupid enough to go back to my apartment. Even if I did, I didn't have a key anywhere. It would be just as dumb to go to my father's place.

I had no friends to speak of.

Besides perhaps Liane at the bakery counter.

She was probably my best bet, but she was old and fragile. And I didn't want to subject her to my shitstorm of a situation.

What did that leave me with?

Just the bakery.

That was high-risk as well.

Certainly right now, directly after my escape, it was the worst risk.

But maybe later, when it was closed, armed with the code to the security system, I could dip inside. I could grab whatever money was in the safe. Then I would have enough to run, to get lost in a way that no one could ever find me.

I walked for another half an hour, trying to come up with other ideas that didn't involve mugging someone for whatever they might have in their wallets, but I found myself completely at a loss.

So the bakery it was.

I just had to wait for dark.

Taking a deep breath, I changed directions, taking myself toward the bakery, knowing that, from where I was, it would take me at least an hour and a half to walk there. Then I could hide out in the alley until it was safe, until I was sure that there was no one there.

Night brought no respite from the heat. If anything, the humidity rose instead, making my tank top stick to my back, my hair getting damp.

The foul stench of the contents of the dumpster had woven itself into the fabric of my clothing, the strands of my hair. I was sure I would never be able to wash the scent from my skin.

But that was a problem for another time.

I saw the bustle of closing. Pete, the bakery's all-around helping hand, brought out the trash, missing me squatting behind the pile of cardboard boxes beside it. He walked Liane out the side door, where she paused long enough to see to the security system before the two of them made their way down the alley and toward their respective apartments.

I don't know how long I wasted after that, paranoia freezing me with uncertainty before I finally got up the nerve to stand, my legs seized with pins and needles as I inched my way to the back door, plugging in the code, wincing at the chime as it opened.

When no one came running out to grab me, I moved inside, closing the door behind me, inching through the back hall, moving into the office, feeling every bit like the criminal instead of someone who could frequently be found in this very bakery, in this very office, well after closing on any given evening.

My pulse was pounding in my temples, in my throat, as I squatted down in front of the safe, feeling my sweaty fingers slide across the touchpad as I plugged in the code.

I reached in, the clumsiest of thieves, knocking half the cash on the floor before grabbing a wad of it, shoving the rest back in, pocketing the money, and locking it back up.

My father rarely checked the books.

And with me missing, there would be less pressure for the money.

I would get safe, then contact my father about watching his back as well, as I had no idea what these men were capable of, if the leverage of my captivity was taken away from them.

With that, I grabbed a couple pastries, and made my way back out.

Paranoia had me constantly looking over my shoulder as I made my way through the city, looking for the bus stop that might take me out of town.

As I walked, I realized a few things.

The cash would run out quickly.

And I had no way to make more.

Not without IDs.

Or my credit cards.

Gut churning, I decided at the first stop, I would make a call to Penny in Cape May, ask her to go and collect my things from the house. I might be able to convince her to move my car as well, even though I knew her vision wasn't great, which was why she didn't personally drive.

If I could go to her house to pick them up, there was no risk of being seen, of being caught, if Lorenzo sent men to Cape May to look for me.

Decision made, I ate my pastries, regretting it immediately after the sugar settled, mixing with the fear and uncertainty, making nausea rise up my throat as I sat in the terminal for several hours, waiting for the next bus out of town in the direction I was heading.

At the first stop, I managed to walk somewhere to grab a burner phone, put minutes on it to make the call I knew I needed to. Even if my throat felt tight at involving Penny in any of this.

If you drove directly there, the drive was just about two and a half hours, but on the bus, it took over six and a half with stops, putting me in Cape May the following morning.

I made my way through the streets of Downtown with my stomach in knots, jumping at shadows, searching faces for anyone who didn't seem like they belonged. Men in suits. People scanning crowds looking for me.

I took two minutes to pop into a coffee shop, exhaustion making my eyelids puffy and my eyes unfocused. But I couldn't just get a room in town. I knew I had to drive out, preferably get out of New Jersey as a whole, put another state between myself and the mafia, so I would need the caffeine to keep me going.

Finally, I made my way toward Penny's, feeling a small, tired smile tug at my lips at her prized snowball bushes overflowing the sweet white picket fence in an array of pinks and purples, whites and blues. She was equally miffed and satisfied every summer when some bold tourist would walk past, snapping off a cutting to take along with them.

Penny's house was everything I loved about this town. The pretty old Late Victorian style home with its shingle-covered gable roof, turrets, and open front porch with its rows of spindles. The house itself was a light green, the accents a soft yellow. It was cotton-candy sweet and meticulously kept despite Penny's advancing age.

I could see my car parked on the street, my first hint at true freedom.

Ten more minutes.

I could grab my stuff, tuck it away, and be gone.

All of this nightmare would be behind me.

As I made my way up the front path, I chose to ignore the tiny twisting sensation of regret in my stomach.

Because it made no sense.

I had nothing to regret.

I'd done nothing wrong.

In fact, I had, arguably, done everything right.

You know, except not resisting that kiss. Except actively participating in that kiss. Except maybe allowing it to replay in my head a few times on the ride down to Cape May.

But only a few times, mind you.

And I tried my best to reexamine it rationally.

The only reason I had a physical reaction was the shock mixed with Lorenzo's alpha-ness, and the fact that I hadn't been close to a man in longer than I cared to admit. My life had been about work. My precious free time was typically spent running errands or trying to catch up on sleep. Or, more often lately, looking for ways to trim excess so there was always more money for my father to funnel to the Costa family.

That was all it was.

Biological.

Nothing to beat myself up over.

Certainly nothing to waste any more precious time thinking about.

That was what I was telling myself as I made my way to the front door, knocking on the frame a few times. Then again, louder.

Penny, though she would never admit it, was getting just the tiniest bit hard of hearing.

When there was no response, I checked the handle, feeling it open in my hand.

"Penny?" I called, stepping inside, closing the door, smelling Penny's familiar potpourri fresh flower scent, something that had never changed my entire life. Likely not hers, either. "Penny, where are you?" I called, moving through the front hall and into the kitchen where you could usually find her making her hundredth cup of tea for the day.

But nothing.

Of course, I hadn't told her the exact time I would get there since all I could do was give a rough estimate.

She was probably up in her room, maybe taking a nap.

I checked the lower floor for my possible belongings, but they weren't around.

On a small sigh, I made my way up the stairs to the darker upper level, the only light on being a small one in the hallway.

"Penny," I called again, going toward the master bedroom at the end of the hall. "Are you here?" I added, wondering if she had slipped out to grab something to eat or something.

"Afraid she's not," an all-together too familiar voice said, pitched low, as the light flicked on in the bedroom, making my heart soar upward even as my stomach plummeted. "Don't bother trying to run, Giana," Lorenzo said, moving closer, his dark eyes heavy-lidded with sleeplessness, but bright with victory. "Chris is downstairs. You won't get far. Might as well make it easy on yourself," he offered, moving closer, arm reaching out.

"Like hell," I snapped, raising my arm, flinging scalding hot coffee at him, then turning to run.

Chapter Seven

Lorenzo

The meeting with Leon Lastra had been frustrating at best.

It was painfully clear within five minutes that the man simply didn't *have* the kind of money my father wanted to squeeze out of him. Why he was so intent on bleeding a stone was completely beyond me. There were other marks, ones who owned bigger businesses, who could be convinced to pay more.

It made no sense to focus so much on such low-hanging fruit.

My father, though, was a man with a lot of ego. If he thought someone slighted him in even the smallest way, that he was being fucked over, or—worse yet—laughed at, he got petty.

Like kidnapping a man's daughter because he wanted a little extra out of someone who already struggled to pay his fees.

The Lastra Family Bakery had been a staple in their neighborhood for generations. It was successful, but no bakery was rolling in endless amounts of cash.

And I couldn't imagine what Leon Lastra could have done to piss off my father, to slight him in any way. It was painfully clear the man was a fan of the mafia, was desperate to be affiliated in a way that wasn't about being indebted to us.

They weren't a rarity, these mafia groupies.

And they came in both types.

Women who wanted to fuck a powerful man.

And men who wanted to *be* powerful.

Unfortunately for Leon, he wasn't someone who had "big earner" stamped on his forehead. He had no chance. And he was the only schmuck who didn't see that.

It didn't bother me that he was desperate and needy.

What did bother me, was the lack of genuine concern for his own daughter.

When he'd found out that we had her, that we were keeping her until he paid, he hadn't batted an eye. He hadn't begged for her back. He hadn't pleaded with us to treat her well, to let him see her, to at least speak to her.

He'd just accepted the reality.

As though she was a pawn that he was willing to sacrifice.

It shouldn't have mattered to me, his feelings toward his daughter, their obviously strained relationship. It wasn't my business. *She* wasn't my business.

But I'd had the girl in my place for just a couple of days, and I seemed to give more of a shit about her well-being than he did when he'd been with her for her entire life.

I'd even called him out on his disregard for her.

"You don't seem too concerned with Gigi's well-being," I'd observed, leaning back in my chair in the restaurant we'd met at because I knew it couldn't be bugged. Because we owned it. Because we kept guards in it twenty-four-seven so that no one could ever sneak in.

We'd learned a lot from all the wire-tapping and raids of our predecessors. None of us were planning on catching a charge because some fed overheard us talking over dinner or in our own damn living rooms.

"That girl," he said, shaking his head. "You must have your hands full with her. Always too much lip, not enough respect. "

"One might argue that those are learned traits," I shot back, annoyed.

"Psh, she's on her own."

"On her own?" I repeated, brows furrowing.

"Yeah, she's a grown-ass woman. There's no talking to her. You know how women are."

"Wait," I said, sitting up suddenly, knocking into the table as I did so, making Leon jolt. "What did you just say?"

"Women. They're more trouble than they're worth."

Women.

Not girls.

Women.

"Leon," I said, feeling my stomach knot. "How old is Giana?" I asked.

"Oh," he said, waving a hand in the air. "Twenty-two. Going on twenty-three."

"Twenty-two?" I repeated, something in me rebelling at that knowledge, unable to accept it.

"She looks younger, yeah?" he asked, nodding. "She gets that all the time. I have some assholes accusing me of abusing labor laws when they see her at work late at night. But she's an adult. And she's got a mouth on her. That she got from her mother."

Giana was a grown-ass woman.

Not even just barely legal.

Which would have still felt gross. If you fantasized about fucking the youngest woman you wouldn't go to jail for, there was something wrong with you.

But she was into her twenties.

There had been a barrier in my mind about her once I got a good look at her face, when I decided she was underage.

Anything thoughts of her physically were behind that wall.

I did think, occasionally, that parts of her personality were mature, but there was no thinking about her anatomy.

Now, though?

A wrecking ball had crashed through that wall.

And all the images of her in my home came back, the parts that had been blurred out before in crisp detail.

Mingle that beauty with the personality I was starting to appreciate, and yeah, there was a tug of desire so strong I almost got up and walked out of the restaurant right then, without having hammered out details with Leon.

As it was, I forced myself to sit through the conversation where he made excuses I'd come to expect, and I had to make a threat that he surely came to the table expecting as well.

When we left, he walked away with an "or else" that he had to deal with.

And I walked away armed with new knowledge.

And each step back to my apartment had anger bubbling up.

I didn't like being lied to in general.

But this reaction felt over the top, even for me.

I was storming into my place without thinking shit through rationally, kicking out Emilio.

And there she was.

In yoga pants that fit her round ass all too well.

With that challenge in her eyes.

With that haughty lift of her chin.

With that smart mouth her father disliked, but I always found intriguing.

Except now, I didn't just find it intriguing. Oh, no. I found it sexy as fuck.

So when she threw that sass at me, I pounced on her, not giving a thought to how it was an abuse of power, how she was trapped, how she might have let me do it just to save herself from retribution.

For a second, that fear gripped my system.

Until, of course, her lips started responding under mine.

It was still a dick move, though. And that realization made me pull away, made me rush toward my room before I could rip off her panties, lift her up on that counter, and fuck her until she was screaming out my name.

It was about five seconds too late that I realized my mistake.

I wasn't just any man.

And she wasn't just any woman.

I had left my captive unattended near an exit.

And like any good victim, when she saw a chance for escape, she took it.

I was right behind her.

She couldn't have gotten too far on those short ass legs of hers.

But by the time I broke onto the street, she was nowhere to be found.

Even after I called in Chris and Emilio, then Anthony, we got nothing. We staked out the bakery for hours, her apartment, her father's place.

It was just before the bakery closed that I realized where she was most likely to go, what her most rational next step was.

If she wanted to get away from us, she needed her shit, her IDs, her money, her car.

They were all in Cape May where she'd left them.

We were there in a couple hours, watching the house.

There was no sign of Giana, but an older lady showed up, packed up Giana's shit, put it in the trunk, then drove the car back to her own house.

It didn't take too much work to get the woman out of the house for a while with some bullshit about "winning" a free dinner at a pricey place in town, to slip in and wait for Gigi to show.

I knew she would.

Then there she was.

A part of me thought she might immediately give in.

The other part was glad when my little hellcat reared her head again, tossing burning hot coffee at me, and making a run for it.

Skin scalded, pain searing across my nerve endings, I rushed after her, grabbing her arm near the top of the stairs. But she whipped around with her free arm, slicing across my wrist with bared nails, sinking in ruthlessly, drawing blood, surprising me enough to release her. I caught up to her again at the landing, grabbing her, slamming her back against the wall, watching as those gray eyes blazed up at me, that haughty fucking chin raising, daring me to put my hands on her.

And, fuck, I wanted to put my hands on her, alright.

But not to hurt her.

At least not in any way that she wouldn't like.

"You done fighting me yet?" I asked, watching the rise and fall of her chest in that plain black tank top she had on. No bra, and the air conditioning had her nipples pebbling up under the fabric.

"Not even close, asshole," she snapped, bringing her knee up.

Luckily, if there was one move I was always prepared to defend myself against, it was a knee to the balls.

My hand shot down, grabbing her knee, yanking up, pulling it wide, pinning it against the wall.

It should have ended there.

Fighting had never been a form of fucking foreplay for me before.

But there was no denying my cock straining against the fly of my slacks, the tight grip of need in my balls.

I shifted closer, my hips moving inward, taking advantage of her vulnerable positioning, pressing my cock against her pussy.

The gasp that escaped her should have been startled, offended, fearful—anything but what it was.

Needy.

Her chest was rising and falling rapidly. There was no way was from the twenty-foot flee from the bedroom. She might have been small but she wasn't so small that such a short distance would wind her.

No.

She was breathing heavy because she wanted me almost as much as I wanted her.

Curious, I thrust my hips inward harder, making a choked whimper escape her.

A slow, satisfied smile tugged at my lips. "So what are you running from, hellcat?" I asked, thrusting inward again, watching her eyes go small as I started to drive her up, toyed with her obvious desire to feel my finger, my tongue, my cock against her wet pussy. "What I represent? Or the fact that, despite that, you still want me?"

Fire blazed in her eyes as her hands planted against my chest, shoving me backward, catching me off-guard, making me almost go flat on the stairs behind me as she rushed off the landing.

Seeing Christopher's shadow near the front door, she darted down the hall instead of out, making a beeline for the kitchen that had a door out into the small garden out back.

I got there just as her hand landed on the knob, pulling it toward her. My palm slapped down on the door, slamming it back into place, my body pressing forward, pinning her against it.

Leaning down, I placed my lips near her ear. "Are you going to answer me, baby?" I asked, my hand slipping around her body, between her thighs, feeling her hips buck back against me as her breath caught, as her hips ground down on my fingers and palm, greedy for more, even if she refused to admit it.

"Fuck you," she snapped instead, but her voice was low, needy, her whole body taut, trying to hold herself back from grinding down against me again.

"You want that, don't you?" I asked, teeth nipping into her earlobe, drawing a whimper out of her as her hips finally rubbed against me again. "Admit it," I demanded, fingers gliding upward, slipping under the waistbands of her pants and panties, then moving downward. "Or I can just find out for myself," I added, fingers gliding down her slick pussy, my cock throbbing at the idea of pushing inside her.

But not yet.

Not until she was begging for it.

My thumb moved to her clit, working her in slow, soft circles until she was rocking against me, making low, mewling noises that made me damn near lose control right then and there.

Impatient, needing to see her reaction, I grabbed her with my free hand and turned her, pushing her back against the door, waiting for her chin to lift, her gaze to find mine.

Only then did my fingers ease down, then slam inside her. I got to watch as her head fell back, as her lips parted on a quiet moan, and her eyes fluttered closed as she took a steadying breath before they opened again, pinning me, all thoughts of resistance gone.

As if her pussy wasn't telling me everything I needed to know about how she felt. She was drenched, already dripping down my palm. Her walls tighten around my fingers, shamelessly demanding more.

But I wanted the words, damnit.

She wasn't getting anything until she admitted it.

"You want more, you're going to have to ask for it," I told her, watching as her eyes slit at me, pissed, but needy—her mind and body at odds.

"Fuck you."

"Eventually, baby. Right now, we're doing this," I told her, flicking my fingers inside her, making her thighs clench together, wanting more of it. "If you will just ask for it, that is," I added, thumb doing one quick graze over her clit.

"Lorenzo..."

"Yes?" I asked, doing another little flick.

Her breath hissed out from between her teeth as her eyes got even more heavy-lidded, as her walls tightened around me again.

"Damnit," she growled, hips moving in a circle.

"One word," I told her. "Just one word and I can put you out of your misery."

"Please." It was said under her breath, a barely audible plead.

But she said it.

I heard it.

That was all that mattered.

I used my fingers to fuck her. Hard. Fast. Relentless. My lips crashed down on hers, swallowing up the hisses that turned into whimpers that became moans as I drove her upward, as my fingers curled inside her, raking up against her top wall and rubbing against her G-spot.

My teeth sank into her pouty lower lip, digging in, pulling, as my thumb swiped across her clit, keeping her body guessing, driving it up, but not giving it the consistency she needed for release.

Not yet.

Not until she was practically crying for it. My teeth released her, my tongue moving inside to toy with hers, finding her eager, desperate even. For more. For everything.

I ripped my lips from hers, my gaze focused on her, watching her eyelids flutter open, cloudy with need.

I finger-fucked her harder, faster, my thumb starting working her clit relentlessly, getting the throaty cries I so desperately needed.

"Lorenzo," she cried, fingernails digging into my arms as her walls tightened hard around me for a second before they started to spasm around my fingers as she crashed through her orgasm.

It stole her moan.

Her breath.

The strength in her legs.

Leaving her gasping, hands digging into my arms, holding herself up as the waves kept crashing.

Her forehead pressed into my chest as she could finally draw in a breath that came back out on a moan as the last wave coursed through her.

And damned if everything in me didn't want to grab her shoulder, push her to the floor, have her take out my cock, bury it in her mouth, give me some of the relief from the clawing desire I'd just given her.

But not yet.

Not even if my body felt like it was crying for relief.

She came back to her senses slowly at first, then all at once, her breathing slowing down, her grip loosening. Then she was slamming backward away from me, her chin raising, her eyes blazing again, angry that she wanted me, that I knew it, that she had responded to me just like we both knew she would.

"I guess I got my answer," I said, knowing I was goading her. What can I say? She was hot when she was pissed.

"I fucking hate you," she told me, jaw tight, lip starting to tremble with her anger as my fingers slowly slipped out of her, out of her panties and pants.

"You might hate me, baby," I said, raising my hand upward, slipping my fingers into my mouth, watching as shock gave way to desire again as I licked her taste off of them. "But your pussy loves me," I told her as my fingers left my mouth. "Now get your ass in the car," I added, taking a step back, reaching behind her to yank the door open.

"No."

"You want to play it that way?" I asked, shaking my head.

"I want you to try to make me," she told me, jaw tight. "I can make a big scene," she added, thinking she had the upper hand.

Her stubborn ass was a glutton for punishment, I realized as she opened her mouth to scream, making me slap my hand over it and grab her, yanking her around so that her back was against me, my arm anchoring around her stomach.

"This is going to happen, Gigi. Like it or fucking not. You don't have a choice in the matter. The only choice you have now is if you are going to behave, so you can ride up front like a human being, or if I need to throw you in the trunk again like spare luggage. You understand me?" I asked, waiting, feeling her body sizzle with anger. "I asked a question," I repeated, giving her a small shake.

To that, she nodded.

"You want to ride in the trunk?"

A head shake.

"Good. Then keep your fucking mouth shut when we go outside."

Really, I should have known better.

Than to take her at her word.

To think her pain in the ass self was capable of playing along. Even when she clearly had no advantage, when we all knew how this was going to play out.

The second we moved outside, she started to scream, making me drag her back inside as Chris went to grab the cuffs and the duct tape.

When I put her in the trunk, her gaze was on me, eyes fucking fuming.

I had a feeling that the second she was free, she was going to try to fucking claw my eyes out.

And I didn't want to know what it said about me that I was turned on just thinking about it.

Chapter Eight

Giana

I would never get that image out of my head.

His fingers.

His mouth.

The way he looked at me while he did it.

God, even the memory was making me need to press my thighs together to ease the aching between.

Even as I swore I hated the man.

Maybe there was some truth about the thin line between hate and love. Well, not love. Obviously. But attraction. After all, what was hotter than anger?

The car took the third hard corner in a row, making it abundantly clear that they weren't being done by mistake, rather trying to make me roll around the trunk, my arms clamped at the small of my back, making my shoulders scream.

He was trying to make a point.

He was always going to come out on top.

And, damn him, that seemed true, didn't it?

It bruised my pride to admit it, but I was no match. I wasn't a criminal. I wasn't born into this. I didn't have the skill set he'd likely learned at his father's knee. While I had been trying to help dig my father out of whatever mess he'd gotten himself into.

I didn't think like a criminal.

I didn't know how to disappear without being found.

And now?

Now, there was no way he was going to let me get away. There would be no unlocked doors. No unmanned elevators.

I was in this for the long haul.

With a man my body responded to even as my mind revolted.

I wanted to say I would cling to my hatred, that I would coddle and feed it, that there was no way I was going to let him get his hands on me again. At least not willingly.

But there was a little voice in my head whispering that I wasn't sure I would have any defenses if he looked at me with those heavy-lidded eyes, talked to me in that deep voice, said those delicious things.

It was weak and pathetic and I hated myself for it. But it was true.

I guess I finally understood the concept of hate sex. In the past, it had always seemed like a weird, fringe thing that only super kinky people were into.

But I was really starting to hate this bastard who was keeping me from my life, keeping me under his thumb—God, that thumb—but that hatred was there, a weirdly tightened coil in my core, something wound too tight, something I instinctively knew would be incredible—unfathomable—when the pressure was released.

All that said, I wasn't sure I could live with myself, assuming I lived through this, if I knew I had been so damn weak, such a slave to my own desires. I'd had no trouble controlling them in the past. In fact, they'd hardly ever been any trouble, more of a little background chatter to everything else in my life that took more precedence.

By the time the car pulled to a stop, and the engine cut off, my shoulders were aching, my thigh muscles sore from trying to brace myself against all the rolling, and I was starting to get a raging headache from all the rampant overthinking.

There was a long pause before the trunk popped open.

I felt a wave of relief when I noticed we were in the same parking garage we'd been in the last time. At least I wasn't being thrown in some basement somewhere.

It wasn't Lorenzo's face I saw when the light streamed into my dark prison, though.

It wasn't even Chris.

Nope, it was Emilio, of all people.

"You've got a lot of spirit in you," he said, giving me that smirk that seemed so natural to him. "I've never seen Lorenzo so pissed off before," he added, reaching in, snagging my legs, pulling them out to dangle over the back of the car.

"Yes, how dare I not be a model prisoner, sitting and waiting for all the menfolk to come to a decision about my fate?"

"Yeah, I get it. I'd be pissed in your position too. This isn't your fault. And this isn't how we usually do business. Let's just hope the next meeting with your old man goes better."

"When is that?" I grumbled as Emilio grabbed my upper arm, helping me out and onto my own feet. But even when I was, his hand stayed there, making sure I didn't get away from him. As if I would get far without my hands free.

"Three days."

"You only gave him three days to find the money he owes you?"

"Plus interest. And he doesn't owe me shit personally," Emilio reminded me, seeming to want to distance himself from the whole kidnapping and imprisonment thing, even as he walked me inside, situating himself in such a way that the lone employee hanging around didn't see the cuffs as we moved into the elevator that Christopher was holding open. He didn't join us, though. Given my earlier escape, I figured he would be stationed at the bottom of the elevator from now on.

Great.

"Plus interest? My father can barely make payroll each week, and you think he can find thousands of dollars *plus interest* for you in three days?"

"Hey, babe, don't shoot the messenger here. These aren't my decisions. And, for the record, they're not Lorenzo's either."

"Yeah. You're all just a bunch of mindless soldiers, right?" I asked as we stepped out into Lorenzo's apartment, the man himself throwing back a whiskey in the kitchen. "No thoughts of your own. Just do what you're told. How pathetic is that?" I asked, looking over at Lorenzo, chin lifting.

"Put her in her room. I'm not in the mood tonight."

"The truth is so inconvenient, huh?" I asked as he made his way across the living room.

He stopped in the opening of the hallway, leaning down, eyes hard. "Watch the mouth, hellcat, or I *will* bring out the duct tape again."

With that, he went off into his room, slamming the door.

I was led to my room, and it didn't escape me that there was now a lock on the outside.

"Turn around," Emilio demanded when I stepped into the threshold. "I will undo the cuffs."

"So you can lock me in my room," I hissed, feeling the cuffs release, my shoulders crying out when I could finally swing my arms forward as I turned to face Emilio.

"Hey, not my fault you fucked up your escape attempt, babe," he said, shrugging, waiting for me to take a step inside, then reaching for the door. "Now you gotta deal with tightened security. I'm on duty tonight, so if you need anything, just call."

At this point, I'd rather starve to death than have to ask these guys for anything.

Really, what had I been smoking to have thought they were all kind of charming before my escape attempt? How was I able to distance the men themselves from the acts they had done? Some of them to me?

Maybe I had a little of my father in me after all.

Maybe I had somehow let myself romanticize these men, had somehow been able to excuse their crime because they hadn't treated me badly after they'd taken me. No one had hurt me, abused me.

But there was one problem with that thought process.

They hadn't hurt or abused me *yet*.

Clearly, if given the order, they would.

That was how the mafia worked, wasn't it?

Family over everything.

Even their own moral compasses.

They would string me up and slit my throat if the boss demanded it.

It wouldn't matter how many things they bought me, how much food they brought me, how well they had treated me if the end was me in a shallow grave somewhere.

Frustrated, I dropped down on the edge of the bed, taking a few deep breaths, trying to consider any exit strategies.

It was about fifteen minutes later, and I was no further along with any ideas, when I heard Lorenzo make his way across the hallway, going into the gym. There was a short pause before I could hear his footsteps on the treadmill, the pace set to punishing. Like he was trying to outrun something.

As committed as I was to hating him, an annoying little voice wondered if what he was trying to do was run away from his desire for me.

But that was ridiculous.

Sure, he had wanted me.

There had been no mistaking that.

But that didn't make it personal.

Men like him probably thought of it as some sort of twisted power play. Make the poor, abducted woman want you, then take advantage of that.

It wasn't personal.

It wasn't about me.

It was about the situation.

He got off on dominance.

And maybe the push and pull, the fighting.

And that made him pretty fucked up, didn't it?

Then again, I was just as fucked up if I was wet just at the memory of that scene in the kitchen, damnit.

"Ugh," I growled, getting to my feet, going into the bathroom, running a shower. Cold. Because I was trying to shock some damn sense into my system.

I went to sleep pissed at myself, at Lorenzo, at the entire situation.

I tossed and turned to dirty dreams about us.

And woke up even more frustrated—mentally and physically—than I had been when I'd gone to bed.

There was a sharp rap at my door, making me shoot up in bed.

The outside lock slid, but the door didn't open.

I guess that was my wakeup call.

My presence was being requested.

A petty part of me wanted to stubbornly stay in my bed. Only better sense dragged me out, realizing that if I refused to follow directions, Lorenzo would come in. Things would get physical.

In a way I was trying to convince myself I no longer wanted. You know, with him being a bad guy and all.

On a sigh, I made my way to the door, into the hall, the living room.

In the kitchen, Lorenzo was unpacking breakfast, little round foil packages that smelled like eggs.

Breakfast sandwiches, I guessed.

My stomach churned, but I didn't reach for one.

"Eat," he demanded, waving a hand to the assortment of bagels.

When I didn't immediately fall into line and reach for a bagel, his gaze cut to me for a moment, making my chin raise, defiant. It was a pathetic stance to take, but it was all I had in the moment.

His hand grabbed a bagel, moving around the island. "It takes thirty days to starve yourself to death, hellcat. I don't think you have that kind of discipline. Eat the fucking sandwich," he demanded, slamming it down in front of me. "Or do you want me to shove it in your mouth?" he asked, innuendo clear in his voice, in the glint in his eye.

"Try it," I dared him, head dipping to the side a bit, a challenge. "I'll bite it off," I told him, watching as his lips twitched.

"Thought we covered this, Gigi," he said, head dipping a little to get more in my face. "You'll get it when you beg for it."

"That's never going to happen."

"Pretty sure you thought that last time too."

"Yes, well, that was before I realized what an evil bastard you are," I told him.

"Oh, you knew exactly what kind of evil bastard I was all along, babe. You just don't want to admit to yourself that you're turned on by that. But you'll come around," he said, giving me an infuriatingly smug smirk as he moved off into his bedroom.

I took the sandwich that Lorenzo had put in front of me, taking a few bites as I made myself a cup of coffee. My gaze went to the unmanned elevator. Hinting at freedom it wouldn't give me now that a guard was stationed full-time at the bottom.

At least he was out of this space. At least no one else was around to witness these interactions between Lorenzo and me.

I heard the shower turn on in Lorenzo's room, and it took actual effort not to imagine his naked body climbing in there.

I don't know how long I stood there, some strange thought niggling me at the back of my mind, something that wanted to be acknowledged, brought forward.

But it escaped me for a long time before I finally remembered.

I had broken out of the building.

And I had looked upward when I turned down the side street.

All the way up.

To Lorenzo's apartment.

Where there had been a fire escape.

A fire escape that I hadn't seen outside any of the windows in the apartment.

It had to have been in Lorenzo's room, though, based on the placement. Not the bathroom. That one had a solid obscured glass window. Not the large windows over his bed, either.

What did that leave?

"Oh my God," I hissed, placing my mug on the counter, trying to gauge how long I had before he would get out of the bathroom.

Maybe long enough.

For me to sneak into his closet, find the window, open it, and climb out.

A patient, rational voice told me to wait, to see if he left, to try it then, when maybe I wouldn't be seen.

But I had no idea if I was going to be given the same freedom as before, if I was going to be locked in my room when he left.

If he locked me up at night, despite the guard at the bottom of the elevator, chances were I wasn't going to be allowed to walk around the apartment anymore.

It was now or never.

On that idea, I ran through the apartment, going into the closet, cringing as I carefully clicked the door closed, as though he would hear it over the water slapping against the tile in his shower.

The closet was as big as my bedroom at my apartment, built-in wooden units lining both sides, suits and shirts and slacks hanging, gleaming leather shoes lined up on the lower shelf, expensive watches in a tray at eye-level alongside an impressive assortment of cuffs-links. There was no way windows were on those sides, with the one wall butting up to the bathroom, and the other lining the hallway.

So it was the small wall directly forward.

With another built-in there.

And an assortment of random items.

My hands went frantically for each of them, pulling, then putting them back into place, knowing one of them had to be false, had to be a lever to unlock the false back, to expose the window.

Desperation was a snake coiling in my belly as my hands fumbled, nearly dropping one of the boxes there before I finally found a lever near the back, and when I pulled it. It let out a hissing sound as the lock released.

Carefully, I grabbed the edge of the cabinet, pulling it away, back and all, exposing another of the apartment's massive windows, but this one with a sill that lifted.

Close.

So damn close.

I pulled the window up, feeling the humid summer air slap me in the face as I glanced outward, making sure the fire escape was there, intact, usable.

As a whole, I wasn't afraid of heights. I'd grown up in high-floor apartments for most of my life. But not penthouse high, that was for sure. My stomach felt wobbly as my hands grabbed onto the slatted metal bottom of the fire escape.

I wasn't entirely sure how I was going to make it down in a rush without tripping, then possibly falling to my death, splattering on the pavement below, but I knew it was my only choice.

My knee lifted as my hands moved further out, trying to grab the rungs.

Just as I was hauling my body weight up and out, a hand closed around my throat, hard enough to cut off my air, making my stomach pitch, my leg falling instinctively.

He hadn't made a single sound.

Or maybe he had, but I had been deafened by the pounding of my own heart.

"You're one hell of a fighter, I'll give you that," Lorenzo said, pulling my back flush against his bare, hot chest. I could feel the remnants of his warm shower through my clothes, making a shiver course through me as his other arm anchored around my lower stomach, holding me completely captive.

I wasn't sure I had ever felt smaller than I felt in that moment.

"How did you know?" I asked, defeat a sinking sensation inside. I'd never get another chance now. I was fully at Lorenzo's mercy, at my father's mercy, at Arturo Costa's mercy: all these men, not one of which had my best interest at heart.

What an awful, helpless feeling that was.

Awful enough that the impossible happened. Tears burned my eyes, making me close them tight as a humiliating, pathetic strobe-like gasping sound escaped me, a surefire tell.

"Hey," Lorenzo said, releasing my throat, his other hand sliding toward my hip, turning me, pressing me back against the wall at my side. "Look at me," he demanded, snagging my chin, forcing it upward.

"Fuck you," I snapped, keeping my eyes shut.

"Look, I'm not mad," he said, voice a little hopeless sounding as a traitorous tear slipped out between my closed lids, trailing down my cheek. "I'm impressed, actually."

"I don't give a shit if you're mad," I snapped, eyes opening, glaring at him.

"Like the fire more than the water," he said, his thumb moving out to wipe the stray tear off my cheek.

"Gee, I'm sorry that my complete and utter helplessness is so distasteful to you. I can't say I am a fan of it either."

"Look, hopefully this will all be over at the next meeting."

"And if it's not?" I asked, feeling my jaw start to tremble. "What then? I start having parts of me cut off? I get my throat slit? A bullet to the head? What happens when my father can't pay, Lorenzo? Because, honestly, if that's my fate, you might as well just let me go. I think I'd rather swan dive off that fire escape than have one of you kill me."

"I'm not going to kill you, Giana," he told me, conviction clear in his voice.

"What then? Your father? Emilio? Chris? That guy who was originally supposed to kidnap me, the one who is more vicious than the rest of you? If your father orders it, I know someone will jump to carry through with it.

"No one is going to kill you, Gigi."

"You don't know that. You can't say that. *You* don't run this family. You don't get to make the calls."

"I make a lot of calls, baby. They might not be as flashy as the ones my father makes, but trust me when I say that when it comes to your life, I can find a way to spare it."

"By what? Sacrificing my father? Indebting me for my entire life? Gee, what a wonderful future I have in front of me."

"Oh, Gigi. You're too fucking young to be so hopeless. We'll figure it out."

"And I'm just supposed to trust you on this?"

"Have I lied to you? I've been as up front with you as possible. You haven't been blindsided by anything yet."

That was true to a point.

Thus far, the only surprises that had come my way had been ones I had brought upon myself.

For a kidnapper, he had been overall pretty decent except when I had provoked him. And even then, he hadn't actually hurt me.

"Making sure I have food and clothes to wear isn't exactly in the same league as pleading for my life," I reasoned.

"I won't have to plead for shit," he said, rolling his eyes at the very idea. Because big bad millionaire mafiosos never had to plead for anything, I guess. "I would appeal to my father's strongest desires."

"And what desires are those?"

"Fear and money," he said, immediately, not needing to give it any thought. "The more people shitting themselves at the mention of his name, the happier he is. And killing you two won't do anything for his bottom line. Keeping you on the books and squeezing you for more cash, that will."

"We don't have more cash, Lorenzo. I don't understand why that is so hard for you guys to grasp. I guess because you've never had to borrow from the food bill to pay the light bill. But there is nothing to squeeze out of us. There's almost nothing left."

"We'll figure it out."

"I'm sorry but that isn't much of a reassurance. And there is no *we*. You and I, we are not a *we*. I will be in this on my own. You will be living in this ridiculous ivory tower, while I make myself cozy in a cardboard box behind the bakery."

"That's not going to happen."

"Oh, my God. Yes, it will. The only way I could pay you more would be if I stopped taking a salary. This is not rocket science. There is no more fucking money."

"Well, maybe you will just so happen to find yourself a wealthy client who has very expensive eclair tastes, and is willing to pay well for it."

"You're out of your mind," I said, rolling my eyes. "What? I'm supposed to believe that you are going to be my silent benefactor in some backhanded plot behind your father's back? What? For forever? Get real."

"Nothing is for forever, Giana. Someday, that position my father holds will be mine. And when it is, you have my word, that I will set you free from this family."

"Your word," I snorted, shaking my head.

"Hey," he growled, snagging my chin again, this time, his fingers nearly bruising they held on so hard, as he forced me to make eye contact. "I stand by my fucking word. You can doubt plenty of things about me, but you don't doubt my word. I wouldn't give it if I didn't mean it. We will work out our temporary fix. Until I can give you a permanent solution. You want it in writing, we can get it on paper."

"Right," I said, laughing. "Because some scribbled note from a mafia prince to some nobody baker will stand up in court."

"I don't like that."

"Being called a mafia prince?" I asked. "Well, too damn bad. I hate to break it to you, but that is exactly what you are."

"I don't give a shit what you call me," he said, shaking his head. "But don't call yourself nobody. You're a somebody."

"Really, in the grand scheme of things, I'm kind of not. I'm not bitter about it. But it is what it is."

"It is what it is," he repeated, gaze intense.

"Yeah. Why are you looking at me like that?" I asked, brows pinching together, unable to read the look on his face.

"I didn't have you pegged as stupid," he said, his words making me jolt back.

"Stupid?" I repeated, letting out a humorless laugh. Stupid? Who the hell called anyone stupid outside of a schoolyard?

"Yeah, stupid. I didn't see that coming. A hard worker? Sure. A smartass? Yep. A royal fucking pain in the ass? Absolutely. Someone who would go down swinging before she'd ever beg for mercy? Damn fucking straight. But stupid? Yeah, never knew that was part of the whole picture."

"What the hell are you talking about?"

"Well, if you think you're a nobody, that people don't see you or don't appreciate you, you're a fucking idiot, kid. Truth hurts. Deal with it," he said, moving away to close and lock the window again.

"Um, excuse you, but who the hell do you think you are to call me stupid? I'm not stupid. I'm a realist. And the reality is, that if I was shot by some mafia boss and thrown into the ocean, hardly anyone would notice. Like it or not, that is how it is. You don't know me. So you can't pretend to know more about my importance than I do."

"Gigi, for fuck's sake. You've been in my house a week. And I can't get you out of my fucking mind. So all these other people, these ones whose lives you've touched on a daily basis, they give a shit. You're important to them. Saying otherwise just makes you insecure, not a realist."

"What did you just say?" I asked, hearing a strange airlessness in my voice.

"That you're insecure. I know. That one stings. No woman likes having that thrown in their face. Even if it's the truth."

"No," I said, shaking my head. "Before that," I clarified, gaze holding his.

His chin tucked a little as he ran a hand across the back of his neck. "That I can't get you out of my head," he said. And if I wasn't completely mistaken, I would swear there was almost a hint of, I don't know, vulnerability in his voice. That seemed so wholly out of place with the overall picture I had of this man, but there was no denying it was there.

"Yeah," I said, voice still breathy. "That."

"I think I've already explained my reasons for that. Hard-working. I like that. I work hard too. The sass? It keeps me on my toes. The fighting spirit, I respect that. Then there's that face. That ass. Those thighs. Those tits. Giana, if you think you're nothing, you don't have a mirror. Or anyone in your life who can see what you have to offer. Remember that."

I was supposed to hate him.

The man had kidnapped me.

He was holding me hostage.

He'd spent the last twenty-four hours giving me an attitude.

He literally held my life in his hands.

Everything pointed to hate.

Except the pressure in my lower stomach.

Except the lightness in my chest at his words, at truly being seen for maybe the first time since my mother's death.

I shouldn't have needed external validation, but Lorenzo's meant more to me than I cared to admit.

Any thoughts of hatred evaporated.

And anything akin to resistance dissolved as well.

My hands were the ones that rose first, one pressing to his chest, the other going around the back of his neck, pulling, urging.

My lips were the ones to claim his.

There was hesitance at first, just a gentle pressure, waiting for rejection, some unsure part of me still not entirely convinced he hadn't been blowing smoke, or simply trying to cheer me up.

Lorenzo's body stiffened at the contact, his lips still under mine.

But just for a moment.

And then, as you might expect of a man as dominant as him, he took over, his hands grabbing the sides of my face, not exactly gentle in their pressure as his lips claimed mine. Hard. Hungry. Demanding. Refusing to accept anything less than full surrender.

This was not a man who did soft, who did gentle.

I wasn't sure I was a woman who wanted that, either.

My nails dug into the skin at the back of his neck as my other hand got greedy, tracing up the corded muscle of his arm, across his strong chest, fingers grazing the crucifix hanging from his neck before moving downward, slipping between the ridges of his abdominal muscles, feeling them tense under my curious exploration.

Emboldened, my hand pressed against the front of his low-slung towel, feeling his hard cock against my palm, my hand closing around it.

A hiss escaped Lorenzo as his body shuddered.

In punishment, his teeth sank into my lower lip, pulling until I let out a small, pained whimper.

His hands moved down, grabbing my wrists, yanking my arms up over my head, pinning them to the wall behind me as his hips shifted inward, his cock pushing against the fabric of my barely-there shorts, making me cry out against his lips.

And damn if I didn't feel his lips smiling against mine before he pulled back, eyes blazing, watching me as he did another slow, deliberate hip thrust, as my thighs parted for the invasion, as my hips bucked forward to invite more of the sensation as he grazed across my cleft.

My breath shook through my chest as he shifted his hands, grabbing both my wrists in one grasp, freeing his other hand to move downward, slipping under the hem of my shirt, fingers teasing the skin of my belly above the waistband of my pants before stroking upward. And I swear little fires sparked across my skin.

His palm closed around my bare breast, squeezing, making a moan escape me as I arched my back, pressed myself against his hand, needing more.

A small smile pulled at his lips as his thumb and forefinger snagged my nipple, doing a roll that was just shy of painful.

"Lorenzo," I whimpered, my hips rocking against him, desperate for more, for everything, for complete and utter oblivion, something I knew he could give to me.

"What do you want?" he asked, voice a gravelly sound that slithered across my skin, sank in, and turned everything inside to mush. "My fingers," he clarified, hand moving down, pressing between my thighs. "Or my tongue?" he asked, giving me a wicked smile.

"Both," I admitted, not caring how needy I sounded. I *was* needy. And he knew it. There was no pretending when he saw me as clearly as he did right then.

A low, rumbling growl moved through him as his hands grabbed the waistbands of my shorts and panties, yanking them roughly down my legs, barely giving me a second to step out before his hand was grabbing my knee, lifting, throwing it over his shoulder.

Then his mouth was on me, tongue tracing up my cleft before circling around my clit.

My hands slapped down on the back of his head, holding him against me as his tongue started to do little flicks against my clit and two fingers plunged inside me, thrusting lazily.

My hips rocked shamelessly against him as his lips closed suddenly around my clit, sucking hard, sending an unexpected orgasm through my system, leaving me crying out, body shaking, hands holding onto him for dear life as my leg muscles weakened with the intensity of the waves that crashed through me.

Lorenzo kept working me through it, stopping only as the last tremor moved through me, as everything became too sensitive for anything else. As if sensing this, he moved away, kissing and nipping down my thigh, then back up, over my belly, working his way upward.

He barely had a chance to get to full height again before my hands were grabbing at the tuck of his towel, pulling, then tossing it away as my other hand pressed into his chest, pushing him up against the window, urging him to sit on the low sill to make up for our height difference as I lowered down to my knees.

My hand grabbed him at the base as my lips closed around his head, sucking him deep, feeling his cock press past the point of comfort, making me choke around him for a second before I relaxed, adjusted.

He didn't let me go for long, grabbing a fist-full of my hair, yanking slowly backward, little sparks of pain racing across my scalp as he slid out of my mouth.

His eyes were small slits of desire as he pulled me upward, making short work of removing my shirt, my bottoms. Reaching down, he snagged me behind the knees, yanking me off my feet as he got to his, carrying me back into the bedroom, tossing me onto the bed as he went into his nightstand, grabbing a condom, slipping it on, then looking over at me as he stood off the side of the bed.

The hunger in his eyes made a fire blaze through my core, spreading outward until my entire body was heated.

Lorenzo reached downward, grabbing my ankles, pulling me across the bed, hiking up my knees, then coming over me, his body pressing me into the mattress as his lips crushed against mine.

His teeth sank into my lower lip as he thrust inside me.

There was nothing slow or soft or sweet about Lorenzo. He fucked like he lived. Hard, fast, demanding.

He moved backward, going up on his knees, grabbing my legs, pressing them together, pushing them against my chest, making me feel him even deeper, a little pinch that shouldn't have felt good, but somehow did.

His hand moved out, grabbing my hand, slipping it between my thighs, using his thumb on top of mine over my clit, helping drive me upward harder, faster, until my chest started to feel tight, until my muscles started to seize up.

His free hand moved upward, grabbing my neck, putting pressure on the side.

"Come," he demanded as my head started to get a little light, as he fucked me harder, as he pressed his thumb roughly against my clit.

And just like that, I did, a deep pulsation that started in my core then exploded outward, stealing my breath, stealing my voice, my back arching, my hand slapping down onto Lorenzo's arm, holding on as he fucked me through it, dragged it out, until the final wave crashed. He slammed deep, body jolting, voice hissing out my name as he came.

I felt in pieces afterward, completely out of control of my body that was suddenly racked with aftershocks—a phenomenon I had started to believe was some lie men told each other to stroke their egos.

Nope.

They existed.

Apparently, you just needed a man like Lorenzo Costa to bring them out of you.

He sat back on his heels for a long moment, head angled back, eyes closed, trying to even out his breathing.

Around the time my aftershocks subsided, he seemed to get control over himself as well, slipping out of me, hopping off the bed, walking back to the bathroom, half-closing the door.

Just as function came back to my body, sense came back to my head, making me knife up in the bed, my heart flying upward, the reality settling in on me.

I'd just slept with him.

What the hell kind of Stockholm bullshit was that?

My stomach twisted in knots as I climbed off the bed.

I didn't stop to think about it, just rushed bare-ass naked across the room, into the hall, across it and into my own, closing and locking the door, dropping down on the edge of the bed, hands covering my face.

"Oh my God," I whispered as my thoughts swirled, all of them slamming into each other, falling down in mid-stride.

It wasn't long before I heard Lorenzo's voice calling my name, a curious sound that got more confused as he called again, making his way into the hallway. I heard him move out into the main area before he came back, stopping outside my door.

He tried the door, finding it locked in his hand.

"Giana," he called, voice low.

Biting into my bottom lip, I refused to answer, knowing I wasn't in any condition for rational thinking—let alone an actual conversation—right then. "Get back out here," he demanded, but his voice was softer than usual, coaxing.

There was no reason to go out there, though.

That happened.

But it changed nothing.

He was still a man with my life in his hands.

And I was a prisoner.

Talking about it wouldn't change the facts.

Better to put the distance between us now.

Because we could never freaking do that again.

As if we realized this at the same exact time, his hand slid the external lock.

It was over.

It wasn't going to happen again.

Chapter Nine

Lorenzo

I barely saw her for the next few days.

I tried to tell myself it was for the best.

Fucking her had been a bad move. It complicated shit. And I liked my sex—and life—decidedly uncomplicated.

That said, I would admit that it felt strange having her in my place, but a ghost. I unlocked the door first thing in the mornings, but she didn't come out until after I left. She must have had amazing hearing, always hearing the swish of the elevator as it came up, because I never caught her in the common area.

A part of me wanted to charge in, demand to hash shit out. But I had just enough self-preservation to keep me from doing it. Which was just as well. The woman deserved a little privacy if she wanted it. Her life had been turned upside down and shaken. She should be allowed to hold onto whatever she could to feel steady.

So I let her have things her way, though I installed some solid locks on the window to the fire escape as well as my closet just in case.

It was better this way.

After the next meeting with her father, I hoped she would be able to go back to her life, likely cleaning up her father's messes, but free.

And I would be back to my business. Which, I had to admit, was suffering since she arrived, since I started making excuses to be home, since I'd had to chase her around the tri-state area.

It would be good to get back to what was important.

Some day, this family would be mine. Keeping it from turning into a complete shitshow before then was important.

Now if I could just get that fucking woman out of my mind, that would be great.

I found myself wondering what she was doing in the apartment when I was out. When I was in, I wondered if she had enough food and drinks in her room since she refused to come out to eat dinner with me. And at night? Alone in my bed? Yeah, let's just say she took the dominant place in my mind then, leaving me hard and frustrated, a strong part of me wanting to charge across the hall and get another round.

It took more self-control than I knew I was capable of not to, to go to sleep unsatisfied.

But it was almost over.

The deadline was here.

"Yeah?" I asked, answering my phone on the second to last ring, not wanting to deal with my father, but knowing I had no excuse not to pick up.

"Bring the girl here at six."

"What?" I asked, confused. There hadn't been any talk about bringing Giana with me to the meeting with her father. And, quite frankly, it was not good that my father ordered she be there. He wanted to make a spectacle of her, to chain her to a chair, to gag her. He wanted a reaction out of Leon. My father had always thrived on the fear he could instill. But it was one thing if the fear was that of the person who had fucked him over in some way. It was a complete other to make Gigi pay for the sins of her father.

"What part of that was hard to understand?" my father asked, tone cold.

"Why would the daughter need to be there?"

"Leverage. If he tries to dick us around, we have her there."

We'd have her there.

My stomach twisted as his words settled in and his meaning became clear.

If Leon tried to stall, if he didn't have what he needed to, my father would order harm to Giana in front of her father.

And if anyone tried to step in—myself included—he would put a bullet in us.

I had no delusions about my father, about his feelings toward me. I was his underboss because I was the hardest worker, the biggest earner, because I had a body count that surpassed anyone but Brio.

I was the best option.

It had nothing to do with fatherly love.

My father wasn't capable of it.

He would take me out if he thought I was making him look bad. He'd drive a spike through me if he knew how I'd been running things behind his back for years.

This was not good.

And my fucking hands were tied.

"Six, Lorenzo."

And with that, silence.

As my heart pounded and my thoughts raced, while I tried to think of a single way to get us out of this situation.

I'd given her my word that I would take care of her. My father slicing off one of her fingers in my presence wasn't exactly me keeping it.

"Fuck," I hissed, grabbing my glass, throwing it at the wall, feeling a small amount of satisfaction as it shattered to the ground.

"What is going on?" Gigi asked, shocking me. It had been days since I'd heard her voice.

Or seen her face, I reminded myself as I turned so quickly that the room spun for a second.

There she was. In a white tee and a pair of short shorts. No bra, judging by her nipples peeking out through the fabric.

I didn't need my cock to stiffen right then, but there was no denying it did.

I sighed as I raked a hand through my hair before turning to grab two new glasses, uncapping the whiskey, pouring us each a double, then holding one out.

"Trust me, babe, you're going to want it."

Hesitantly, she moved forward, reaching out for the glass, careful not to brush my fingers with hers as she took it.

"My father hasn't paid," she said, not sounding surprised, but the hollowness in her voice was a knife to the gut.

"The meeting is at seven," I told her. "At my father's house."

"Oh."

"You need to be ready by six."

"Okay."

"Giana," I called when she turned, to go find something more appropriate to wear.

"What?"

"It's not good that my father wants you to be there tonight," I told her, trying to ease her into it.

I should have known better. Giana wasn't stupid. She knew more about the mafia than she let on. She knew how shit worked.

"He plans to use me against my father if he doesn't pay," she said. To her credit, she didn't tear up. But I saw her fear. It was in the tightness in her jaw, the way she jutted chin up to hide the tremble of her lower lip.

"That's my thinking," I agreed.

"In what way?" she asked, swallowing hard, and I didn't want to think of all the awful things that were likely running through her mind right then.

"I imagine roughing you up."

"That's it? Just slap me around?"she asked, rolling her eyes. "Come on."

"Babe, I don't know. I wish I had an answer for you, some reality to prepare you for. I just know that my father is unstable when he feels he is being slighted. And he can be a real dick. I haven't personally seen him order anyone to hurt a woman, but do I think he is capable? Yes. There is very little I don't believe my father is capable of."

"What have you seen him order done to men?" she asked, biting into her lower lip to stop the quivering.

I'd never been a man who comforted people. That was not what I did. But there was an almost overwhelming urge to walk over there, to wrap her up, and assure her that there was no way I would let anything happen to her.

But the reality was, I could no longer make that promise to her. Not if I wanted both of us to make it out of this shit alive.

"Most commonly, the clichés stand. Broken kneecaps. Shattered hands. Severed fingers. Or," I started, swallowing back the bad taste in my mouth at this one, "tooth extractions."

I was capable of a lot of wicked things. I could beat a man near to death without batting an eye. But there was something about pulling teeth that turned my stomach.

"I've had a dentist do an extraction before my Novocaine kicked in," Gigi admitted, cringing a bit at the memory. "I could live through that again. I mean, people used to pull their own teeth out with pliers before dentistry came about. I wouldn't die from it."

"No," I agreed, nodding. "You'd make it."

"They used to saw off the limbs of soldiers in the civil war. That's where the term 'bite the bullet' comes from," she added, as if inserting that fact somehow made the reality easier to swallow.

"I see what you're trying to do here, babe," I said, shaking my head. "But no amount of mental preparation is going to make it any less horrific if any of those things happens."

To that, she nodded, her chin dipping to hide the sudden swimming in her eyes.

"Can I ask something?" she started, taking a shaky breath.

Yeah, babe."

"Can you do it?" she asked, looking up, blinking back the tears.

"What? Why? Why me?"

"Because I know you wouldn't want to. And there is some comfort in that, I think. Kinda like we were both in that shitty position together. I don't think I could handle it if I knew it was some guy who was taking pleasure in my pain."

That was a big ask.

Everything in me said I couldn't do it.

I didn't hurt women, as a rule.

And the thought of hurting this one in particular made it feel like someone was pouring lava into my chest.

"I will do everything I can to be the one to do it," I agreed, though. After all, she was the one calmly accepting her potential torture. Could I really deny her the choice of who would deliver the blows? It was a small favor given the situation. "And I think it would be something that would escalate. So if you can put on a show like I'm really hurting you when I am using half-power, we might be able to avoid something worse. If you think you can fake it well enough," I added, knowing my father wouldn't buy it if she was trying some scream queen audition.

"I'm a woman, Lorenzo," she said, snorting. "I know I can fake it well enough."

With that, she tossed back her whiskey, moving forward to place the empty glass on the counter in front of me.

I knew what she was doing.

Trying to create distance again.

But this time, not from the future torture.

From past pleasure.

And I knew I should have let it go.

Let her have what she needed in the moment. I was a huge part in how fucked up her life was right then. I owed her what little comfort I could give her.

But as she made her way into the opening of the hallway, I found myself calling her name, watching as she turned, brow raised.

"Yeah."

"You didn't fake shit with me," I told her, taking a sip of my drink.

To that, she lifted her chin higher, and turned back away, knowing there was no way to deny it.

I tossed back the rest of my drink, trying to mentally prepare myself for the evening. But there was no use. There was no way to prepare yourself to potentially cut a part off of someone you were beginning to give a shit about.

Give a shit.

That was all it was.

She had been in my space, in my life, for a while now. I gave a shit if she was harmed.

That was all it was.

That was all it could be.

"Whoa," I said a few hours later when I could hear a click in the hall.

There she was.

In a red dress and black heels.

Why Emilio had someone pick up dress clothes for a woman being held against her will in the spare room of my apartment was beyond me.

"I figured, if he wants a spectacle, might as well go hard," she said, that stubborn chin of hers jerking up, ready, defiant.

She looked like a woman ready to take on the world.

Or New York City's *Capo dei Capi.*

Which was really the same thing.

"You look good, babe," I told her, trying to remind my body that we decided not to touch her again.

"If he wanted sniveling and simpering and begging, he chose to have the wrong woman kidnapped," she added, eyes hard.

You had to appreciate her spirit.

It was the sexiest thing about her.

"Good," I said, nodding. "Keep that mindset. We might make it out of this thing tonight," I said, grabbing my keys. "Ready?"

"Yep," she said, the word snapping out as her back straightened.

"We're going to do everything we can to avoid anyth—" I started to assure her as we closed into the elevator.

"Don't," she cut me off, shaking her head. "I think we both know you can't make any promises tonight. I'd rather not get hopeful about some scenario that isn't going to happen. It will undo all the prep-talking I did while getting ready," she said, staring straight ahead at her reflection in the mirror as the doors opened.

She looked like what she was.

A woman on a mission.

Stone fucking cold.

A part of me itched to slip my hands up her skirt, to warm her up.

But she was right. She would fare better if she kept her guards up. The dress, the heels, the makeup, it was all warpaint. Taking any of that away might shake her confidence, make the whole thing worse.

My hand went to her lower back, making her body jolt at the contact, but not move away, as I led her into the parking garage.

There was no fighting, no trying to get away. We both knew we were beyond that now.

Hopefully, this would all be over by the end of the night.

And no permanent damage would be done.

It was a short drive to my father's brownstone, but my stomach worked itself into painful knots all the same, my mind unable to think of anything but the fear and pain in her eyes if I was ordered to turn on her.

My father had three of his guards around. With Christopher and Emilio there for me, despite not being expressly told to follow.

Leon would be shitting himself walking in. Or maybe he was just delusional enough to think he could charm the lot of us, and work his way back into our good graces.

At my side, Giana was ramrod straight, but her gait was calm and confident as we made our way up the front stoop. She didn't even bother to glare at my father's guards who were openly eye-fucking her before we disappeared inside.

"The fuck is this shit?" My father's voice boomed through the house, high-pitched and irritating, and my gaze went to Giana to see if she was surprised by the lack of depth there.

"The fuck is what shit?" I asked, facing my father as he came down the hall.

"What? We don't lock up prisoners anymore?" he asked, giving Gigi a cold once-over. She did the exact same thing, but slower, picking all the pieces of him apart, examining them, finding them lacking. Judging by the way his jaw started to tick, he saw this as well.

"She wasn't resisting, but if you wish it," I said, digging into my breast pocket where I'd tucked the cuffs in case she got cold feet between my apartment and the brownstone.

I slid them open, and Giana turned to face me, holding her wrists out in front of her, letting me click them on.

I tried to catch her eyes while I did it, but she refused to look at my face.

"Is Leon here yet?" I asked.

"He's not supposed to be for another half an hour," my father said, turning and walking into the dining room, leaving all of us to follow. "Why did you bring Emilio and Chris?" he asked, moving to the liquor cabinet.

"They pull guard duty when I need to handle business."

"I have my own men here."

"I see that," I agreed, then walked over to make my drink. My father was not someone who played host. And maybe in his position, I wouldn't either.

"Sit down," he demanded, glancing at Giana. "No, the other side of the table," he commanded as he took the head. He wanted her in the back near the wall facing the doorway, so her father would see her when he came in. My father wanted to watch Leon sweat. He got off on that shit.

I didn't wait to be instructed, taking the spot next to Gigi. I figured if I was the one right next to her, I would be the one my father commanded to put their hands on her if it came to that.

"So how has our little prisoner been behaving?"

"She's been a model prisoner," I lied easily, as I had been doing to him for years, my whole life, even. "Quiet as a mouse," I added, watching as Emilio and Chris bit into their cheeks to keep from smiling. "You'd almost think she enjoys imprisonment," I added, seeing Gigi's brows draw together slightly, not understanding why I would make that statement .

Until my father spoke, of course. "Well, where's the fun in that?"

I didn't know much about how my father interacted with women. My mother up and disappeared when I was young, so I never got to really study their dynamic.

I had no delusions about my father, though.

Chances were, my mother hadn't disappeared.

She was dead, tossed in the ocean or the woods somewhere.

That was how my father handled problems. With a bullet and a grave.

I had always assumed he would see women as a problem. He was simply validating something I had thought all my life.

He was rough with women.

Yet another thing I thankfully hadn't inherited from him. Maybe I had never treated women seriously, had always thought of them as temporary, but I had never treated one poorly, let alone hurt one.

"Always good to have fewer problems," I said, shrugging. "We always have a lot going on."

To that, he grunted, toying with his drink.

"So what do you think? Did the stupid bastard scrounge the money up, or what?" he asked, seemingly to the room at large.

But it was Giana who spoke up, surprising us all.

"I wouldn't count on it," she said, glancing over at my father.

"Your life isn't worth a couple grand?" he goaded.

"To him? Probably not."

"Oh, I would probably even pay a couple grand to get him back," he said, waving his glass at me.

I could feel Emilio's gaze on me, angry for me, but I had long since stopped being offended by my father's lack of regard. I just needed to stay in his graces enough to keep my position, so that when he died, I got the family. Everything else? It didn't fucking matter anymore.

In a strange way, I felt like Gigi and I were kindred there. I wanted my family legacy, she hers. And we would put up with damn near anything to get that for ourselves.

Time ticked slowly, marked by the grandfather clock wedged in the corner, that had been in our family as long as anyone could remember, but—like the rest of the place—in need of some love.

But my father just didn't have any of that to give.

Then, finally, we could hear the front door opening, making all of us—save for my father—straighten.

Beside me, Gigi took a slow, deep breath. I shouldn't have noticed the way it made her breasts strain the front of her dress, but I would be a liar if I said I didn't.

Leon walked in, the carefree gait of a man who was invited to dinner, not one who owed money to a mafia boss. He even took a second to offer my guards a nod and tight smile before making his way into the room, focus intent on my father.

"Lastra," my father greeted. "Do you have my money?" he asked, not one for small talk.

"Well," Lastra started and I could feel my eyes rolling already. "I have some of it. Unfortunately, it seems like our safe was robbed a few nights ago," he added, and my gaze went to Giana, knowing it had likely been her, to get what she needed to get out of town, to get away from us. That said, if it had been any significant sum of money, I was sure she wouldn't have gone down to Cape May to collect her things. At least not right away. If it was anywhere near what Leon owed the family, she would have been able to sat pretty for days or weeks in a nice hotel room somewhere before taking that chance. Whatever she got from that safe was likely only enough to get her through a few days comfortably.

"You're telling me things that aren't my fucking problem, Lastra. I don't care if you had to steal your grandmother's brooch she brought over from the old country to get me my money. If you had to rob a fucking bank for it. We already discussed this."

"I know, I know," Leon said, grabbing the back of the chair across from me, actually lowering himself down as though this was a normal social call.

It hadn't escaped me that he hadn't so much as glanced his daughter's way.

"We told you what would happen if you didn't pay this time."

"I have some of it, Art. Quite a bit of it, in fact," he went on, tapping fat fingers on the tabletop. "I can get the rest within a week. Two tops."

"In two weeks, you would owe me for next month," my father reminded him.

"Yeah, but you know me. I'm always good for it. Have I let you down yet?"

To be fair, that was true. The money eventually always got scrounged up. If it hadn't, Leon would have been dead years ago. My father was just sick of the runaround. It was always a problem, always late.

I had a sneaking suspicion the only reason it was ever paid in full at all was due to Giana finding a way to swing it. And with her in our possession, Leon had no fucking idea how she had managed it all those years.

What a poor fucking excuse for a man.

It would work out for everyone involved if I just put a bullet in him. Then Giana could be freed, and she and I could put our deal into motion. Then my father would never have reason to look at her again.

Win/win.

Except, I was pretty sure there was a part of my father that got off on Leon's ass-kissing, his desperate desire to be an associate of the family's. It made him feel bigger, since the community as whole knew what a dick he was.

Arturo Costa didn't have the respect the old dons did, back when they always protected their neighborhoods and made sure their people were taken care of. Back then, there was loyalty and admiration from the community. They kept their eyes cast down when they saw something illegal, and they kept their mouths shut when the cops came around.

That wasn't the kind of empire my father had.

The neighbors feared him, wanted him out of their nice neighborhood, wanted his leering guards with their ass-pinching fingers off the stoop and sidewalks.

So he had to get his adoration elsewhere.

From small men like Leon Lastra.

"Boss," one of my father's guards said, stepping into the room.

"Can't you see we're busy here?" my father shot back, reaching into his jacket, producing a gun, placing it down on the table—a silent threat, one that Leon didn't outwardly react to. For all I knew, my father pulled a gun on him often.

"It's Paulie. Says you wanted to see him."

My father had forgotten all about it. That truth was plain on his face, at least to me, someone used to a lifetime of his half-truths or full lies.

"Yeah, yeah. But tell him he has to be quick," my father said, rising to his feet.

The guard left for a moment, and then there was another figure moving into the room. Freakishly tall and thin to the point of gauntness, Paulie's suits hung off of him like a scarecrow's in a field

My father had stacked his books full of questionable characters. There was none I disliked as much as Paulie—a man with a strangely monotone voice and shifty eyes.

He worked as a debt collector, had likely graced Leon's door more times than he could count over the years.

His stare was on my father as he moved in the room, seemingly ignoring us all.

I thought nothing of it until Paulie reached into his pocket, his port-wine birth-marked hand producing a fat envelope he passed to my father.

But right in that second, everything about the air in the room shifted.

And it all radiated from the woman sitting at my side.

She'd been stiff before, but she was brittle now. One touch would splinter her.

My gaze lifted, curious, finding her focused on Paulie's hand, her lips parted, her eyes round, her breathing ragged.

Most worrisome of all, though?

She was shaking.

Hard enough that her teeth were clacking together.

This was a woman who had been kidnapped, who had been chased across state lines, then caught , bound, and dragged back.

She'd never shown me fear like this.

She always showed me fire.

Spirit.

Beside me now, she was shrinking into herself, becoming small right before my eyes. It was right then that I realized how little I knew about her connection to the family, about her interactions with major players.

Had Paulie been sent to threaten her? To press her for the money owed?

It wouldn't surprise me. Paulie didn't give a shit who he had to lean on to get the money he was owed. Even if that meant scaring small women.

Still, the reaction seemed over the top for her, this woman who had given even my father a little lip.

There was a short, whispered conversation between Paulie and my father before Paulie turned, seeming to notice everyone gathered around for the first time.

His gaze went right to Giana. And those shifty eyes warmed. His lips curved into some semblance of a smirk.

Yes, clearly some sort of history. Bad on her side, pleasant to Paulie.

His gaze roamed over Gigi for a long moment before shifting to her father who rose to his feet, holding out his hand to be shaken by Paulie's.

"Long time no see, Leon," Paulie said, further confusing me. "What's it been? Five? Six years?"

There was something in his words, an undercurrent that I couldn't quite make out, heavy with meaning hanging thick in the air.

"Yes, somewhere around there," Leon agreed, giving the man a hearty handshake before dropping it.

My gaze shifted to Giana, finding her gaze on her father, disbelieving, then shifting to Paulie's hand once again.

I was so distracted by her reaction that I missed whatever occurred between the two men before Paulie was saying his goodbyes and walking out of the room.

There was a pause, then the slam of the front door.

And, somehow, that seemed to penetrate through whatever fog was swirling through Giana's mind.

It happened so fast.

I was watching her and I couldn't have predicted it, couldn't have stopped it.

One second, she was sitting beside me, confused, shocked, completely and utterly still.

The next, she was on her feet, her handcuffed hands reaching across the table, grabbing my father's discarded gun, lifting, aiming, and emptying the magazine.

Into her father.

Her fucking *father*.

There was collective cursing from all of us in the room, the rushing in of my father's men.

My hands immediately went for Giana's, pulling the gun from her shaking hands, putting it down on the table at my side.

"What the fuck just happened?" my father asked. It was rare for him to sound shocked, but there was no denying it in his voice right that moment. It was in all our minds, in fact.

What the fuck just happened?

There was no need to rush to Leon's body. Clearly, Giana had spent some time in a range in her life. Because all but one of the bullets had landed in her father's chest cavity. He was dead before he hit the ground. Still, Chris went over, bent down, checked for a pulse, and gave us a head shake before standing.

"*Fuck*!" my father snapped, reaching up to rake a hand through his hair. "Get her the fuck out of here for a minute. I can't think straight with her shaking like that," my father demanded, his guards moving forward.

"I got it," I said, holding up a hand.

"Basement," my father added as I grabbed the small chain between Giana's hands, pulling until she fell into step with me.

I wanted to reach for her.

I wanted to pick her up, carry her against my chest.

There was something genuinely broken in her right that moment. And part of me responded, wanted to grab some glue, and put her back together.

But no one could know that.

No one could see that.

It was a surefire way to sign her death sentence. And things were already bad enough for her right then.

I pulled her down the hall, into the kitchen, then down the first step before reaching for her, and lifting her up to carry her down.

Her body was strangely loose through all of this, as limp as a child who's deep asleep.

The basement was partially finished, the area around the landing and to the left was a game room with a pool table, card table, a massive TV, and a full bar. A couple leather armchairs were sitting in the opening.

Guard chairs.

Because the other side of the basement wasn't just where the furnace and water heater were situated.

It was where my father had a holding room set up.

For people he wanted to question.

People like Giana.

Fuck.

No.

That couldn't happen.

I had to somehow convince him that I would be the better choice. Maybe spout some shit about having gained her confidence, that she would give me the truth with less fuss.

Which was true.

But it would also allow me to take whatever truth she fed me, and twist it, to make my father think twice about how he would handle the situation.

I moved in through the security door, feeling the cool and damp already start to penetrating me. It seeped in through the cement floor, the cinder block walls.

My father had the furnace and water heater closed off in their own space, likely doing so to prevent any prisoner from ripping some piece of it in desperation, and using it for an attack. The rest of the space was sparse, unfinished floors and walls with a wooden beam ceiling. And a couple sets of shackles attached to the wall.

My stomach twisted, at the idea of putting them on her, but also at knowing I didn't have much choice.

I bent down, carefully placing Giana on the floor, grabbing one of the lower shackles, attaching the cuff to one of her ankles, leaving the other free.

"Giana," I called, voice soft, reaching for her chin, lifting it, waiting for her gaze to find mine. "What the fuck just happened?" I asked when she finally looked at me.

Chapter Ten

It was the hand.

That hand.

That one I remembered well.

All too fucking well.

It was a hand I had described in acute, painful detail to a female police officer while my legs were spread in stirrups.

I was one week shy of my sixteenth birthday. My mother and I had been spending time after school planning on a way to make it a big, happy affair. On a tiny, sad budget.

That was what I always remembered from childhood. My mother constantly trying to find ways to cut corners, to make a dollar stretch as far as possible. It didn't matter how rough a year we had, she always had found ways to make Christmas and Easter and birthdays something special. Maybe I'd never gotten name brands or expensive electronics like some of the kids I went to school with, but I had beautiful memories of brightly-colored packages on Christmas morning, of simple park birthdays full of amazing baked goods and close friends.

We'd never had much by way of family. My mother had grown up in foster care and had never found her forever family. Until she met my dad. She always said that, if nothing else, she would forever be thankful for me, and for the parents she gained through marriage, and for the grandparents as well.

Unfortunately, my great-grandparents passed before I was old enough to remember them, and my grandparents only made it to my early teens.

So all she had left to feel thankful for was me. And she showed it. I don't know if I knew anyone else who had as close a relationship with their mother as I did. She was who I confided in when I had a crush, who I cried to when said crush rejected me, who I went to for fashion advice, who I went to movies with.

She was my best friend in the entire world. And I was hers.

As a kid, I never stopped to wonder why she clung so tightly to me, why she would often come in my room to watch shows, and "just so happen" to fall asleep in my bed with me instead of going back to her own.

I don't ever remember hearing my parents arguing, but as an adult, I knew they must have, knew that the bitterness between them didn't just happen overnight, that there were many cross words that must have created it slowly over time.

And the older I got, the more I could see how much she had protected me from him. Not because he abused me, not because he was ever outwardly cruel to me, but because his cold indifference would have been just as hard to come to grips with as a small child.

He never wanted to be a father, and he didn't feel the need to act differently.

So my mom worked hard to be both parents for me, even while I shared the walls with my father as well.

He was never around, anyway.

So we clung to each other.

And we had decided on flower cupcakes for the party, had picked out her sweet, light pink sundress that I had always admired as my outfit, had sat and written out invitations in my mother's beautiful, flowing penmanship, had even found the perfect park with an actual koi pond and a pergola so we wouldn't melt in the heat.

It was all set up.

We had been working on little specifics. Like the music to load onto my iPod, if four pizzas would be enough, if we should paint our nails red or yellow—or a combination of the two—if I should wear my hair up or down.

We never would hammer out those details.

We never would have that party.

I would turn sixteen.

But by then, my mom wasn't around anymore.

It was a normal night.

My mother and I had stood brushing shoulders in our tiny kitchen, chopping up vegetables for a stir-fry, deciding on peanut sauce since my father wouldn't be home. He hated all things peanut butter. My mother and I binged Reeses when there was enough leeway in the budget for us to buy a big bag and do so.

We had eaten dinner in front of the TV in the living room, watching *Gilmore Girls* reruns for the thousandth time, having always connected to the mother/daughter dynamic, loving the small-town vibe even though we both agreed we were city women through-and-through.

Then, my mother got one of her migraines, having to take one of the pills that made her sleepy and loopy, so she went off to her room to rest in the dark, and I did the dishes and went to my room to listen to some music, still trying to perfect that playlist of mine.

I fell asleep on a mixed CD a friend had given me.

I woke up to it still playing on a loop.

But I wasn't alone like I had been when I fell asleep.

And it wasn't my mother in the room.

Or my father, for that matter.

No, it was a stranger.

Tall and an almost emaciated sort of skinny, something that made his suit hang off his body, looking like a skeleton dressed up for Halloween.

There was nothing significant about his face, except his eyes seemed black and too close-set.

He was just like any average guy you might see on the street or in the store.

But he damn sure didn't belong in my bedroom.

My mouth opened, ready to call for my mother.

But even as my lips parted, I could hear her.

Already screaming before the sound abruptly cut off.

This man wasn't the only one in the apartment.

And someone was doing something to my mom.

I wasn't naive.

I knew all the terrible ways a man could hurt a woman. I just... I just never thought it could happen to my mom.

Or happen to me.

But then this skinny man was moving across my bedroom floor, was making his way to where I was still stretched out on my bed.

I wanted to scream.

I wanted to run.

I wanted to fight.

But it was like something had clicked off in my brain. It was like the connection between my mind and my body was misfiring.

I couldn't scream.

I couldn't run.

I couldn't fight.

I couldn't *move*.

Not even when he got to the bed.

Not even when his hands moved out, pulled off my clothes, touched me, pulled off his own clothing.

The clearest memories I had of that night were of the aftermath.

It was how I distinctly remembered how the bed bounced as he moved off of it, how I finally managed to move, curling up on my side, wrapping my arms around my legs. How tears had soaked my pillow without me having been conscious of crying in the first place, how cold my room was, making goosebumps bead up across all my exposed skin.

It was the man's hands as he methodically pulled his clothes back on.

Underwear. Pants. Shirt. Belt. Jacket.

It was his one hand, in particular.

With a big, red birthmark covering it.

I knew the shape, the shade, where it ended and began.

It was the most vivid memory I had as I lay in my bed, crying, in pain, even after the man left.

At some point, I was aware of my mother in my room, her lip split, her eye black and blue, her hair a mess, wearing only a t-shirt when she'd gone to bed with sweatpants on as well.

"It's okay, baby. It's okay. I'm here. We are getting help."

And we did.

The police showed up.

My mother and I were brought into the hospital.

We were separated.

I was given some sort of patient advocate as the all-female team came in, scraped under my fingernails, trimmed them, took pictures of my body, put me in stirrups, and prodded already sore spots.

It was then that I told the police about the birthmark. I'd even taken her pad, drawn a hand, and colored in the spot, so I knew she would get it right.

It never occurred to me at the time, but my father never came to the hospital.

Eventually, my mother and I huddled together in the back of a cab and rode home, both in silence, but clinging to one another, neither of us able to talk about it yet, to vocalize the horror. Just there for each other. Just in it together.

We went back into the apartment, and she settled me on the couch, knowing I couldn't go back into my room, not going back into hers either.

She made us tea, but never drank her own.

She put on *Gilmore Girls*.

She put a blanket over me.

And then she sat in the chair at my side, eyes glued on the front door of the apartment, seeing something I didn't, thinking thoughts I never considered because I was so confused with my own. Thoughts of stolen innocence. Thoughts of feeling unsafe in my own home. Thoughts of how I was going to explain this to my friends. How anyone could ever understand.

"I should have talked to my mom," I told Lorenzo, feeling tears clinging to my lashes. It had been a long time since I let myself remember that night. It never got any easier when I did.

"You were a little girl, Gigi," Lorenzo reminded me, hand touching my knee, giving it a little squeeze. "And you had just been through hell."

"I know that."

And I did.

On a rational level.

But people, well, we were rarely rational. We were emotional people.

And as horrible as the last part of my story was, the hardest was the next part.

Because my mom knew something I didn't.

I hadn't known that at the time.

I hadn't asked.

And maybe she wouldn't have told me if I had.

But she knew something.

Something so horrible that when I had fallen asleep, she'd taken a kitchen knife, went down the elevator, gone onto the front steps of our apartment building, and slit her wrists.

On the steps.

Because she didn't want me to find the body.

In fact, she was found just ten minutes after it was too late.

I didn't wake up for ten hours.

Then, finally, there my father was.

Face grim.

Eyes strangely hard. And in the aftermath, I had attributed that to his way of grieving.

"Mom killed herself," he told me, not bothering to sugar-coat it, ease me into this new, harsh reality.

Mom was dead.

And the only person who truly loved me was gone.

The only person who could possibly understand how I felt after the attack was done.

And nothing, absolutely nothing would ever feel the same again.

I spent my sixteenth birthday in a therapist's office, curled up in the chair, hugging my legs, putting a wall up between us, as the kind woman said things about how some people process trauma, about how my mother's way of processing didn't have to be mine, about how there was always someone to help, about how there were medications if I needed them, that I had people there for me, people who loved me.

I knew the grim truth, though.

There wasn't anyone who loved me left.

I was alone in the world.

I didn't think medications would help me process that.

I didn't think therapy would either, so I stubbornly refused to go after a month of sessions.

Instead, I went back to school. I worked in the bakery. I slept on the couch. And I rather obsessively drew that birthmark on lined pages of my school notebook.

Dozens, hundreds of times.

They scattered around the apartment.

My father picked them up and threw them away.

"He knew about that birthmark. He'd seen it every day for months," I told Lorenzo. "There was no way he didn't know it when he saw it. He looked right *down at it* upstairs. And he wasn't surprised to see it there."

The reality of that still made it feel like someone had a hand around my throat, like they were cutting off air.

It all came tumbling back as I sat there while my father shook hands with my rapist.

My mom staring at the door.

That hadn't been kicked in.

The police said the locks hadn't been tampered with, that we must have left it unlocked.

We hadn't.

I knew we hadn't.

I had locked it myself, slid the knob on both the deadbolts my mother insisted we install when there had been a slew of burglaries in the building several months before.

The door had been locked.

And no one had tampered with it.

And my mom sat there staring at it for hours when we got home.

Because she knew.

She knew someone had unlocked it.

And it wasn't either of us.

Maybe she knew more than that too. Maybe she recognized the man who had attacked her. Maybe she knew about the birth-marked man. Maybe she had met him, had shaken hands with him in the past.

Other things came back too.

Like how that month, magically, the cable didn't get shut off. The phone didn't ring off the hook with creditors looking for their minimum payments so they would leave us alone for three weeks.

My father ordered in dinner almost every other night.

He bought a fancy new watch.

He got a new wardrobe full of suits like his mafia friends.

"I wonder how much I was worth," I said to Lorenzo, shaking my head, too numb to feel shocked by the revelation. "I wonder how much he thought my mom's life was worth. I bet it wasn't much," I added, taking a shaky breath. "I always knew I meant little to him. But I guess just... not *how* little. He'd let someone take something important from me for a full stomach, for a new watch, for fucking chicken parmesan and lobster rolls."

"Gigi—"

"My mom knew. And she just... she couldn't live with that reality. Christ," I said, scoffing. "I don't blame her. I think if I had known too, I would have been out on the steps with her."

"You're not going to kill yourself, Gigi." There was so much conviction in his voice. Like he would take the knife out of my hand if I reached for one. Me. Someone who meant very little to him in the grand scheme of things.

"Oh, why not? Your father is going to have me killed anyway."

"You don't know that. We don't know how this changes things. I can fix this."

"You don't know that."

"I do. I know that. I've been fixing messes with this family for over a decade. I will figure it out. You're not getting killed for this. I'll fucking fix it, Gigi," he added, voice firmer, sensing my disbelief.

My gaze dropped for a second, looking down at my hands, picturing how easily I had reached for that gun, had aimed it, had shot.

"I killed my father."

"The son of a bitch fucking deserved it," Lorenzo said, making my head lift, finding anger simmering in his eyes. For me. For what had been done to me.

It struck me suddenly that since my mother passed, I'd never really had someone on my side. Someone willing to fight for me.

If someone had told me that the person that finally would be on my side would be the underboss of New York's biggest mafia family, I would have had a good, long, much-needed laugh about it.

Yet here we were.

I felt I knew Lorenzo enough at this point to know that look on his face.

Determination.

And that he was a man of his word.

He would do everything in his power to fix this.

If there was a way to do so.

"Hey," he snapped, grabbing my chin again, yanking it up high, like I always did when I was being stubborn. "Don't give up on me now, do you hear me? Where's that hellcat who wanted to bash my brain in with a bottle of whiskey? I need her back. Just for a little while longer. Because I am going to need to leave you here. And I am going to need to go up there and fix this. Don't crumble on me now."

"I don't crumble," I told him, jaw getting tight. I knew he was baiting me. And that I was biting. But I guess that was the point, wasn't it?

"Prove it," he demanded, eyes bright.

I didn't see it coming.

But he leaned forward as his hand slid from my jaw to my cheek, slipping down to the side of my neck where he liked to rest it, and his lips pressed to mine.

But it wasn't hard and demanding, like I expected from him.

No.

This was something I didn't think he would be capable of.

Soft and sweet.

It was like a warm drink to my system, working through me, warming me from the inside out.

It was over far too soon, though, leaving me cold and alone in the basement as Lorenzo stood, walked to the door, gave me one final glance, then walked out, closing the door behind him.

I could hear him talking to someone through the door, making my stomach twist.

I could trust Lorenzo. He was proving that more and more by the moment. And if I could trust Lorenzo, I could trust Emilio and Chris. But Arturo? Arturo's men? Definitely not.

"It's me," a voice called through the door.

"Who?" I called back, trying to keep my voice low.

"Chris," he answered.

"Maybe I would know that if you ever spoke to me," I shot back, hearing a small chuckle in response.

"Hang tight," he told me, voice barely above a whisper. He must have been talking to me between the crack in the door, paranoid we might be overheard. "We got this."

I wanted to believe them. I wanted to trust that their confidence wasn't misplaced, that they could somehow spin this conversation into something positive.

But I had finally met Arturo Costa.

And he didn't seem like the kind of man who let people get things over on him.

For the supposed "boss of all bosses," he was a surprisingly small man. In both stature and nature. He clearly got off on my father's ass-kissing. He loathed it when I didn't cower before him. Then there was that oddly weak, higher-pitched voice.

I guess movies and TV—and, let's face it, Lorenzo—had skewed my perception of what mafia men were supposed to look like and act like.

It seemed like Arturo understood this preconception, too. I guess it was why he was so ruthless. Because he knew it was the only way a man like him could command respect.

Except it wasn't respect at all.

It was fear.

And being made to feel fearful made people angry; it didn't inspire loyalty.

So maybe Lorenzo and Chris were right. Maybe they could work this out, after all.

I couldn't let myself get too hopeful, though.

My gaze shifted around the cold, empty side of the basement.

This was not the place for hope.

This was where it went to die.

A shudder moved through me as I wondered how many men had lost their lives right where I was sitting, how much blood had been bleached from the floors, how many people had begged for their lives while being chained to a wall.

I wasn't naive enough to believe everyone made it out of this place alive. I wasn't even naive enough to be sure I would.

At this point, though, I was more worried about the things that could happen before death than the act of dying itself.

If Arturo was a small and weak man who used fear as a motivator, if he employed rapists and child molesters, if he didn't have the respect of his own damn son, who knew what could happen to me down here.

And Christopher would be powerless to stop it.

Closing my eyes, I took a deep breath, resting my head back against the wall, suddenly wishing I had put on pants and a normal shirt for this event.

At the time, I thought the dress and heels would make me feel more sure of myself, that they would work as some sort of shield between me and the men I would be faced with. I figured I would be going back to Lorenzo's penthouse after the meeting.

Now, I was just cold. And exposed.

Upstairs, I could hear the muffle of male voices, the movement of feet, the slamming and shuffling and dragging that must have been my father's body being moved.

I probably should have felt some remorse then.

For what I had done.

I wasn't a killer.

I had a gun out of fear, because I lived alone, because my father had been connected to the mob, because I had been weak and defenseless once, and I didn't ever want to feel that way again.

And, yes, I had taken that gun to a range and learned how to use it, finding something cathartic in doing so, something I needed in my stressful little life.

But I hadn't ever shot a living target before.

I was sure I never would.

Or that I would at least hesitate to do so, to possibly take someone's life.

And I damn sure figured I would feel regret or pain or sickness over doing just that.

Yet here I was. Just twenty or so moments after shooting my own father dead one floor above, and I felt none of those things.

I felt vindicated.

I felt justified.

I felt stronger.

Stronger.

Yes, that was the feeling.

I'd been beat down so much in my life, by people, by circumstance. I don't know if I ever realized just how *small* I felt until right then, when I felt bigger, stronger.

Maybe this was why people got into lives of crime. Maybe this feeling could be addictive. Especially if you had been denied it your entire life.

I took a deep breath, smelling must and stale air and the wet that created mildew in all corners of basements.

I was in a mafia boss's holding room. Chained to a wall. My hands cuffed.

And I'd never felt quite as powerful before.

Maybe Lorenzo would be able to smooth over what I had done to my father. Maybe he would get me free, with minimal damage to show for my time spent here.

But as I sat there, I made a solemn vow that I would never—fucking never—feel weak again. Be used again. Be manipulated and under-appreciated again.

I would never be made to feel small.

I didn't care what it might take to secure those things for myself.

I didn't care if I had to kill every single Goddamn member of the Five Families to earn my freedom.

Maybe Arturo Costa had seen a small, easy target when he'd ordered me kidnapped.

What he didn't realize was that in doing so, he'd freed me.

And he had no fucking idea what I would do never to be caged again.

Sure, maybe Lorenzo would save me.

If not, though, well, I was going to have to save myself, wasn't I?

Chapter Eleven

Lorenzo

My father was having his very own version of a panic attack when I made my way back upstairs, every inch of me wanting to jog back down the steps, grab Giana, and make a run for it.

Two things stopped me.

We would never make it.

And everything we had collectively been through at the hands of our shitty fathers would be for nothing if we ended up with bullets ripping through our bodies.

I had to be smart.

I had to keep my fucking feelings out of this shit.

My father was pacing the dining room, his hand gripping the gun Giana had used to kill her father, the other raking through his thinning hair.

"Jesus fucking Christ. Goddamn it. What the fuck just happened in here?" he mumbled to himself, clearly starting to spiral.

And if he got past the baffled phase, he was going to get angry.

We needed to move and fast.

Seeming to hear my internal monologue, Emilio gave me a tight nod, moving off to the stairs, to jog up the stairs.

"Where the fuck is he going?" my father demanded, waving the hand with the gun outward, making one of his men flinch. Everyone who knew Arturo Costa—no matter how loyal they might be—knew to be fearful when the man was losing control of a situation.

"To go steal some luggage," I explained, voice calm, reasonable, not too authoritative, because he would lose his shit if he realized I was taking control of the situation he should have already gotten a hold of. "Figure those assholes next door would question a rolled-up carpet," I added, knowing I was scoring points by dissing the neighbors. Those "assholes" were actually a nice, older couple who had lived in their brownstone since my grandfather bought his.

"Those fucking nosy bastards. Probably already called the cops," he said, eyes wide, panic intensifying.

"They're deaf as shit. You told me that the last time someone popped off by accident when they were cleaning their gun."

"Right. Yeah. Probably thought it was just thunder if they did hear it."

That was unlikely. No one confused gunshots for thunder. For fireworks? For a car backfiring? Sure. But not fucking thunder.

"You still have that giant suitcase from your trip out to Chicago, right?" I asked, cringing at the memory of that shitshow. The Chicago families weren't like the New York ones, weren't quite as under the thumb as my father's ego wanted them to be. It had been ugly, with all sides leaving pissed off and losing respect for one another. If I ever got my place as *Capo dei Capi*, that was yet another thing I needed to try to repair.

But one thing at a time.

"It's up there somewhere," he agreed, back to pacing. "This blood is never going to come the fuck out."

It would have, had he bothered to get the floors redone, like they'd been needing for over a decade. But with the protective finish worn down? He was right. We would need to sand it down ourselves, or rip the floor up entirely.

"Found it," Emilio said a moment later as I stared down at Leon Lastra's body, still coming to terms with the fact that Giana had been the one to take the bastard out. Sure, he deserved it. But that was some Biblical shit I had not seen coming.

The luggage was really more of a medium trunk, ornate and leather, which likely cost a fortune. We were in crisis mode, though. We would deal with replacing it some other time. Luckily, my father had very little attachment to possessions once they weren't shiny and new anymore, so he didn't even flinch as Emilio dropped it down next to Leon's body, clicking it open.

"It's big, but..." Emilio started, making me sigh.

"But so is he," I agreed. "Fuck. Go get some trash bags and an ax," I demanded of one of my father's men who took a moment to give me a grim look before rushing off.

It wouldn't be my first—or last—dismemberment. And the shock of it wore away once you did it the first time.

There were plenty of tricks to the trade, though, things you learned through personal trial and error.

Serrated blades didn't cut through bones easily. Slashing didn't cut a bone.

Your best bet was a weighted blade, like a machete or ax which would help break the bones when you swung them with enough force.

Of course, a chain saw was always a great choice. But the neighbors would definitely hear that. At least an ax was quiet.

My father's man returned a moment later with a box of black bags and a heavy ax, handing them both to me, stepping away, message clear. He wanted no part of this dirty work.

I'd been shoveling shit all my life in the name of this family. What was one more disgusting act?

I took one of the bags out of the box, set it open on the floor, then removed my jewelry, putting it down on the table. Everything else I had on would need to be burned, but I'd preferred to keep my crucifix which had been a gift from my mother, and my watch worth down payment on a very nice car. With that done, I wrapped the head, legs, and arms in black bags to try to minimize splatter, and I got to work hacking.

By the time I was done, sweat was slicking every inch of my body, with blood spread up my arms and down my face, but Leon's body was in enough pieces that I could shove the rest of him in the trunk relatively easily, stick the rest of the bags in there, and let Emilio zip it up.

"If there is a tarp anywhere, it would be good to have that for my trunk," I told my father, who had been staring at me like a demon that had just crawled out of the pits of hell. I probably looked just like one, too. And I realized in that moment that my father had not even needed to do one-tenth of the evil shit I'd needed to do in my life. Because he liked impersonal kills with a gun. He liked delegating the ugly work.

I'd never known that luxury.

He'd been tossing every horrifying, disgusting job at me since I was eighteen years old.

"Emilio and one of your guys can handle it, handle it," I added. Normally, I wouldn't trust my father's men, but with Emilio there, I knew everything would be handled correctly, even if that meant it took twice as long. "I would do it, but I am covered in evidence right now," I added, waving a hand at my ruined suit, my bloody hands and face.

"Right. Yeah. That will work. And the others can get to work at ripping up the floor, burning the wood and clothes."

Thankfully, the fireplace was one of the few things that worked in this place, mostly for just this reason. You never wanted to leave a trail of anything in this lifestyle. We lit fires all year round. This wouldn't be cause for concern to the neighbors.

I stripped out of my clothes, wiped any wet blood off my face with the fabric, made sure my wallet and keys were removed first, then watched as they threw my clothes into the fire, leaving me there in my boxer briefs in the middle of the dining room.

"Go take a fucking shower," my father snapped, lip curling; knowing him, likely pissed that he'd never been fit, that he never would be, that everything about me was an external exertion of power, while nothing about him was.

"What else needs to be done?" I asked, needing to know his plan, that if I was going to walk away, he wouldn't rush downstairs to deal with Giana.

"I need to watch the fire to make sure everything gets burned down," he said, going for the liquor cabinet again.

That was exactly what he would do, too. Get drunk and watch the fire.

I just needed ten minutes.

"You know what to do," I told Emilio as I walked past. "Don't skip any fucking step, no matter how frustrating it gets. Or annoying your company gets," I added, voice lower.

"Don't worry about me. I've done this with you more times than I can count. Nothing will trace back."

With that, I made my way upstairs, going into my childhood bedroom to wash off with ancient soap, making sure I scrubbed every inch of me five times over, getting under my nails and in my hair, until every inch of me squeaked.

Only then did I get out, dry off, and find an old t-shirt and running pants in my closet that still fit even if they were a little tight across the shoulders, arms and close to floods at the ankles. But they were clean and evidence-free; that was all that mattered.

I bleached the tub and the floor, then made my way back downstairs, finding half the dining room floor already ripped up, boards cut up and sitting in black bags, waiting to be burned.

"Leave," my father demanded as soon as I walked into the room.

"What?"

"Leave. I'm done with you for the night."

Done with me.

That was a rich way to put it.

I'd just saved us all from indictments.

But *he* was done with *me*.

"There's still—"

"Did I fucking stutter, boy?" he snapped, using a tone I hadn't heard from him in a while. One that said if I pushed, that gun in his hand would be pointed at me. And his men would be cleaning up another mess.

He was unstable.

But that was all the more reason I needed to stay.

To make sure he didn't go downstairs, didn't take it out on Giana.

"Get out of my mother fucking house, so I can get some goddamn peace," he snarled, grabbing his bottle, heading toward the stairs.

Good.

That was good.

My father liked to drink, but it always hit him like a handful of sleeping pills.

If he was heading upstairs with a bottle, in another twenty minutes, he would be out cold.

I could leave now and come back, to be there when he sobered up to discuss the Giana situation.

And until then, I knew Chris was down there to make sure none of the other guards went in.

It was fine.

I actually had one more dark mark to etch into my soul before the night was over.

I put up with a lot when it came to our family.

Men with their addictions, their bad habits, with their rage issues.

But I would not tolerate a fucking child rapist.

That was just not going to stand.

Decision made, I caught a cab back to my place to grab my second car, one I rarely used because it was flashier than what I typically drove. But it was wheels. And it had a nice, roomy trunk.

I wasn't planning to take him far, anyway.

I just needed to get him out of his apartment, into my trunk, then across town to the butcher's shop.

I needed a little time with this particular bastard.

As a whole, I didn't enjoy having to beat men whose only crime was having a family emergency that ate away at the money they saved to pay us. It was a necessary evil. A duty I carried out because this lifestyle didn't work if you weren't able to stomach doing terrible things to bring about the wanted result.

But once in a while, when there was a particularly annoying asshole you knew beat on their wives or kids in their spare time? Yeah, you could enjoy that shit a little more than usual.

There were only a handful of times I had craved the bloodshed, though, and thought of pained screams as music to the ears.

In fact, I was pretty sure this would only be the second time that I grabbed someone, knocked them cold, tied them up, and threw them in at trunk—only to carry them down the stairs and string them up in a basement—and done so with absolute fucking *glee*.

"What the fuck do you think you're doing?" Paulie asked, finally coming to, doing so slowly at first, then all at once, finding himself suspended from a meat hook in the ceiling, the cuffs biting into his wrists from hanging while unconscious.

He had a giant fucking egg on the side of his head from where I'd needed to whack him several times to keep him down while I moved him around, got him strung up.

From the looks of that thing, he had to have a killer migraine jackhammering through his head right about then.

I liked that more than I should have, too, as I leaned back in my fold-up chair, a small table situated next to me, laid out with a bunch of fun little tools I'd stolen from the butcher shop above. All kinds of little tricks of the trade. It was rather disgusting, if you thought about it, what kinds of tools were used on dead animals.

But they sure as fuck came in handy when dealing with the very-much-alive Paulie, a different kind of beast, one that didn't deserve to keep walking the earth alongside decent people.

"Well, Paulie, I have learned a few disturbing things about you this evening," I told him, finding a roast needle, turning it around in front of my face where he could see it, and come to his own conclusion about how I intended to use it. Whatever he was thinking, it was much worse.

Sometimes it wasn't as flashy as something stabbed into a testicle or an eyeball.

A roasting needle driven into an eardrum had a certain finesse to it.

"Your father is going to have your head for this," he added, yanking at the cuffs, trying to get the hook out of the ceiling since I'd had the forethought to make sure I closed the loop so he couldn't just slip right off of it. He was a tall guy. It really was a shame that he didn't dangle. Cuffs biting into the wrists was a throbbing, insistent kind of pain, one that you couldn't ignore, no matter how long you found yourself trapped in them.

I put down the roast needle, reaching instead for a skinning knife.

"My father is very much concerned with this family's reputation, Paulie. We like being known as brutal, ruthless, torturous murderers," I told him, getting to my feet. "But we aren't too keen on being seen as child molesters."

"You don't know what the fuck you are talking about. I'm no child molester."

"I know sick fucks like you can get it twisted sometimes," I agreed, slipping the blade of the knife under his top button, cutting it clean off. One thing you had to admire about butchers —they took pride in their equipment. There wasn't a dull blade in the entire shop. Parting his shirt, I ran the very tip of the blade up his front, his chest. Really, it took no pressure at all to make the blood bead up on the surface. Superficial, just a hint of my intentions in case they weren't already clear enough. "But just so it gets clear to that fucked up thing you call a brain, fifteen-year-old *girls* are still fucking children," I told him, dragging the tip of the blade across his collarbone, feeling my lips curve up when he hissed at the searing pain.

"You mother fucker," Paulie growled, trying to pull up a knee, kick me in the balls.

But his fear was making him slow.

And I ducked out of the way before he could make contact.

Not that it would have stopped me.

I was beyond pain in that moment.

Revenge for yourself was sweet. I always thought it was the epitome of highs.

But revenge for someone else, someone smaller and weaker, someone who couldn't have saved themselves no matter how hard they tried? That was some next-level shit.

I understood why there were tribes of women in the world who spent their lives tracking down and killing rapists.

What a fucking rush.

"She was *begging* for it," Paulie declared, making me turn away, going back to my tray to trade the skinning knife for the fork.

Turning, there was no hesitation.

I dug those prongs deep into his stomach, careful to miss any major organs, not wanting this over that quickly.

Giana's pain deserved more than a quick death for her rapist.

I was going to drag this out until the walls were dripping in blood. Until parts of him were dangling off.

Then I might go ahead and let him bleed out.

"First of all, no, she wasn't," I told him as I yanked the fork back out. "Secondly, even if she did, it's still rape, you sick fucking bastard," I informed him, going a bit lower, putting the fear of God into him. Or, maybe more accurately, the fear of the devil, since we both knew his soul was bound for the fiery pit. Getting anally fucked with a barbed wire bat, if there was any justice in the afterlife.

"You don't understand—"

"You're goddamn right about that," I agreed, reaching for the lamb cleaver before turning back, testing the weight in my hand.

"We were owed!"

"So we take the money. We take the blood of the man who owes us money. We don't spill the blood of the wives. We don't take the innocence of the fucking *children*. You should have known that. Now you're going to learn the hard way."

By the time my phone rang in the plastic bag I'd tucked it into to make sure there would be no chance I'd have to replace that as well as the suit I'd already lost, Paulie looked more like a prop in a horror movie than a man. Bones sticking out of skin. Intestines dangling. Piss mingled with the vomit on the floor, diluting the bright red of the blood.

I took a moment to strip and wipe off the excess blood, then went to scrub up in the sink before moving to uncover my phone, checking who I'd missed.

Emilio.

With a curse, I checked the time, wondering how much I had let pass, what was going on with Chris and Gigi.

It wasn't as bad as I thought.

Just shy of two hours.

Not long in the grand scheme of things, but Paulie had felt every moment of it.

"Yeah?"

"It's done."

"Okay. I know you've had a similar night to the one I've had, so I am going to need you to call Brio and get him over to the shop."

"Who?" Emilio asked, sounding exhausted. I didn't blame him. I was sure that once the adrenaline wore off, I would be drained as well.

"Our other guest this evening. Things came to light. About certain hands. And underage bodies."

"Oh, fuck," Emilio hissed. "Alright."

"Yeah," I agreed.

"Does he know?" he asked, clearly meaning my old man.

"No. Took a bottle to bed."

"Those two were tight."

"I have zero tolerance of this kind of shit."

"Yeah, no. I get it. I agree. I'll call Brio. I'll get a cup of coffee and help out. If you can be up, so can I," he said, proving again that he had it in him to work harder, just chose not to for a boss he didn't respect.

Me, on the other hand, he would endure two murders and body disposals for.

"Appreciate it," I said before hanging up, then put my phone back in the bag before moving around, collecting up instruments, taking them to the sink.

I bleached them and soaped up as much of my body as I could, grabbing some old uniform pants and a jacket from a dusty box in a corner to slip on before making my way upstairs to put the tools back into the dishwasher, setting it to run again, then making my way back down with some industrial cleaners the guys used to clean down the shop each night.

By the time I had everything set up and ready for them, they were coming in the back door, shuffling down the steps.

Emilio first, half-empty iced coffee in his hand.

Brio next.

He was just shy of my height, a little thinner, but fit in a more wiry way. He kept his black hair buzzed, had a sharp jaw and onyx eyes. He had an array of black and gray tats snaking up his arms and across his neck. He'd never gotten the memo about dressing for the family, wearing jeans, a black tee, and black Tims. He looked more like a gang member than a made man in the mafia, but Brio had never been someone to give a shit about appearances.

He moved toward the door first, hands in pockets, casual as can be about a corpse clean-up. He should have been, with how many corpses he'd created that needed to be dealt with.

He glanced in the room, head nodding, before turning back to me.

"That's a good amount of damage. Respect that," he said, grabbing for the latex gloves I'd found upstairs, taking the box of black bags.

"At least you don't need to cut this one up," Emilio said, sighing, drawing Brio's attention back to me, again, impressed. The sick fuck.

"I'm hurt I wasn't invited to the festivities, I'm not gonna lie," Brio said, clucking his tongue.

"The night really wasn't supposed to take this turn," I told him, shrugging, feeling the weight of my arms from all the hacking and slicing and lifting of bodies.

"You always did know how to make shit interesting," Brio said. "Is something going on that I need to know about?" he asked, pinning me with those icy eyes of his.

"Not that I know of. Yet. The way shit is going lately, just keep an ear for your phone, yeah?"

"Got it," he agreed, ducking into the room.

Emilio stood with me for a moment, finishing his coffee. His gaze cut to me as Brio's voice carried to us from the other room.

But he wasn't talking to us.

He was talking to the body.

He did weird shit like that.

"I heard you like touching little girls," he murmured, and I could hear him dragging a chair across the floor, likely trying to get the meat hook uncurled, so he could drop the body. "Got off easy, man. Did you know there are five basic types of torture? You got sharp, blunt, cold, hot, loud. Sure, sure, there are millions of little subsets within each group. Hot water. Fire. That sort of thing. So many ways to spend *so* many hours. We would have had lots of fun, you and me."

"Jesus Christ," Emilio hissed, shaking his head. "I hope to fuck that bastard never gets pissed at me. He'd revive a man just to rip out his teeth one-by-one."

"Oh, shit. Sorry 'bout that man. Guts just fell right out. Guess I gotta be more careful with ya."

"Do something," I demanded, barely holding back a laugh at the look of horror on Emilio's face.

"I think I'm owed hazard pay for having to dispose of something with that crazy bastard."

"You got it," I agreed, nodding my head.

"Go clean up fully. We got this. Then get your girl out."

"She's not my girl," I insisted, shaking my head.

To that, Emilio moved into the doorway, looking at Paulie's mutilated body, then back at me.

"You sure about that?"

"Oh, man," Brio interrupted. "He didn't cut your tongue out? Shit, man. That would have been my first move. Harder to scream when you're choking on your blood, y'know? Missed opportunity, there."

"Yeah," I said to Emilio, trying to block out Brio's insane ramblings. "This was business. He made the family look bad. Got away with it for years. It's not personal."

"Aw shit, little boss man," Brio said, standing upright, facing me. "Even I know this shit is personal. I mean, where *is* his cock? Oh, wait, shit, is that it?" he asked, pointing. "I thought it was a finger. Damn. No wonder he was such an asshole, packing that pencil dick. But yeah, boss man, me? I do this shit. You? You don't do this shit. So you doing this shit, that's personal. Own that shit."

With that, he turned his focus back to Paulie.

"Keep an eye on him," I told Emilio quietly.

"You have no worries with this," he told me, shrugging. "We know what we're doing. Go handle the rest of this, so we can all get some much-needed rest."

With that, I did, heading home for a quick shower and change after checking with Chris to make sure no one had tried to come and relieve him of his duties.

Luckily, everyone was working on laying the new floor, and had forgotten about the woman in the basement.

Which was good.

I grabbed a cup of coffee and made my way back to the brownstone, taking a deep breath, steeling myself for whatever might come my way.

Or so I thought.

"Where the fuck have you been?" my father asked when I made my way in through the house, glancing over at the new flooring that was carefully being put into place by men who were not qualified to do so, their suits getting rubbed bare in the knees from crawling around, their fucking gold jewelry dangling. It was a sight. If I were less tired and stressed, I'd have had a good chuckle over it. "I was just going to talk to our guest about her actions last night," he added, already reaching for the door to the basement, making his way down.

He might have always had a poor tolerance for liquor, but the bastard rarely dealt with hangovers. Which made him a lot more on his game than I was currently feeling.

I had to shake it off.

This was the most important part.

The only part that mattered.

I didn't even trip over that thought like I knew I would have just a week or so before.

Because back then, it was saving the family's face that was most important, making sure the other families—especially the Espositos and the Lombardis—had no reason to try to make a power move, take over the top family position.

I didn't know when that stopped being the main motivator.

Fuck.

Sure I did.

It started right there in my closet. Right before I even put my hands on her. When I felt a tug somewhere inside, something new and interesting and, yeah, fucking terrifying, if I were honest.

There had been hints of affection before then, having appreciated her attitude and fighting spirit right from the jump, but in that closet, when she showed me something soft under all that hard, that was when the change started.

It had only continued to grow since then.

I just didn't realize how big it had gotten until the night before. When, for the first time, I was genuinely worried I wouldn't be able to get her out of this mess.

Right then, panic had gripped me, a tight sensation in my chest and throat, a sloshing in my stomach.

It was then that I knew I would move hell and earth to get her free, to get her justice. And to give us a real shot at something.

Not as debtor and collector.

Not as a kidnapper and hostage.

Just as a man and a woman.

I wanted to give that a shot.

I had a feeling there was something there.

A future.

But to have that, I had to fix the present.

And, I reminded myself as I gave Chris a nod, watching as he moved out of the way, the present was far from fixed.

But we were close.

So close.

Or so I thought.

My father opened the door to the unfinished side of the basement, and I could hear the rattle of the chain as a half-dozing Giana jolted awake, eyes swollen, but from exhaustion, not tears.

No, she hadn't been crying.

There was a strange swelling of pride inside at that.

I had no idea if that was because I was happy she had that much spirit, or if it was because she trusted me that much, or a combination of the two. But it was there, a floating sort of sensation in my chest.

Her gaze slid up my father's body, her chin jutting up as she got to his face. She didn't look at me, and I got the feeling it was because she didn't want it to seem like we had any sort of connection. Which was good. My father would be pissed if he thought someone respected me more than him.

"What was your name again?" he asked, glaring down at her, trying to intimidate her. And if that didn't show you what a little fucking man he was, I didn't know what did, trying to scare a small woman less than half his age.

"Giana," she told him, no tremble in her lip, no tremor in her voice.

"Giana. You fucked up last night," he told her.

"Or did I make things easier?" she asked, shrugging one of her shoulders.

"How the fuck could killing a family friend make anything easier for me?"

"When did he ever pay on time?" she shot back. "And I can assure you, Mr. Costa, that when he did, it was only because I made sure it happened. My father was never good with money. I think he was very impressed with you," she added, and I could hear the hint of disgust in her voice, but only because I was beginning to know her well enough to. I knew what she was trying to do. Stroke my father's ego. And it was killing her pride to do it. But she was doing it. And I felt another wave of pride. "He was always trying to emulate you. Buying things we both knew he couldn't afford because he wanted to be more like you."

"He was a decent man. Flawed, but decent," my father said, chest puffing just the slightest bit. "Which makes me wonder how wicked his daughter must be to shoot him in cold blood with no provocation."

To that, Giana took a deep breath, giving him a version of the truth I had a feeling she had been working on all night, making sure there was no way any part of it could be taken the wrong way.

"I used to think the same thing about my father," she told my father. "That he was decent, just flawed. Which was why I always nudged him to do what was right and pay his debts, no matter the personal sacrifice he might have to endure. It's important for your word to be honorable. But last night, sitting at your dining table, I realized I was wrong all these years. He wasn't a decent man. He was the lowest kind."

"And what kind is that?"

"The kind who betrays his own family."

Christ. I could have written this speech for her.

Family over everything.

That was the code we lived and died by.

"How did he betray his own family?"

"Last night, you had a guest come in while we were all having our... meeting," she fumbled on that word, choosing it carefully.

"Yes. An associate of mine."

"Well, I'm sure you have no idea about this. I think people can hide their sins pretty well when they know powerful, moral men would be angry if they uncovered them."

"Are you talking about Paulie?" my father asked, the name making Giana cringe for a second before she shook it off. "What are his sins, then?"

"He rapes children," she told him, gaze going up to hold my father's. "He raped me when I was fifteen."

"There are a lot of men in the world who have a taste for young women," my father said, shrugging, suggesting that it could have been another man.

But I was reading more into that. Into the almost defensive way he said it.

Shit.

Fuck.

Goddamn it.

He knew.

He knew what Paulie had been up to.

He looked the other way.

Or he outright allowed it.

Either way, shit just went from bad to worse, and I had no way to get that information across to Giana.

So she went on.

"That's true, unfortunately. But I remembered something very specific about this man. A port wine birthmark on his left hand. I even drew a picture of it after the rape. I had told my father about it. And last night, he shook the hand with that very birthmark on it. He knew, Mr. Costa. He knew that Paulie raped me as a little girl, that one of his friends had raped my mother. Worse yet, I think my father *let* him do it, gave him a key to our apartment to do it."

"That's quite the little story you've created in your head. I'm sure if I invited Paulie over here to talk about it with us, he would say he had nothing to do with that event."

This is the part where things were going to get even more touchy.

Because he couldn't call Paulie.

This was not going to be good.

As if sensing the train of my thoughts, Giana's gaze finally met mine, her brows pinching at whatever she found on my face.

Shock.

Fear.

Resignation.

Those were all things I was feeling right then.

She could have seen any—or all—of them.

"That's not going to be possible," I told my father, making him half-turn to look at me.

"What's not possible?"

"Having Paulie over."

"Why not?" my father demanded, words a snapping sound, already sensing I was about to say something he didn't want to hear.

"Because he's in a couple garbage bags being transported to a safe location."

"A couple of garbage bags?" my father repeated, not great with subtlety.

"I always believed our family was against pedophilia. I didn't want him disgracing our name. I handled it."

"Who the *fuck* gave you the order to do that?" my father shouted, loud enough for Giana to shock back.

I couldn't blame her.

My father's anger was of the explosive sort.

If you weren't prepared for it, it could be scary.

I, however, had been on the receiving end of his rage since I was a kid.

I wasn't worried about his words, his tone.

What mattered right now were his actions.

"He was our best collector. He brought in more than all of the others combined. Are you out of your fucking mind?"

"He touched children."

"Who the fuck cares what he did if he got the job done?" he roared back, making my stomach twist.

It was one thing to believe your father was scum. It was a complete other to learn that there wasn't a word to describe how disgusting he was. That he could look the other way to children being abused.

This was the man I'd pledged loyalty to.

I didn't see the gun coming out.

I should have expected it, but I was reeling from the revelation.

I sure as fuck felt it when the bullet ripped through my shoulder, though.

Giana's screech pierced my ears as the pain gripped my system, as Chris burst into the room, and the men upstairs came running across the floor, down the stairs, and in as well.

"Who the fuck do you think you are?" my father raged, waving the gun, making his men jerk around, not wanting to be on the receiving end of a bullet meant for me. "You think you're the boss of this family?" he asked, expecting an answer, needing me to admit I wasn't.

"I thought I was following through with the oaths this family has made."

"You don't get to make those fucking decisions. Those are my fucking decisions," he raged, flipping the gun in his hand, whipping me across the face with it.

And I had no choice but to stand there and take it.

In the mafia, if you raised hands to a made man, you signed your death warrant.

That was just any old made man.

You simply didn't raise a hand to a boss.

That didn't happen.

Sure, he might kill me for what I'd done.

But if I put hands on him, I would be dead for sure.

I was placing my bet.

Taking the beating so I might live.

And my father had always been good with a beating.

It was harder now that I was taller than him, bigger and stronger than him. But he managed to make up for those shortcomings with a boundless amount of rage.

It wasn't long before I was tasting blood, and felt the tell-tale crack of a broken rib, the sharp pain that accompanied it.

A part of me couldn't help but wonder what Giana was thinking as I stood there with my arms at my side, taking a beating.

Did she think I was weak?

Did she think I was afraid of my father?

Or did she understand what was happening?

As the gun collided with my jaw, I finally swallowed my pride enough to glance over, finding her shifted up onto her knees, the chain straining against the wall because she had tried to move closer, wanted to do something.

Her wide eyes were on mine.

Fearful.

Concerned.

For me?

For her?

Maybe I would never know.

Because my father's rage only seemed to grow when I didn't cry out, didn't curse, didn't beg for mercy.

"Get on your fucking knees," he demanded, making me suck in a deep breath as I moved to do so.

I wasn't a man who truly understood fear.

Fear did nothing.

Acceptance of inevitable fate was a prouder way to go, in my humble opinion.

I could feel the cool of the cement through the knees of my slacks as I carefully went down closer to Giana, as I reached discreetly into my pocket, pulling what I was looking for out, tucking it into my fist, waiting for the opportunity to give it to her, to give her a fighting chance.

If I didn't make it out of this, I wanted her to be able to.

Emilio would find a way to help her. He would know I would want that.

I lifted my chin, staring up at my father, who somehow managed to look like an even smaller man at that angle.

"You are not the mother fucking boss of the Costa family, boy," he roared, lifting the gun.

I'd seen him shoot many men in my life.

From a car.

From a street corner.

From a window.

Across a room.

He didn't often do up-close-and-personal killing.

I was starting to see why.

His fucking hand was shaking.

Hard enough that the gun was trembling, and his aim was for shit.

Maybe I could make that work to my benefit. Turn just right at the exact right second. Get a graze instead of a direct hit.

I doubted he would shoot me when I was down. It wasn't a power move. His men were watching.

"You want to be a *Capo dei Capi*, you need to kill the current one," he added.

In that moment, it sounded a lot like an invitation to my ego.

But it wasn't that easy. It never was. If I killed my father to take his place, the other families would decide to kill me for my disloyalty. And then they would all go to war to pick the next *Capo dei Capi*.

If I went that route, there was no way I was going to make it out of this.

At least I stood a chance that my father wouldn't feel the need to be lethal.

"Family over everything," I countered, shaking my head. "Always," I added.

They were good final words, if this was the end.

The men would repeat them.

My father's reign would be questioned.

Especially if he killed me after them.

There was a rumbling sound coming from my father before his finger slid to the trigger.

My hand moved outward slightly, looking like I was bracing myself.

When his gaze didn't follow the movement, I slid the saved item out of my hand, passed it to a confused Giana, feeling her slide it into her own fist, hiding it.

There.

It was done.

Come what may.

Chapter Twelve

The handcuff key was still cool in my palm when the shot rang out. The sound was deafening in the small, enclosed space, making my ears ring so loud that I didn't even realize I was screaming until I heard Arturo snap, "Someone shut that bitch up," a second before a palm slapped across my cheek, the hot pain seeming to snap me out of my shock, making my gaze fly to where Lorenzo was sprawled on the ground, bleeding from a gunshot wound right above his left ear.

Oh, God.

No.

No no no no.

This couldn't be happening.

He couldn't be bleeding to death right in front of me.

It wasn't until right that moment that I realized he had started to mean something to me, despite my efforts to keep him at a distance.

He'd been good to me, considering.

He'd sided with me against the family.

The biggest taboo of all.

And then he'd... he'd murdered the man who had raped me.

Who did that?

He told his father it was about the family's honor, but I knew that wasn't all.

He'd done it for me.

He'd killed for me.

He'd gotten the revenge I wanted, but knew I couldn't stomach to get for myself.

And then his final act before staring down the barrel of his father's gun was to hand me a handcuff key, to grant me my freedom when the opportunity presented itself.

"Get him the fuck out of here," Arturo growled, waving down at Lorenzo's body.

Arturo's guards were the first to the body, grabbing him, lifting him, hauling him out of the room.

Chris stayed with me.

While Emilio and Chris and some of the other guards I had met while stuck at Lorenzo's penthouse technically belonged to Arturo, it was clear to me that their loyalty was to Lorenzo.

Once Lorenzo and the guards were gone, Arturo stormed out too, followed by his remaining guards, leaving just me and Christopher.

We both stayed in numb silence for a long couple of moments, hearing all the movements upstairs. I was pretty sure I heard Arturo going up the stairs to the top level, could hear his men getting back to work on the dining room floors.

Only then did Chris turn to me.

"Was he still breathing?" I whispered, my heart thudding so hard in my chest that my ribcage hurt.

"I don't know," he admitted, sounding remorseful about it.

"Is Arturo going to kill me?"

"I don't know," Chris said again, shoulders falling.

"Are his men going to rape me?"

"No," he told me, straightening, chin lifting, a stubborn move I knew well.

"You can't say that for sure."

"I'll be standing right outside this door."

"For what? Forever?" I asked, shaking my head.

"If necessary. And there's Emilio too," he added, shrugging. "Lorenzo would want us to do this."

My heart shrank smaller in my chest, felt like it was drying out, becoming brittle.

"What happens now?"

"My best guess? Arturo hits the bottle. Which means he will pass out for the rest of tonight."

"Will his men leave?"

"Some of them. When they're done with the floor. The ones who stay will move outside so they can piss off the neighbors by smoking and bullshitting all night. If you hold off until then, I can get you upstairs. Use the bathroom. Get you something to eat and drink."

My bladder was screaming.

I was going to get a raging UTI at this rate.

But what choice did I have?

"Okay," I agreed, nodding. "Thank you, Chris."

"You didn't belong in all this shit anyway."

"And if it weren't for me, none of this would have happened."

He didn't deny that, because we both knew it was the truth, as hard as it was for me to swallow.

If Lorenzo was dead, it was my fault.

I wasn't sure how my conscience was going to accept that, come to grips with that.

It wasn't the time for it, anyway.

Now was the time for survival.

And, eventually, freedom.

That was what Lorenzo wanted for me.

I would honor that.

"I have to go outside the door. In case anyone comes down," Chris said, sounding regretful.

A part of me didn't like the idea of being alone. The other part wanted solitude, needed to process all that had just happened, what it all meant, what the next move was from here.

"Okay," I agreed, nodding. "Thank you."

He gave me a tight nod and moved outside the door, closing it behind him.

Alone, the cool of the room settled deeper into my bones. But what sent goosebumps over my skin wasn't the cold, natural dampness of the basement.

No.

It was the puddle of darkening blood on the floor near my foot.

I scuttled back from it, leaning back against the wall again, feeling the relief on my ankle shackle once I gave it slack.

Tears flooded my eyes unexpectedly, blurring my vision, cracking open something deep inside.

I didn't bother fighting them, too tired to try. Instead, I leaned my head back against the wall, letting them flow freely, dropping down onto the bodice of my dress, darkening the material, soaking it as the time went on.

Eventually, they dried up. But not before they made my cheeks raw, my eyelids puffy.

And between the swollen eyelids and the sheer exhaustion that had been weighing on me finally won out, making my eyes flutter closed.

I dreamed of Lorenzo.

The same, yet different.

We were in his penthouse. But there were no guards, no locks on doors meant to keep me in.

Because I was there by choice, walking across his apartment with bare feet, carrying two mugs of coffee, handing one to a waiting Lorenzo leaning back on the couch, still in his loafers, slacks, and button-up, but his jacket was draped over the back of the sofa at his side.

He gave me a head tilt, eyes soft, and motioned me to him with the fingers of his free hand.

I went to him willingly, happily, settling in close at his side, feeling the weight of his arm settle around my shoulders, pulling me closer still.

It was the safest I ever felt in my life.

The warmest too.

The most content.

I woke up shivering, teeth chattering with the cold, my stomach churning painfully, my neck screaming when I tried to lift my chin from my chest where it had bobbed while I was asleep.

I wanted to go back to sleep.

I wanted to fall back into that dream.

I wanted anything but this hopeless reality.

"Hey," Chris's voice called, making me jolt, looking to find him moving toward me. "Come on. We have five minutes," he said, kneeling down to un-cuff my leg shackle.

I don't know why I did it.

Why I didn't just let him in on Lorenzo's last act of kindness toward me?

I guess because my conscience couldn't take any more good men catching bullets because of me. If he knew, he would be a sort of accessory. If he didn't, he was an innocent bystander.

So while he worked on the shackle, I lifted my hands to my face, pretending to block a yawn, slipping the key into my mouth, tucking it under my tongue.

The metallic taste was like a shock of caffeine to my weary system as the shackle finally fell.

Chris stood, reaching downward, grabbing my forearm, pulling me onto my feet.

"Christ. You're freezing," he realized, reaching out to chafe my arms, such an unexpectedly sweet gesture that I felt a small smile pulling at my lips despite the dire circumstances.

"I'm alright," I assured him, even if the cold felt like an ache in my bones at that point.

"If we have a minute, maybe I can get you something hot to drink," he told me, dropping his hands, moving in front of me. "Wait," he said, stopping me after two feet. "We need to get those off," he told me, motioning to my feet.

With that, he took off my heels, tucking them back over by my space, before we continued on, heading up the stairs.

Each step made my stomach drop, made my heart flutter, sure someone was going to come charging out of nowhere, screaming at me to get back in my basement.

But no one came.

But even as we broke into the kitchen, Chris doing a quick glance around before he decided the coast was clear, leading me toward a room off of the kitchen.

"Guest bath," he told me, shuffling me inside. "I'll get the food. Take a second to warm up."

Fat chance of that since Arturo—like his son—set the air conditioning to arctic, so the air was blasting through the vent to the side of the sink.

It didn't matter, though. I wasn't going to freeze to death.It was inconvenient and uncomfortable and maybe I did run my hands under hot water before I exited the room, but I was going to be fine.

Chris was waiting with me with a cup of coffee in one hand, a bottle of water tucked under his arm, and what looked like leftover pasta in a paper bowl, a ton of parmesan cheese shredded on top.

"Go on," he said, nodding toward the door, glancing around, paranoid.

I didn't need to be told twice, I flew down the stairs as fast as I dared, worried about them creaking.

Chris followed behind more slowly, bringing everything over to me.

I reached for the coffee first, taking a long sip.

"Eat this," Chris demanded, taking the coffee, setting it down, and handing me the bowl as he set the ankle shackle back into place, giving me a regretful glance as he did so.

"It's okay," I assured him, nodding. He didn't need to feel guilty.

I was going to get myself out of this.

Like I had needed to get myself out of everything else in my life.

In the end, it always came back to me.

If I could single-handedly keep the bakery from bankruptcy, if I could keep my father from getting his kneecaps busted, if I could escape kidnappers, if I could pick up a gun and take the life of my own father, I could get myself free.

This time for good.

My heart would crush at leaving the bakery behind, knowing that if I was gone, the bank would eventually have to take it. And knowing the neighborhood, it would get turned into some truly tragic trendy coffee place with no such thing as old charm, homemade treats, or friendly service from people who genuinely took pride in their work, in the community.

My grandfather would understand given the situation.

Maybe someday, in a new city, far outside the reach of Arturo Costa, I could start again. Maybe I could open a new bakery, name it after my grandfather. No, I didn't have the leather-bound recipe book in his handwriting anymore, but I had the recipes memorized, had them saved in my email in case something ever happened to the original.

It was not the same.

But it was something.

It would still honor his memory.

And it was something positive to look forward to after all this negativity, all this cold, all this uncertainty, all this pain—both old and new.

I waited until Chris looked away, spitting my cuff key into my hand, tucking it under my thigh, then setting to work on the pasta as best I could with the awkward cuffs in the way.

When I finished, he took the bowl, disappearing while I finished my coffee, took one sip of the water, not wanting to put too many fluids in if I didn't know when my next bathroom break might be.

"I'll keep this with me outside the door. You can just call me if you need a sip. Eventually, Arturo is going to remember you need to eat, drink, and use the bathroom. He's not new at this. He's just..." he trailed off, waving his hand.

"Okay," I agreed, nodding, not sure if that filled me with a little hope, or a lot of dread. "Thank you again."

"He'd want it," Chris said, looking grim, making my stomach clench.

I wanted to ask.

If he knew anything, if he'd heard anything.

But, somehow, I also didn't want to know.

It was better not to know.

At least until I was far away from all of this.

Because I wasn't sure that if I learned he'd survived, I would still be able to do it. Pack up. Run off. Start over.

I was pretty sure a part of me would need to see him, would feel indebted to him, would maybe even want to stay with him, get that warm feeling back I'd gotten in a dream.

It was ridiculous. On a rational level, I understood that. But there was no denying the desire was there either.

I had no one left in the world.

If I had him, somehow, I think that would supersede the more rational side of me.

No one wanted to be wholly alone in the world. Even if all he would ever be was a person who had known what I had been through, that would be something, someone, more than I had now.

But I knew the smartest thing to do was run.

The only thing to do was run.

So it was better not to know.

At least that was what I spent the next several hours trying to convince myself of between little snippets of boredom-induced sleep while the house was quiet.

I think I heard it the second Arturo's feet hit the floorboards, though. I knew I heard the water running down the pipes as he brushed his teeth. I heard his footsteps on the stairs as he made his way into the kitchen. I heard the bleep of the coffee pot, the sound of the fridge opening and shutting.

I heard him move over toward the top of the stairs, felt my breath catch in my chest.

"Who is down there?"

"Chris," Chris answered, and I couldn't imagine how tired he must have been. I had been catching little cap naps on and off. I had a feeling he didn't.

"Bring her up to use the john. Toss some food at her. Then stick her back down there. I have shit to do today."

Thank God.

I nearly cried in relief.

With that, Chris made his way in, undoing my ankle, giving me raised brows.

"You have to be exhausted," I observed.

"I'll be fine."

"Once we come back down, you should try to sleep. Even just right outside the door if you don't want to leave."

"I'm not going to leave. Not until there is someone I trust to replace me."

Was it good or bad that Emilio hadn't shown up?

"But you have to sleep."

"I'll figure it out," he insisted as we heard the door slam upstairs.

"Was that him leaving?"

"Probably. Come on. Let's stretch those legs. I think we need to scrounge up some triple antibiotic for that ankle too. It's getting raw. Those shackles are filthy."

I felt a shudder move through me, thinking of the sweat and blood and who knew what else from an unknown number of men were on those cuffs.

"Why doesn't he just deal with me now?" I asked as we sat at the kitchen table, a spare blanket wrapped around my shoulders as I ate plain oatmeal and tried to pretend it wasn't disgusting. It was food. That was all that mattered.

"He probably isn't sure yet how to handle it."

"Because he wants to keep making money off the bakery?"

"Seems like it might be part of it."

"I can run the business with the owner in absentia," I told Christopher, getting a raised brow from him. "I've looked into it. It seemed smart to know my rights when my father was involved with people who frequently make people go missing. There are all kinds of loopholes about how if I have a key and access to the accounts and such, I can keep it running until he returns."

"Doesn't seem like a forever sort of plan."

"No. When someone is missing for ten years, you can file for them to be declared dead. After another ten years from then, they will do so if they never show up. So that's a twenty-year plan."

"And after twenty years?"

"After twenty years, I am the sole beneficiary to my father's will." I knew that because my mother had insisted on him drawing up the documents when she'd been alive still. Just in case.

"Well, that sounds like a good plan then. Tell that to the boss like you told that to me. He might be hot-tempered, but he is all about the money."

Right.

The money.

The money that would likely be doubled just because of the hassle I caused.

Money I would never be able to produce.

Not without Lorenzo and his deal.

Even then, though, I would be looking over my shoulder, waiting for the next minion of Arturo Costa's to catch me alone and accost me simply because he could.

As much as a big part of me wanted to stay, wanted to work it out, wanted to be able to continue the legacy my family had created, the other part of me knew I would never feel safe, would never feel comfortable with the arrangement.

I had to go.

But it would make everything easier if I could have that meeting with Arturo, give him my reassurances, spout off all these facts I knew, agree to his terms.

Then walk out of this house a free woman.

No trying to find a way to escape.

Then, once I was sure I wasn't being followed, hop on a bus or train and get the hell out of here.

Sure, I had the same problem as I did when I had tried to escape the last time. No money. No cards. No nothing. Unless one of them was willing to go into Lorenzo's apartment to grab them for me. Let's face it, the chances of that weren't great.

Still, this time, the possibility of living on a street sounded preferable to being under the thumb of a ruthless mob boss.

I would figure it out.

I always did.

That was my superpower.

"When do you think he will make time for me?"

"Honestly? Hard to say," Chris told me, shrugging his tired shoulders. "He won't forget about you completely, but it might be a day or two before he makes the time for you."

"Okay," I agreed, taking a deep breath, trying to prepare myself for that possibility. "I'm really regretting this fashion choice," I admitted, looking down at my dress. "That basement is freezing."

"I'll leave the door open as much as I can. Let some warmer air in. Plus you won't feel so alone."

"You're a good guy. Has anyone told you that lately?" I asked.

"You just did," he told me, taking my bowl over to the sink. "Go hit the john one more time. Here," he added, going under the sink to grab me a fresh cleaning rag. "You'll feel more human if you can do a little washing up," he told me, shrugging, grabbing another rag. I figured for himself since he hadn't had a chance to go back to his place to shower or change either. The two of us were going to be pretty gross if this went on another day or two.

Whore's bath completed, I made my way back down the stairs with Chris behind me smelling like dish soap and stale coffee.

My ass immediately objected to the hard floor as I lowered down.

A day and a half passed.

Chris left the door open much of the time, and he was right. It felt better seeing another person, even if that person was sitting in a leather chair, dozing off for twenty-minute spells at a time.

I knew how unsatisfying that kind of rest was. Because that was all I was getting as well, always jerking awake when my head would fall forward, my chin hitting my chest, sending a shooting pain up the back of my neck.

Eventually, after a few hours of that, we both resigned ourselves to groggy consciousness, him giving me a regretful look as he slid the door closed when there were footsteps on the floor above.

Arturo didn't come down to see me that day, that night.

So, as was becoming our ritual, when he went to bed, I was brought up to use the bathroom, gratefully brushing my teeth side-by-side with Chris when he found some extra brushes and paste in the linen closet, washing all my important parts when he left to grab us food.

We sat in companionable silence, jumping at every noise, as we ate.

Maybe I should have run away then.

But there was no window to sneak out of in the bathroom.

And un-cuffing myself and trying to escape in front of Chris put him in a bad position. He would either have to let me go, in which case he would be in major trouble with his boss. Or he would have to try to retrieve me, which would bring the other guards in on it, would make things messier. And I was not so vain as to think I could escape Chris as well as the two or three other guards that were always hanging around. And then what would become of me?

I couldn't take that chance.

If I did need to escape, I had to be smart about it.

But I told myself I would try to get through a meeting with Arturo first.

If that failed, then I would make my escape.

Until then, I had to learn to accept the confinement, the endlessly slow hours of the day, the helplessness. And be thankful for Chris's kindness, his loyalty to Lorenzo even when there seemed to be no proof that Lorenzo was alive.

The piercing in my chest at that was enough to make me nearly miss a step on the way down the stairs, Chris's quick reflexes the only thing keeping me from falling down the steps, and both of us from being found out.

"Hopefully not too much longer," Chris said, giving me a weary smile that neither of us was buying.

Anything akin to hope died around the third day of absolutely nothing from Arturo Costa. Like he had forgotten me entirely.

To be fair, he spent most of his days and nights out of the house, seemingly coming in just to charge up the stairs to his bedroom.

Invariably, I would hear one of his guards inside the house, going upstairs, coming back down, and talking on the phone, ordering food.

You notice a lot of things stuck in a quiet house, listening to all of its secrets.

Like the fact that Arturo probably had an enlarged prostate given how often he got up to use the bathroom each night.

Like there was the telltale skittering of mice somewhere in the basement.

Like the boss of the Costa family, apparently, had a nut allergy, judging by the way the guard who ordered would always make sure the meals were nut-free.

Like one of the guards let himself in the house in the middle of the night to watch—of all things—reruns of *I Dream of Jeannie.*

Like the other guard, apparently, sometimes snuck away at night to go screw some girl a block over.

I cataloged all of this, clinging to each bit of information because it was all I had in the world at that point.

On the fourth day, I heard footsteps on the stairs.

I should have been filled with dread, should have had my stomach tightening, my heart hammering.

What did I feel instead?

Relief.

Because, one way or another, I was going to get out of this goddamn basement.

Maybe that would be freely and with Arturo's blessing.

Maybe that would be under the cover of night while I snuck out.

Or maybe it would be with parts of me in garbage bags.

But it was out.

Out was all I cared about at that point.

"Christ. When was the last time you showered?" Arturo's voice called, making me stiffen, having an idea I knew what was to follow. "Go home. Clean up. You can't represent this family looking like that."

And there it was.

The order I expected.

I was completely on my own now.

Christopher would come back. Of course he would. But maybe it would be too late at that point. And if I survived this meeting, I would likely have a new guard, one who didn't care if I ate or used the bathroom. At least temporarily, until Chris could get him to leave.

I took a deep breath, making sure the handcuff key was safely tucked under my tongue, looking up as the door slid open.

Arturo Costa looked rough.

Dark circles framed his eyes even though he had seemed to spend most of his time in bed. His skin was pale, his face bloated. Likely from all that crappy food he'd been ordering. And not to mention all the alcohol I was sure he'd been drinking.

"What? No pleading for your life?" he asked, voice low, almost bored-sounding.

I couldn't help but wonder if that was because Lorenzo wasn't around. Clearly, Lorenzo was the workhorse of the family, was the one who handled the day-to-day operations of a massive criminal empire.

Arturo was the sort to sit on his throne and look down at all the peasants, not the sort to actually work. He thought he was above all of that. But now he had no choice but to deal with it all.

Good.

I was glad he was struggling.

I hoped he hated every moment of it.

"I'm too cold and tired," I told him, letting my voice be a little weaker than I wanted it to.

I was a woman with some pride. I had been doing so much my whole life, handling everything for everyone, never breaking under the pressure. It killed me not to be able to lift my chin, to give him direct eye-contact, to let my attitude slip into my voice.

But men like Arturo Costa, they liked women small and weak and subservient.

I had to play my part if I wanted to survive.

"Well, that will make you think twice about trying to involve yourself in business that has nothing to do with you."

Nothing to do with me.

Meanwhile, I had been the one kidnapped because of said business.

Asshole.

"Am I going to stay down here forever?" I asked, going ahead and forcing my lower lip to tremble.

"That depends."

"On?"

"Many things. You are currently the reason I will be out of a not unsubstantial sum of money every month."

"I was actually thinking about that," I started, then launched into it, making sure not to sound too sure of myself, mumbling a lot, kneecapping my sentences.

In the end, he was quiet for a long moment.

"Why would you know all of that?" he asked, suspicious.

"My father would sometimes leave town without notice for days or even weeks," I claimed. It was pure and utter bullshit, but I damn near believed myself when I said it. "I was always worried about our business, about our debts," I added, looking up at him.

"He was never very reliable. I will think about it," he told me, turning, making his way to the door.

"For how long?"

"However the fuck long I want to think about it. Couple days. Couple weeks. Get comfortable. I'm not done punishing you for what you've done. You need to learn your lesson before we can talk about the next steps."

With that, the door slammed, locked.

I really thought I had him.

I thought I was convincing enough.

Maybe I had been.

But then I'd made a mistake.

I'd questioned him.

To men like Arturo Costa, the world revolved around them. Your time meant nothing.

Shit.

Days? I could handle days.

Weeks? I wasn't so sure about that.

And I didn't think I could handle months, either, if those months were going to be filled with men coming in to punish me.

He had made the decision for me, then.

I had to escape.

The question was just how. And when.

After Arturo went up to bed, of course.

I had a key to the cuffs on my wrists, but the shackle on my ankle had a bigger lock.

I couldn't claim to be a master at picking locks, but I had needed to open my apartment door with a bobby pin more than a few times when I rushed out of the house too quickly, forgetting my keys as I went.

I didn't have a bobby pin, though.

But once I got the cuffs off, I might be able to rig the key up or parts of the cuffs up to get in the keyhole.

Or I could see about trying to work the pin out of the wall.

On that thought, I listened for a moment, making sure there was no one else about to charge in, then turned, inspected the wall.

Someone had reinforced the cinderblock around the hole they'd made, smooth cement grabbing at the sides of the rusty pin.

If I had something to use to knock it around, I might be able to loosen it.

But I didn't exactly have any tools.

The sound of rapid footsteps on the stairs had me turning back, my heart going into overdrive.

I didn't have a lot of time to build my anxiety, though, because the door was pushing open, and someone was walking in.

He was tall and fit, but on the thinner side, with dark hair, dark eyes, tattoos peeking out from the neck of his black t-shirt.

The t-shirt was what was weird.

Not only a t-shirt, but jeans. Tims.

I'd seen a lot of men associated with this family, they always dressed in suits, they always looked like they were on their way to very important meetings.

Was it a good or bad thing that this man looked like he was about to go commit some crime?

He was good looking and on the younger side, closer to Lorenzo's age than Arturo's.

"Who are you?" I asked, hearing a weariness in my voice that betrayed my exhaustion, my fear.

"Brio," he told me, coming to a stop a few feet away. "You and me, we were supposed to meet before this," he told me, squatting down, resting his forearms on his knees.

"You were who was originally supposed to kidnap me," I decided, remembering Lorenzo telling me that the guy he'd replaced had been vicious.

That was who I was looking at.

A man that made a man like Lorenzo feel morally superior.

Great.

That was just great.

"That's me," he agreed, giving me a small smile. "I got rid of that pedo's body too," he added, like this was the most normal, natural conversation to have. About a tortured and murdered man to a woman who was chained to a wall in the basement of a mafia boss's house.

Hell, maybe to him, it was.

"Oh, really?" I asked. "Um, thanks."

"Little boss man did the work. Looks like he enjoyed himself doing it, too. Cut his cock off," he added, nodding, clearly impressed with the brutality of Lorenzo's actions. "But he skinned it first. That's just," he said, bringing his fingers up to his lips to do a chef's kiss, "perfect. Wish I had thought of that one before. Peeled balls before. But the cock, that is a boss move," he told me. "Oh, he cut that ugly ass mark off the bastard's hand too. Real carefully. Got every millimeter of that thing. Shoved it in his mouth. Real masterful work. Wish I could have been there."

"Did you come here to tell me the body is taken care of?" I asked, confused.

"Nah. Actually, might be in trouble if that shit gets around too much. Don't worry about me, they need me too much to stick me down in a basement to rot. Just came to take my shift. Figured I'd introduce myself."

With that, he moved to stand, turning, going to make his way back to the door.

It was then that I saw something sticking out of his back pocket.

Something in a brown wrapper with red, white, and blue writing.

A Snickers bar.

"Hey, Brio," I called, making him turn back.

"Yeah, doll?"

"Could I maybe have that?" I asked, pointing with my cuffed hands. "The candy bar," I added, going ahead and letting my voice get small again. "I'm so hungry," I said, eyes wide.

"Oh shit. Forgot I had that. Got a bad sweet tooth. Yeah, sure, here," he said, tossing it to me, giving me a smile when I managed to grab it out of the air.

"Thank you."

"Don't mention it. Hey, nice shoes," he told me, jerking his chin toward my heels before walking out, closing, and locking the door.

I wasn't actually hungry.

And while I did love a good Snickers bar, had earned one with all the shit I had been through, I didn't want it to eat.

No.

Something had just clicked when I'd seen it.

See.

I could get free.

I could run.

I could give up my entire life.

I could live in fear that Arturo's ego might mean he would look for me.

I could do that.

But why should I have to?

Why should I—the only person in this entire situation who was innocent in every way—have to settle for that?

Why did Arturo, the guiltiest of all of us, get to get off Scot-free?

This man with blood on his hands?

This man who would look the other way when he had a rapist on his payroll?

This man who would ruthlessly stick a gun in his son's face and pull the trigger?

The answer was simple.

He shouldn't.

He shouldn't get away with it.

I couldn't *let* him get away with it.

Really, I had very little left to live for.

So while there was a lot of risk in trying to take down a man like Arturo Costa, it wasn't like I had a husband or kids or even a pet to leave behind that might miss me. And even if I died, I'd have done so taking out one of the worst human beings anyone had ever had the displeasure of crossing paths with.

That was a legacy worth leaving behind.

Lives would be spared.

Businesses like the bakery would get a reprieve while the family scrambled to figure out the new power dynamic with the boss and the underboss dead.

Yeah.

I could take an eternity of punishment in hell with a smile on my face for making this one final decision, doing this one thing that would positively impact so many lives, that would bring the scales of justice back into alignment.

Killing the *Capo dei Capi* of New York City.

With the fucking peanuts in a Snickers bar taken from one of his men.

It was almost poetic, really.

I just had to figure out how to get the peanuts into his system.

And, of course, how to get out of the...

Wait.

Nice shoes.

That was what Brio had said.

I'd forgotten about them until that moment. Chris had taken them off of me, and I'd never needed them again since most of our trips upstairs were in secret.

I remember when I had opened the box back in Lorenzo's apartment—something that suddenly felt like a lifetime ago; I swear I'd been a different woman then—that they were a weird choice. With their clunky Mary Jane strap with an oversize buckle. But, then again, I hadn't seen a fashion magazine since before my mother died, so what did I know about fashion trends?

But, yes, a buckle.

A real metal buckle.

Stretching my leg out, I carefully grabbed the edge of one heel with my bare toes, pulling it closed, inspecting the buckle, pulling at it, feeling a sense of satisfaction when the edges of the metal weren't soldered together, just curled against each other, letting the whole thing pull apart to one long metal piece.

If I had the shoe, I had everything I needed to get the shackle off.

At least I hoped.

From there, I just had to find a way out.

With Brio standing guard, I knew there was no way out there unless he left his station.

But there was another side of this unfinished half of the basement. And chances were, there had to be a window out.

Most people couldn't fit through a standard basement window, the type that wasn't an egress. But this was one of the very few times where being small truly came in handy. Maybe I had never been allowed on certain rides at the theme park, but I had always been the one who could crawl in air ducts to save abandoned baby opossums, who could climb inside the storage cabinets every week at work to wipe them out properly.

I could fit through a basement window.

If I could get something to climb to get close to it.

And then I could get inside. Carefully. And slip the peanuts into something I knew Arturo consumed every day, pray he didn't see or taste them. Then get back in the basement, get back in my shackles, make it look like I'd never left. No one could ever suspect me.

Then, during all the confusion with police and such, I could slip right back out, disappear for a short period of time, then possibly get back to my old life.

Free.

For the first time in my entire life.

Yeah, that seemed worth all the risk.

Decision made, I hid my makeshift lock picks just in case someone came in, and I set to eating my candy bar, but spitting out the peanuts, piling them on the floor, then crushing them under the heel of my shoe into a fine powder before scooping the dust up and hiding it in the candy bar wrapper, shoving that in the toe of my shoe before tucking them a few feet away again.

Then I waited.

And waited.

And waited.

Arturo came home, went upstairs, the guard ordered the food on his way back outside. Then, finally, the house quieted down.

On the other side of the door, Brio seemed to be watching something on his phone, some show or movie with a lot of gunshots and yelling.

Good cover sounds.

I reached for my shoes with a sort of calmness washing over me. I guess this was what they talked about when people did incredibly dangerous things but for a good cause, how they never even thought twice about it.

I sure as hell didn't as I freed my wrists, struggling a bit with my leg shackle because I was trying not to make too much noise.

But it gave, and something inside of me fizzled with actual excitement as I carefully placed it down, reaching for the wrapper full of peanuts, folding it carefully, and tucking it between my lips.

Standing up made my body hiss in objection after being in a cramped position for so long, but I ignored it as I inched across the cold floor, making my way toward the door to the other side, using my little lock pick set to unlock the door, cringing as it clicked. But on the finished side of the basement, there was some sort of shootout taking place on Brio's phone, covering the noise as I slipped to the other side, carefully closing the door.

This side of the basement was what I expected. The furnace, hot water heater, piles of discarded cardboard boxes, wilting in the dampness.

And, yes, a window.

Without bars.

Adrenaline coursed through me, making me feel like I was buzzing as I moved around the dark space, looking for something to stand on, nearly laughing in relief when I found a freaking step ladder.

A step ladder.

In a room with a window.

I guess Arturo was so cocky that he never thought anyone could get as far as I did. Maybe he had reason to be that confident, because no one ever had.

But I guess he hadn't really pissed off a woman enough before.

I placed the step ladder, then reached up, carefully pulled open the window, looking out into the small backyard for a minute, making sure no guards were around, then clamping my lips harder around the wrapper, and hauling myself out.

My arms were shaking, my body sweating, excitement, fear, and exhaustion a strange concoction in my system.

It felt like it took forever.

But it was all over in maybe two minutes.

And I was out.

A part of me wanted to make a run for it.

But the backyard was fenced on three sides. And the only way out was down the side and past the guards. Even if they weren't the fastest of guys, I was pretty sure they could get me, could haul me back. And then I didn't want to think about how Arturo would make me pay, and ensure that I could never get away again.

So I crab-walked toward the back window, glancing in, then taking a steadying breath, heading inside.

Silence.

Save for Brio's phone that I could hear even a floor above. If he heard movement above him, he would just figure it was Arturo or one of the other guys.

I had no idea what Arturo consumed aside from the whiskey he drank and the food he had ordered in.

But there was one thing that was true of the father as well as the son.

He started the day with coffee.

Decision made, I went over to the coffee maker, finding that Arturo, again like Lorenzo, made up the pot the night before, so it would brew before he got up.

The fresh grinds were in the filter.

Almost giddy with excitement, I shook the peanut dust into the grinds, mixing them up a little in case someone decided to check the machine—which seemed unlikely, but, apparently, plotting murder made one paranoid.

Finished, I tucked the wrapper back into my mouth, not wanting anyone to see it, to suspect anything since it likely shouldn't have been in the house at all.

With that, I made my way back outside, realizing as I got to it that getting back in a basement was a lot harder than getting out.

In the end, I had to lie flat on the ground, slithering backward like the snake I guess I was that night, lowering myself down, legs dangling for a heart-dropping moment before I finally felt the step ladder, then stepped down.

I took the extra moment to put everything how I found it, sneaking into the other side, locking myself back up, and spending the next hour or so trying to get my buckles back into shape.

They looked all wrong in the end, but I hoped that these men wouldn't be the sort to look too closely.

Then I sat and waited.

Exhaustion disappeared, replaced with something that made me all sorts of wicked.

Excitement.

Anticipation.

Freaking *glee*.

I couldn't even consider sleep, my whole body was buzzing, adrenaline bouncing off my nerve endings as I leaned back against the wall, waiting to hear the house wake up.

On the other side of the door, at some point, Brio turned off his phone, maybe catching a little forbidden sleep like Chris had done the other nights.

A smile pulled at my lips as I heard the coffee pot beep as it finished brewing. And again when I heard Arturo's feet on the stairs, completely unaware of what was going to happen.

I should have felt guilt.

I guess normal people would have.

But I couldn't help but wonder how many men and women had started their days just like Arturo was starting his, completely oblivious that everything was about to change, losing their lives—or the lives of loved ones—because Arturo willed it.

He'd caused countless deaths.

He'd brought unfathomable amounts of terror into the hearts of others.

I felt no guilt.

Not even as I heard him take his cup upstairs, likely drinking a big gulp before getting into his shower.

In his locked bathroom.

Out of sight of anyone who might be hanging around with an epinephrine pen.

The excitement dimmed, the glee turned into something like disappointment, like defeat, when minutes passed, when nothing seemed to happen.

Tears sprang to my eyes, wondering what the hell my choice was now.

Trying to make a run for it?

What were my chances?

How could I start over with no money, no IDs?

Maybe I could go to the police.

Tell them my story.

Point fingers.

See if they would make me disappear.

My hands reached up, wiping the tears off my cheeks.

I don't know how long I sat there like that, biting my lip to keep the sobs in, face getting raw from the saltwater.

I was barely aware of the footsteps above, casual at first, then running, barely even registered the shouting.

But then there were frantic feet on the stairs, up, then down again.

The door flew open, bouncing against the wall.

And there was Brio.

His eyes were a little wild, but everything else about him calm, focused, as he made his way over toward me, producing a key, reaching for my ankle.

"You got to go, doll."

"Go? Go where? Where are you taking me?"

"I'm not takin' you anywhere. No one is. You're gonna get up, go up those stairs, and get fucking lost, you hear me? You run. And you don't look back. And you don't say shit about ever being here, you got that?"

"I, ah, yeah," I agreed, nodding as he fished for a handcuff key, freeing my wrists.

"Let's do it," he said, pulling me onto my feet, taking off toward the stairs, jogging up them.

Was I wrong?

Had it worked?

Had it just taken them this long to find him?

Hope swelled under my ribcage as I made my way into the kitchen.

"Out the back. And disappear, doll. Don't fuckin' look back, yeah?"

"I, yeah," I agreed, but he was already going through the front hall, jogging up the stairs.

I knew I had to run.

I knew I had to disappear.

But for some reason, I stood there for one extra second, looking around.

And then I saw it.

A wallet on the table.

I rushed at it, grabbing it, stuffing it down the bodice of my dress, and doing exactly what Brio said.

Getting out of there.

I didn't run right away.

I walked casually around the house, then down to the street.

I was nearly at the corner when I heard the sirens. Another couple seconds before the police cars came barreling down the street.

Turning, I saw them screech to a halt out front of Arturo's brownstone.

I took one second to watch, to see the ambulance pull up.

But I was pretty sure it was too late.

That was why they had to get rid of me.

Because the cops were coming.

And they couldn't have a prisoner in the basement.

Then I did it.

I ran.

And ran.

And ran.

I found myself in a crowded park, people glancing at me sideways for wearing a bright red evening dress and no shoes in the early morning, but I ignored them, let them think I had just done a walk of shame, reaching into my bodice to produce the wallet.

Arturo's.

There was his face on the driver's license, staring back at me, accusing me.

"Rot in hell, asshole," I grumbled at the picture as I reached into the fold to pull out a wad of cash.

Two thousand.

That would get me safe.

I could figure it out from there.

Don't ask me why I didn't just drop the wallet in the trashcan and make my escape from the city. I don't know the answer.

All I know is that I didn't do that.

I sat on a bench, flipping through the wallet.

And that was when I found it.

The letter.

And the picture.

I read it once, twice, three times, before the words started to sink in, to penetrate, to make sense.

Then I reached for the picture again, not wanting to believe it, but there was no denying it.

I sat there for a long time, long enough that my ass started to hurt, staring down at what I just found, trying to decide what it meant, if anything.

But it did mean something.

And, I guess, I wasn't running away after all.

I had one more wrong to right.

And then I would be done with this fucking family once and for all.

Chapter Thirteen

Lorenzo

Apparently, one does interesting things when they are coming out of the drugs used for a medically-induced coma.

Like demand someone turn the lights on, when the problem was your eyes were still shut.

Like ask for someone to stop spinning the room when the room was, of course, stationary.

Like offer to ruthlessly murder the shitty husband of the nurse who had been telling the other nurse that he'd been cheating on her for six months.

I remembered exactly none of this, but was told all of it by a smiling Emilio as he stood at my bedside, looking worn out, eyes baggy, skin pale, clothes wrinkled.

"How long have I been out?" I demanded.

"Just over a week," he told me, eyes pained. "It was touch and go. They didn't give you a great odds. Thank fuck you're a stubborn bastard," he said, giving me a weak smirk.

"Where is she?" I demanded.

I didn't know much when I was out.

Of the actual world.

A lot of people wake up from their comas saying they heard every sentence uttered to them, felt every brush of a hand, tried so hard to get back to the surface of their consciousness.

That was not me.

I guess maybe because of all the drugs.

I knew nothing of the world around me.

Not the constant beeps of the machines I was hooked up to. Not the squeaking of the nurses' shoes. Not Emilio's demands I wake the fuck up already and fix this mess.

All I knew was blissful unconsciousness. And dreams of Giana.

The soft brush of her hand. Those gray eyes. Her voice calling out my name.

I spent seven days in my head alone with Gigi.

But I was in the real world now.

And I needed to know where she was, if she was okay, when I could see her.

"We don't know," Emilio admitted, wincing, bracing for the impact of my rage.

"What the fuck do you mean you don't know where she is?" I roared, folding up in the bed, the machine at my side starting to scream.

There was hardly a blink before I could hear those squeaky shoes rushing in, a pretty blonde nurse coming in at my side, looking at the machine, pressing a hand to my chest.

"You need to stay calm," she told me, voice firm.

"I need to sign myself out," I shot back, ripping the monitor off my finger, the tube out of my hand.

"You really need to see the doctor. He is on his way in. Mr. Costa, you were shot in the head. You had surgery. And you were in a coma. You need to take it slow."

"I know what happened. And I know I need to get the hell out of here," I told her, regretting my tone when she shrank back.

Let's face it, they knew average people didn't get shot in the head.

They likely heard all about who I was.

"He's not going anywhere until he gets looked over," Emilio assured the nurse. "But maybe tell the good doc he better get in here within the next five minutes, okay?" he asked, tone heavy with meaning. *Or else.*

The nurse rushed off, leaving us alone in the stark white room, the sun streaming in through the large windows.

"I need you to talk," I told him, pushing the button to fold my bed up. I hated to admit it, but I was a little light-headed, a little off. "Where is Giana?"

"Look," Emilio said, face grim. "A lot of shit has gone down since you passed out. And I need you to cooperate with these doctors. Because I need to get your ass out of this bed, out of this hospital, in a suit, and in front of the families. As soon as possible."

Emilio was rarely serious, never grave.

But he was both of those things right that moment.

I had no idea what had happened, but I knew I had to trust him, that I had to make sure I was able to function, then get the hell out of there, so he could fill me in.

"Okay," I agreed, nodding.

"He's on his way in," the nurse called, barely pausing in the doorway before rushing off.

"I know. We'll send a basket in apology," Emilio said, shaking his head. "Always such a charmer, Lorenzo," he added, reaching for his phone, blowing off a series of texts.

I wanted to press him, but then the doctor was there, spouting off a bunch of shit about my surgery, about how lucky

I was, about possible complications, about therapy should I need it, about follow-up visits with a neurologist as well as my primary care doctor.

I yes'd him to death, then asked for my papers as Emilio ducked downstairs, coming back with a suit in a dry-cleaning bag.

I moved on frustratingly unsteady feet into the bathroom, took a two-minute shower in the minuscule enclosure, brushed my teeth, and shrugged into the suit.

Most of the other injuries from my beating had healed over in the week since I had received them. But the freshly shaved line down the side of my head and the bright red wound there were going to take a while to get used to seeing in the mirror.

It was a small problem, though.

And from the sound of things, I had big issues to deal with.

"Alright. Talk," I demanded as soon as we were half a block down from the hospital.

We should have gotten somewhere more private, but the walking wasn't feeling so great, so I was taking the opportunity to lean back against the wall, take it easy on myself.

"Your father is dead."

"What?" I hissed, feeling like someone kicked me in the chest, all my air was gone. "How?"

"Anaphylactic shock," he told me, shrugging. "His men found him when he was late for a meeting. He'd started his shower, but was on the floor dead beside it."

My father's death meant fucking chaos for the families.

Especially since I wasn't around.

"Who is trying to rise up?" I asked, following him as he led me over toward his car on the side street.

"Espositios and Lombardis are making noise. The D'Onofrios and the Morellis are being patient, waiting to hear about your condition. Like I said, though, it wasn't looking good. So the Morellis, last I heard, were ready to step in. If for no other reason, than to keep the others in place."

"Get me to the brownstone," I demanded as he pulled off into traffic. "Did you already inform everyone I woke up?"

"I got the word around to the D'Onofrios and Morellis, but I was holding off on the others."

Good.

They might have heard that, and come to pick me off on my way out of the hospital.

"My father's men?"

"Anxious, at best. I figure there are more skeletons in the closet than we realized, and everyone is shitting themselves that you will do to them what you did to Paulie."

"How the fuck did that get out?" I snapped, glaring at him.

"Don't look at me. Your father managed to spread that around before he died."

My head was spinning with all this information, with all the possible repercussions to this shift in power, to all the things I needed to do to ensure my position, to keep peace among the Five Families.

But still, it circled back to one thing.

One person.

"I need to know what happened to Giana," I told Emilio as he turned down the street toward my father's—now my— brownstone.

"I don't know," he admitted, shaking his head. "The guards panicked, called the cops. I don't know if she was let go, or if she escaped in the chaos. I talked to your father's guards. I talked to Chris. No one knows what happened. She was just gone."

"Was there blood?"

"No. No," he insisted, voice firmer. "I looked. No crime scene was cleaned up. She just wasn't there. I think she just slipped away in the chaos."

"I need to find her."

"I will get someone on it. If we can spare them."

"We will spare them," I told him, not caring if it meant I would be less protected as I made my move to take the position of power, as I plotted to become the *Capo dei Cap*i.

"Okay. I will get someone on that. I think Chris will volunteer. Sounds like they bonded over the days when he was on guard. Your old man kicked him out. That was when all this shit went down. He has been beating himself up about it since."

"Alright. Yeah, in that case, put him on it. And Anthony. We need to open the books, get him in. I need more men I know I can count on around here. Old alliances need to be evened out. And I want Terry taken care of," I told him, thinking of my father's consigliere, a man I wouldn't trust as far as I could throw him.

"Taken down a notch, or taken care of?" Emilio asked, parking, glancing over at me.

"Fucking taken care of," I told him, opening my door, climbing out.

"Boss," Christopher greeted me, rushing forward, blocking my body at the right as Emilio moved in at my left.

I didn't love the idea of having the men I trusted most in the world literally shielding me from possible bullets, but I also had to accept that this was my life now.

I was no longer an underboss.

And being the boss meant you had bodyguards at all times, like it or not.

We rushed up the steps and into the house, most of the family gathered around.

I saw several looks around the room.

Some showed relief.

Others fear.

And still others, uncertainty.

The ones with relief were on my short list for positions closest to me.

The fearful ones needed to be interrogated.

The uncertain ones would just need to have their loyalty inspired. It shouldn't be hard considering they'd put up with my father's shitty leadership for so long.

"You," I said, pointing to several of the fearful and uncertain ones. "On the streets. Listen around. We're not worried about the Morellis or the D'Onofrios. Work any leads you have on the other families. Get it out that I am back and I am fine and I am taking my father's place. You," I went on, pointing to some of the relieved ones, thankful for their acceptance. "We need to gut this place, get all the useless shit boxed up, and get rid of it. And anything even slightly incriminating, questionable, all the weapons, everything else, we need to sort and deal with. I need to know what my father didn't make public knowledge. No surprises."

"Me?" Christopher asked, chin jerking up. "You know what your job is. Find her," I told him, giving him a hard glance, getting a nod before rushing off.

"I need ten guards here at the house. Everyone else, I need you making the rounds at our local businesses, drop in, tell them we are giving them this month off from their debts until I can meet with each of them personally to make sure the rates have all been fair. Yes, fair," I affirmed when brows pinched. "My father leaned too hard on some, and not hard enough on others. We are fixing that. But they don't need to know that.

Just tell them what I said. And otherwise, business as usual. Except you now come to me with your problems. Coffee," I told Emilio as the others decided who would stay and who would hit the streets. "What did the cops and coroner say about my father?"

"Accidental consumption of peanuts. Though no one has any idea how. You know how your father was about nuts."

I did.

I never even tasted peanut butter until I was an adult. He made some rule about how the people who owed us debts couldn't touch or eat nuts the day debts were collected each month. He was anal about it. Which made sense since he had a severe allergy, and almost died twice.

Why he hadn't gotten to an epinephrine pen was beyond me.

That said, I wasn't exactly sad about it.

I saw it in his eyes as he pulled that trigger.

He meant to kill me.

He might have sent someone to finish the job had Chris not called Emilio, getting him to stand at my side night and day in that hospital.

So good riddance to bad rubbish and all of that.

"How are you feeling really?" Emilio asked as I leaned back against the counter, taking a breath.

"I have a headache. And I'm hungry. I just need to get my strength up. Another day or two, and I will feel normal again."

"Glad to hear it. I know you have been waiting for this day for a long time. Kinda sucks that you were in limbo for a good part of it instead of being able to jump right in."

"It's alright. I'll catch up.

"I know you will. You were born for this."

"How many of those guys do you think have secrets like Paulie had?" I asked, cracking my neck.

"That particular secret? I hope to fuck none. But I don't know. I guess you never do. But that's why we have Brio," he declared, handing me my coffee.

"Speaking of. Where the fuck was he? I didn't see him out there?"

"I'm not sure. I know your father's guys said they saw him the night of his death, but not since. Then again, I wasn't keeping tabs on him either."

"Okay. Well, call him in. We need his particular skill set."

"On it. We have to order food in. There's nothing here to eat."

"Alright," I agreed as the house started to burst to life, everyone going into rooms, taking everything that wasn't bolted to the walls down, looking behind pictures, checking inside clocks, drawers, under loose floorboards.

Anything questionable got brought to me.

Dozens of guns of unknown origins were put up on the table to be gotten rid of. I didn't know what might have been done with them, and I didn't want my father's sins on my back. Or rap sheet.

Money was, of course, left with me to squirrel back away when no one was looking. Though everyone who was busting their ass was going to get a stack or two before they went home for the night.

I wasn't above bribing loyalty if I needed to at first. Money always has been and always will be a powerful motivator.

I had trouble sleeping those first two nights.

I wanted to say it was because there was so much to do, so many people to see, so many fires to be put out.

But in the quiet moments when no one was around to command something from me, I could admit the truth to myself.

I was having trouble sleeping because I had no idea where she was, if she was okay, if she even knew I was alive.

Christopher had made no progress.

If she had gotten away on her own accord, she had done so completely. She hadn't shown up at the bakery, at her apartment, at her father's place.

She was a ghost.

And I felt her haunting me in those quiet moments when sleep was supposed to claim me. I needed rest. Food and coffee had managed to keep me going, built my strength up, but I knew I would be for shit if I didn't get some sleep.

I had a sneaking suspicion, though, that I wouldn't get a full, restful night of sleep until I knew what became of her.

Even if that meant she had started a new life out in California and wanted absolutely nothing to do with me.

Or, at least, that was what I was telling myself.

Even though a part of me knew I needed her there at my side.

My brain flashed back to the basement, to the terror on her face. But not for herself. For me.

She gave a shit.

She cared.

She wanted me to live.

I knew that, had I not gotten shot, if I had gotten her out of that basement, even if she went back to bakery, we would be pulled back together.

Something had started there.

Something neither of us was ready to give up.

"It's done," Emilio told me first thing the next morning.

He'd taken up residence in my old childhood bedroom, staying close, and I was surprised how little I resented the intrusion.

After all the shit that had happened in the past few weeks, I was glad to have someone I could trust right there when I needed him.

We'd sworn in his little brother Anthony a day before, and he had shown his loyalty by agreeing to go out and kill my father's old consigliere, Terry.

Eighteen was young by most standards, but I had blood on my hand for the first time at seventeen. So did Emilio. This was our world. We all had to age up faster than most men.

Besides, Terry was a reasonably easy mark. Older. Slower. Arrogant enough to think he wouldn't be a target.

"Did he have anything to report?" I asked. "We should probably have him over for a drink."

"He's actually on his way over. He said he figured something out, but didn't want to talk about it on the phone."

"Wouldn't be surprised. Terry was always up to something."

"How's the head?" Milo asked, rummaging through the fridge.

"Getting better."

"Are you going to be a pain in the ass about going back to the doctor?"

"No. I was in a rush to get out of there. I have questions. Need to know when I can hit the workout equipment again. I will go stir crazy locked up in here."

We'd agreed that I needed to stay inside at least until some of the intel was in about the other families. Especially since I wasn't at one-hundred-percent yet.

"Well, at least you can finally rip all this hideous shit out," Emilio said, waving an arm out at the house in general. "We will find a crew we can trust. Have Brio breathe down their necks while they work. They will be too afraid to do anything like eavesdrop."

"Yo, Milo," one of the guards out front called in from the door. "Your brother is here."

"Yep, let him in," I called. "He doesn't need an invitation here."

With that, there were muffled voices, a door closing, and a sound I wasn't able to place right at first.

But then it hit me.

High heels on hardwood floors.

High heels?

My gaze slipped to Emilio, finding his brows drawn together too, coming to the same conclusion.

We both turned to the doorway just as Anthony and—unexpectedly—Chris moved inside, faces both mirror images of surprise and uncertainty and a small bit of eagerness.

"What?" I asked, looking between them. "Did I hear heels?" I added.

The two men shared a look then both moved to the sides of the doorway, opening it up for our other guests to walk through.

Giana.

And my mother.

My mother?

"Your lady here has been a busy woman," my mother declared into the shocked silence of the room.

I barely remembered her voice, so lost in time, having been so young when she had disappeared. It wasn't soft and warm like Giana's, but rather cool and smooth and confident.

Which matched her appearance—tall, slim, dark-haired, sharp-featured, green-eyed, wearing a simple black dress and heels.

I should have felt a rush of joy, of relief, maybe even of sadness over the lost years when I thought she was dead. All I could feel right then, though, was surprise, confusion, a complete lack of understanding of what I was seeing. It overtook anything else that had been moving through my system with this new piece of shocking information.

"Someone needs to talk," I declared, barely recognizing my own voice as my gaze shifted to Giana.

The relief was like a wave through my system, knocking away the tension that had been bunched up in every muscle thanks to the uncertainty of her whereabouts, my fears about her safety.

She looked amazing.

Better than I remembered.

She didn't dress like my mother, rather wearing a pair of black jeans and a charcoal tee, her long, dark hair free.

No cuts, no bruises.

She seemed fine.

Great, even.

But there was something different, something in her eyes that hadn't been there before.

I couldn't place it at first. Until her chin raised up and her gaze leveled with me.

That was a confidence that hadn't been there before.

But what had brought about the change?

"I went to follow through with my order," Anthony supplied. "To make my bones," he added.

To kill Terry.

"But there was a problem. I was too late. Christopher was already there."

"Why were you there?" I asked, gaze moving toward him.

"Well, my job was to find Giana. And I did."

"Alright, for fuck's sake, let's stop with the dramatics," I said. "Someone give me some straight answers."

"I guess that is my place, darling," my mother said, giving me a careful smile. "Yes, Anthony was supposed to take out Terry. And, my love, I very much approve of that decision on your part. But he was too late. Someone else had already stuck a letter opener in that sneaky bastard's carotid. No," she said when my gaze went to Chris. "Your lady friend here was the one who did it."

"What?" my voice hissed out of me, not able to accept this reality. "How... why?"

"Yes, great questions," my mother agreed, but turned to Emilio. "Milo, sweetie," she said, giving him another of those unsure smiles. "You are all grown. Nice belt buckle, by the way," she said, shaking her head at the rooster with the word "Cocky" written under it. "Can you get me a cup of coffee? This is a long story," she said, moving forward to sit down across from me. "Don't you want to say hello to your girl, Enz?" she asked, the old nickname like a punch to the gut, realizing how many years I had missed hearing it, believing she was dead, while all along, she had been very much alive.

My gaze lifted, finding Giana's gray eyes on me, that confidence just a little shakier. My arm lifted, ushering her closer. There was a moment of hesitation, of uncertainty, before she moved across the floor, let me wrap my arm around her waist and pull her down onto my lap.

"I thought you were dead," she told me as soon as she settled.

"I almost was," I agreed, squeezing her. "What happened?"

"Well, I thought you died. And I was alone. And I would have to get myself out of that basement on my own."

"So, that's what happened. You escaped that night."

"Well, yes. And no," she told me, giving me a wobbly smile as Emilio handed my mother a coffee, and me what looked like a glass of whiskey. I had a feeling I was going to need it.

"How yes? And how no?" I asked.

"Well, I had the handcuff key you passed to me. And when Christopher was sent away by your father, I made a plan to get out through the basement window."

"You're probably the only person over ten years old who could fit through that fucking thing."

"I did. Just barely."

"But then how did you not escape?" I asked, reaching up, brushing her hair behind her ear so that I could see her face better.

"Well, I got out," she told me, nodding. "But I didn't run. There was no way to run, with the guards out front. That was the only way out. I'm not that great of a runner, for obvious reasons. So I had another idea."

"And that was?"

"You know something funny?" she asked instead of answering directly.

"I could use something funny right about now."

"All my childhood, I remembered my father getting pissed off if my mother and I made anything with peanut butter in it. I always thought it was just a preference thing. But as I was sitting in that basement, I remembered overhearing my father snapping at my mother when he came home and there were Reeses wrappers on the table. He said something about how she knew he couldn't be around that shit when he had his monthly meeting. It never clicked until I heard your father's guard ask the restaurant to make sure the meals were nut-free. Your dad was allergic. And I just so happened to get my hands on a candy bar while in the basement."

"What?" I asked, my voice a hushed whisper. Because it didn't seem possible.

"He had to go," she said, shrugging. "For you. For me. For everyone in this damn city. He had to go. And I had a way to do it. So I did. And then I snuck right back down to the basement, put my cuffs back on, and waited, so that no one could ever suspect me, so that if I got free, I was truly free. No more looking over my shoulder all the time. When the police were called, I was shuffled out so no one found me chained in a basement. On my way out, though, I stopped for one minute to grab your father's wallet. For money to disappear for a while."

"Okay," I said. "I need to know how you got from the basement to my mother's side. And, for that matter, standing over Terry with a bloody letter opener," I said, reaching up to pinch the bridge of my nose, feeling a headache coming on.

"Are you okay? Should you be under all this stress? You were just shot in the head," she reminded me.

"Babe, my dad is dead, my mom is alive, and I am suddenly the boss of all bosses. There's no way not to be stressed about this. But I need to hear it, so give it to me straight. How did you find my mom? How did you get her out? Where is Terry's body? I need the details," I told her, giving her knee a squeeze.

Then she gave them to me.

Chapter Fourteen

Giana

It was absurd, of course.

So absurd that I didn't trust my eyes, didn't want to believe what the images meant in the long term.

But there was no denying it, either.

There was the letter. It was a nothing letter, really, some rambling nonsense about some house that some guy named Terry had inherited when a great uncle died. Along with that was a newspaper clipping of a house that had once belonged to the sheriff, that had been used to also serve as the town's only jail. Cells and everything in the basement.

It wasn't until the very end that something became significant.

"I was going to sell it. But I was thinking. That bitch can't up and leave you, take your boys like that. And we both know you'd never get custody. Just saying. It's an option. If you don't like the other one."

It didn't take a genius to know the other option was to kill her.

And, why wouldn't he kill her? That was the most rational—in a screwed up way—answer to that situation.

But, as I now knew about Arturo Costa, he was just a small man with a big ego and a lot of ugliness. He needed to be in control in all things in all ways.

What a blow to the pride it must have been to have a wife that hated you so much that she wanted to run and take your kids with her, likely never to see you again.

He couldn't let her do that.

And he was too little of a man to simply handle it.

No.

He was the sort of man who wanted to make people suffer, who got off on that control.

So while the rational side of my head refused to accept that anyone could lock someone up for years, I had a feeling it was exactly the kind of insane thing Arturo was capable of.

And maybe it wasn't even that crazy.

Every year or so, some story would hit the news about a missing woman being found in some creep's cellar, sometimes having been there for decades, bearing and raising children while never seeing the light of day.

People could do some sick things.

Men who wanted power over women, well, they could do the worst things of all.

Like trapping a wife in an old jail just to know she could never get away from you, would likely be forced to endure visits with you over the years while she sat there, her life rotting away, her boys growing up without her.

I sat in a makeshift cell for just a couple days, and I could feel insanity tugging at the corners of my mind.

I mean, if you had told me just two weeks before that I was capable of using someone's food allergy against them, to *kill* them, I would have said you were insane.

But people became a little more feral when treated like animals.

Some ingrained killer instinct had kicked in.

I couldn't fathom in what ways my head would be screwed with if I had been kept down there for weeks, for months, let alone years, let alone a huge chunk of my life.

I guess I would find out, though.

What other choice did I have?

Arturo was dead.

If there was no more boss, why the hell would his wife be kept alive when she could clearly could point fingers about her imprisonment?

I wanted to be free.

But, I imagined, so did she.

Maybe I should have gone to the cops.

But if there was one thing I was starting to question, it was their ability to do anything about this reign of terror that Arturo had inflicted upon the city.

Palms could be greased.

Or people could be afraid for their lives, for their loved one's lives, so they didn't go after the Families.

I freed myself.

I could free her.

And then I would be done.

I would be able to rest easy.

Okay. I would probably need a shitton of therapy before I could rest easy. But one day. It was a goal worth working toward.

Decision made, I grabbed some shoes and a couple basic self-care items, so I could look less homeless as I hopped on a train out of the city, then took three more trains and two buses before I finally found myself on the block where I would find the simple red brick building.

From the outside, it looked like any other house in the area. It was kept well, the lawn was mowed, the windows were clean. There was nothing suspicious about it. And I guess that was the point. No one would ever walk past that house and suspect someone was being held captive in the basement.

Not wanting to attempt anything in the daylight, I spent some of the precious money I had to get myself something normal to wear, so people didn't keep looking at me sideways. It was hard to miss a strange woman in a bright red dress first thing in the morning. On a weekday. In a small town.

Changed, I made my way back toward the house.

From what I could tell, it was empty.

No one had come or gone all day. No lights were on inside.

Getting close, there did seem to be a radio playing, but when I glanced in the backdoor, it was just sitting there in the kitchen unattended.

I made short work of the kitchen door, having a self-satisfied smile at the fact that the mafia seemed to believe that their reputation alone would scare off anyone who dared poke around their property.

The inside of the house was as bare as I had been expecting. The furniture looked dated, likely belonging to the dead sheriff. Everything was neat, but cobwebs graced the corners, dust covered various surfaces.

Paranoia had me inching my way through the house, walking on tiptoes across the hardwood, wincing anytime one of the boards squeaked.

I did three laps around the house, heart pounding harder and harder each passing moment, trying to find a way into the basement.

Circling back, I found a door in the kitchen that I originally wrote off as a pantry, but when I pulled it open, found a steel door behind.

I could pick a normal lock. A prison cell lock? Not so much.

Turning back, I carefully opened all the cabinets and drawers in the kitchen before finally finding what I was looking for. An almost comical round ring full of keys.

"I swear to all that is holy," a female voice called as I started down the stairs, "if you don't bring me something other than stale bread and sun butter this time, I will claw your fucking eyes out, Terry."

I shouldn't have been able to smile. It was a terrible situation. This woman had been held captive for a huge chunk of her life. But a smile tugged at my lips at realizing that Arturo hadn't won. She refused to lose her spirit. You had to respect a woman like that.

"Who the hell are you?" the voice asked as I made it to the bottom landing.

The woman in the picture had been younger, her dark hair flawless, her body womanly and soft, but fit. This woman was years older, of course, her gray roots were growing in, her body was made thin from, apparently, only being allowed to eat sun butter—not *peanut* butter—sandwiches. Which sort of confirmed my idea that Arturo hadn't just locked her up and thrown away the key, that he came to visit her.

"My name is Giana," I told her, giving her a wobbly smile as I looked at the cell that had been her home for so long.

There was the expected metal bunk, stainless steel toilet and sink, and a little cement cubby with a drain in the floor that served as the shower.

No privacy.

Nothing soft save for the blanket on the bed and a pillow that made my neck hurt just thinking about it.

The shelf was lined with books, which looked to be the only form of entertainment this woman had been allowed.

"Giana," she repeated, brows pinching. "Since when does Arturo hire women? He's terrified of us."

"He didn't hire me. He stuck me in a basement," I told her. "I got out," I said, waving a hand. "When I found out you were in a basement, I decided to get you out before I am done with this fucking family for good."

"How did you get out? I know that basement. There was no way out."

"I had some help," I admitted, pain stabbing in my chest at the memory of Lorenzo passing me the key. "I'm sorry, I don't know your name."

"Celeste," she told me, offering me a strained smile.

"Celeste," I repeated. "I just need to figure out which key it is, and I will get you out of here," I told her, walking over to the door.

"Why would you risk this? Arturo will kill you when he finds out. But not before he plays with you first."

"Arturo won't be playing with anyone," I told her, grumbling when the third key didn't fit.

"Wait. What? What are you saying?"

"That Arturo Costa is dead."

"You're sure about that?"

"I did it, so yes," I told her. "Got it," I said with a smile as the key went in and turned, making the metallic shriek of the door fill the empty space.

Celeste didn't immediately move to walk out. And I guess when you were caged for so long, there had to be some uncertainty about leaving your prison.

"You, a little girl, killed the *Capo dei Capi* of New York City?" she asked, disbelieving.

"I'm not that little. And, apparently, a woman can only be beat down so long before she starts fighting back. Luckily, men like Arturo never think women like us are capable of being a threat to them. I slipped peanut dust in his coffee," I told her, still finding it hard to wrap my head around that. It almost felt like it had been another person who had escaped that basement, done the deed, then locked herself back up.

"Okay. You are going to need to start from the beginning," Celeste told me, finally taking a few tentative steps forward.

So then I did, going through the whole ordeal.

"He killed my boy?" Celeste asked when I was done, eyes swimming, making me realize mine were as well.

"I can't say for sure, but I think so. It... it didn't look good. And I feel like if he was alive, he would have found a way to get back to the basement, or get me out."

"He was a good man, my son?" Celeste asked, needing to know. It had to kill her knowing her sons had become adults without her being there to see it. She'd likely worried herself sick that they might have turned into their father without her there to guide them to be better men. "He had to be to try to save his girl."

"I wasn't his. Not really," I told her, even though that stabbing sensation inside intensified.

"You would have been. If you two had a chance."

"You don't know that."

"I know these kinds of men. Women are background noise in their lives. Until the right one comes along and makes them pay attention. Enz was paying attention to you. If life was fair, you would have been his girl. What about Santi?"

"Santi?" I repeated.

"Santiago. Santi. Lorenzo's brother. Is he alive?"

"Oh," I said, feeling bad that I didn't know his name. "Yes. I mean... as of the last I heard Lorenzo talk about him. He didn't say much, so I don't know much. But his brother never joined the Family. He got married young and had a little boy. That's really all I know. He will be so happy to see you, though."

"I'm a grandmother," Celeste said, trying to wrap her head around that. "I barely got to be a mother, and now I am a grandmother. I guess I look the part," she said, reaching up to rub a hand down her hair. "What is happening with the Family? I want to go see my boy. He's all I have left. Is it safe?"

"I honestly don't know. I got out, found out about you, and came here. I have no idea what is going on there. If Arturo and Lorenzo are dead, who gets to be the boss?"

"War will break out," Celeste told me, calm, confident, knowing more about the mafia than I likely ever would. "The Five Families will all vie for power. Terry will likely try to take the position. But he won't keep it. He's not the kind of man who inspires loyalty."

"What about Emilio?" I asked. I knew that Christopher, the other guards I had met, even Brio seemed lower on the food chain. "Lorenzo always treated Emilio like an equal."

"If he wanted it, he could try for it. But if adult Emilio is anything like young Emilio, he doesn't want that. Can we go upstairs?" Celeste asked, gaze on the steps. "I haven't seen anything but this basement for longer than I care to think about. It would be nice to see something else. And maybe see if there is anything to eat up there."

With that, we made our way upstairs, Celeste finding an old block of cheese in the fridge, taking bites out of it like it was a sub as we walked through the house, Celeste claiming that there would be money hidden somewhere, that we would both need all we could get until she got back to the city, and I got wherever I was going.

We eventually found some, stashed in a faux book in the study. *Crime & Punishment.* A little joke on Terry's part, it seemed.

"How much?" Celeste asked, sitting down on the couch with a groan, not having touched anything soft in years.

"Looks like ten thousand," I said, shaking my head. I'd never touched ten grand before, but here it was, sitting forgotten in a book in a nearly abandoned house like it was no big deal.

"You take most of it," Celeste said, rubbing her feet on the carpet.

"What? No. We will split it."

"No need," she said, shaking her head. "I don't give a shit what goes on with the family, but I am Arturo's wife. And him being dead means I get everything. At least everything legal. I just need enough to get me there. And a lot of food on the way," she said, giving me a weak smile.

"I can't imagine how—"

"Well well well," a male voice said, making my stomach drop, making Celeste's head whip to the doorway where a man I wasn't familiar with stood, gun pointed on her. "What do we have here?"

"Terry," Celeste said, smile cold, eyes level with the man who had been her warden for so many years. If I lived a thousand years, I was pretty sure I would never be as badass as Celeste as she slowly unfolded from her position, seemingly unconcerned about the gun pointed at her. "Came to deal with the loose ends before you make a play for power?" she asked, making her way closer to him.

"You should have been taken care of years ago."

"Probably," she agreed. "Yet here we are."

"Who the hell is she?" Terry asked, jerking his chin toward me, but his focus was on Celeste who was still advancing on him, slowly, like a cat. Did she plan on trying to take him down? Sure, she was a tall woman. But years in a cell with bad nutrition had made her thin. I couldn't imagine she would overpower Terry. He might have been older, but he was bigger.

"Oh that? That's the woman who killed Art," Celeste declared proudly, almost like a mom would.

"What? No."

"Tell him, Giana, darling."

"I, ah, yeah," I agreed, nodding, playing along, hoping she had a plan. "That was me. Peanuts in his coffee."

Terry glanced at me for the first time, surprised, confused.

It was the shortest of glances.

But long enough.

Celeste darted to the side, hand reaching out, closing over the handle to a letter opener.

The rest of it seemed to happen on fast-forward.

Celeste lunging.

Terry yelling, deflecting, getting a cut to the side of his hand that had the gun flying out into the hallway, sliding across the floor, out of reach.

It was seconds, it seemed, between when Celeste lunged, and when the letter opener flew from her hand as she went down, Terry coming down on top of her, hands going around her neck.

Her body writhed; her hands punched, slapped, scratched.

To no avail.

He was going to kill her.

Right there in front of me.

Her gaze cut to me, her eyes darting to the side, making me follow their direction, seeing the letter opener.

I didn't think.

I didn't consider my body count, the dark marks on my soul, which circle of hell I would be suffering in for all eternity.

I rushed over, ducked, grabbed the letter opener, charged forward, and stabbed it into the side of Terry's throat.

"God, I was covered in blood," Celeste said, snapping me back to the present, shaking her head as she looked at her son. "I never thought I was going to get it out of my hair. In fact, that was what I was attempting to do in the kitchen sink when this lovely young gentleman showed up," she went on, reaching over to pat Christopher's hand.

"How the hell did you end up there?" Lorenzo asked, completely at a loss. His eyes looked small and pained, and I couldn't help but worry about his condition, what directions the doctors had given him that he was likely already disregarding.

"It's funny how much a woman in a bright red party dress and blue flip-flops stands out in a crowd," Chris said, giving me a warm smile. "It wasn't hard to track her. And once I knew what town she was heading to, I knew where she was going. Terry used to talk about that fucking house all the time. When I got there, it was a mess, blood completely covering those two," he said, shaking his head. "Looked like a horror movie."

"So you cleaned it up," Lorenzo guessed, knowing his men had been trained well.

"Started to. Then Anthony showed up," he said, smirking. "It was like a fucking party in that place. Between the two of us, we got the body out of there, cleaned everything up. But it wouldn't hurt for a team to go back and do another scrub."

"Noted," Lorenzo said, nodding. "I appreciate it."

"Doing our jobs," Anthony said. "Well, not exactly," he admitted. "I was supposed to be the one doing the killing."

"Killing?" another voice asked, making us all look up, finding Brio walking in through the house toward us, smile a little devilish. "I missed more fun?" he asked, coming into the space. His gaze cut to me, and that smile grew warmer. "I told you those were some nice shoes there, doll," he said, walking over toward the coffee pot.

"Nice shoes?" Lorenzo asked, looking at me.

"No," I said, shaking my head at Brio's back.

"Yes," he countered, turning back, taking a long, slow sip of his coffee.

He'd intentionally drawn my attention to them.

He knew the buckles could be used to escape.

"The candy bar too?" I asked, watching as his lips twitched.

"Nah, doll, that was all you. Took me a while to figure it out, too. You're fucking slick, G."

"But... why?" I asked, shaking my head. "Why wouldn't you just... take the shackles off? Why did you want me to do it myself?"

"Figured when little boss man here up and went missing with Milo, that he didn't die like his old man was hoping. And I saw the way he ripped a man to shreds for you. I wanted to see if you were the kind of woman who deserved the boss, which was what he was going to become. Figured if you could figure out how to get out of that basement, then you could handle being with him."

"Brio, man," Emilio said, pressing a hand to his heart. "I had no idea you were such a romantic," he teased.

Brio ignored that. "Killing the capo, though, that was," he said, bringing his fingers in to do a chef's kiss, "perfect. I never should have doubted you."

"Alright," Lorenzo said, shaking his head. "So, let me get this straight. Brio told you how to escape," he started. "You escaped, poisoned my father, then went back down into the basement, and locked yourself back up."

"I didn't want anyone to think it was me," I told him, shrugging. "I thought you were gone. And I figured that if your father was gone too, they might just let me go. And I could go back to my life."

"And then you found evidence that my mom was alive, then went to save her, stabbing Terry in the neck in the process?" Lorenzo asked, tone getting more and more awed as he went on.

When it was recapped like that, it was pretty awe-inspiring, even I had to admit that.

"Racking up two bodies in a week. Gotta respect that," Brio piped in, almost gleeful about my body count.

"Three," Lorenzo corrected. "Emptied a mag into her old man. That's what got her in the basement in the first place."

"Three? Fuck, man. Marry her," Brio declared. And, what's more, he wasn't joking.

"Speaking of that," Celeste said, moving to stand. "I think these two could probably use some time together. You," she said, looking over at Brio. "How about you take me to go see my other son? And meet my grandson?"

Within ten minutes, new orders had been sent out to most of the other men, and Lorenzo was walking up the stairs with me. One hand was pressed to my lower back, but it didn't escape me that his other hand was gripping the railing hard.

He tried to be strong, but the man was just out of the hospital after getting shot, after being beaten. He needed to rest.

"I'm fine, Gigi," he told me as we got into his room, seeming to sense my train of thought.

"You were shot in the head. You're not fine."

"I'm not one-hundred-percent," he admitted, dropping down on the edge of the bed, looking over at me. "But I will be there soon enough. Until then, there are just some minor, annoying side-effects. I'm fine. Better now that I know you're okay," he added, reaching out, snagging my wrist, pulling me forward. "Was having trouble sleeping not knowing where you were, if you were okay. I failed you."

"You didn't fail me," I said, rolling my eyes. "What were you supposed to do that you didn't do?"

"Save you."

"Well, that would have certainly saved me a lot of trouble," I admitted, smiling at him, my hand raising, carefully tracing above his new scar. "But I think I proved I can take care of myself."

"Knew it the second you cold-cocked me with a whiskey bottle," he told me, smirking. "You alright?" he asked, getting more serious.

"Not a scratch on me, incredibly," I told him, forcing a smile. I was a bit too worn out for a real one. I wasn't sure the last time I got any real sleep.

"Not what I meant. Had a lot of shit go down the past few weeks. You weren't raised in this. It's got to have some impact."

"It probably will," I admitted. "Once I have a shower and some food and some sleep. But I figure you're rich enough to pay for all the therapy I am probably going to need," I said, smiling a little.

"Anything you want," Lorenzo told me, unexpectedly serious, the words more like a vow than anything.

"I was joking," I insisted. "I'm not expecting anything."

"No? You should be," he told me, shrugging.

"I didn't do what I did because I wanted something. Aside from my freedom."

"Well, see, we have a problem there, hellcat."

"What?" I asked, stiffening. "What do you mean?"

"I'm afraid you can have anything you want. Except your freedom."

"Wait a minute—"

Lorenzo's chuckle cut me off. When I looked down, his green eyes were dancing. "Christ. Look at that attitude. Were you going to shoot me with my own gun?" he asked, patting his holster under his jacket.

"I still haven't written the possibility off," I told him, even though we both knew that while I was, apparently, capable of a lot more than I could have ever known, killing him was not on that one of those things. "What do you mean I can't have my freedom?"

"Well, you are free to come and go. To go back to that bakery to work. Whatever you want to do."

"But?"

"But... you come back here at night," he finished, giving my hip a squeeze.

"What? In the basement?" I asked, heart starting to trip into overdrive, having an idea what he was saying, but a part of me needed to hear him spell it out for me.

"In this bed," he clarified. "With me," he added, pulling me closer, then down to straddle his waist, hungry hands starting to roam.

"We don't know each other that well," I insisted, even as every part of me wanted to believe we could make something work.

"We know enough. I know enough. And we will learn more as time goes on," he told me, fingers starting to pull up the back of my shirt. "Say yes," he demanded, a hint of vulnerability in his voice.

He wasn't a man who showed that often, but he had given it to me a few times. The real side of him. The raw part.

Those parts of me responded to it, too, knowing that there wouldn't be a single person on this earth who could ever possibly understand what I had been through over the last few weeks more than Lorenzo. And, what's more, I didn't want anyone else to try.

"Okay. Yes to trying. No to what you are doing with your hands right now," I objected, feeling his fingertips tease the sides of my breasts. "I need to shower," I added, cringing at how much I needed that luxury—a long, hot, soapy shower, and a date with a razor, too, I imagined.

"Mmhmm," he agreed, lips buzzing against my neck as he made the sound. "We can shower. Later. We gotta get dirty first."

There was no way to fight that logic, now, was there?

If there was, I didn't want to figure it out.

So we got dirty.

Then we got clean.

And then we started this strange, scary, wonderful new life together.

Epilogue

Lorenzo - 1 Day

"Go back to bed," Giana snapped at me as soon as my foot stepped into the kitchen.

"Got shit to do, babe," I said, walking up behind her, wrapping an arm around her waist, leaning down to bite into her neck. "No rest for the wicked," I added, my fingers slipping down to press between her thighs.

Her reaction was immediate, her back leaning into me, her ass wiggling against me, her head falling onto my shoulder as a little mewling noise escaped her.

I was just starting to get used to that sound. I wanted to hear a fuck of a lot more of it in the coming days, weeks, months, years, decades if things went the way I wanted them to.

Because Brio was right.

If there was ever a woman who could handle this lifestyle, it was one who fearlessly racked up a body count in just a couple days.

Sure, we had a lot to learn about each other. That would come. But I knew the basics. Her hard-working mindset, her loyalty, her stubbornness, her attitude, her pride, the movies she liked, the food she preferred, her history with her family, the way she curled into me at night.

We'd laid some groundwork.

The rest would come.

"You need to take it easy," Gigi scolded me, even as her hips did a roll, getting more friction for her needy pussy.

"I took it easy for a week," I reminded her, pressing my hard cock against her.

"A *coma* is not rest," she insisted, trying to laugh, but my finger did another swipe against her clit.

"I slept for a week. That's rest. More than you've gotten," I added, releasing her, turning her, lifting her up onto the counter. Her thighs parted for me as I moved between, my cock pressing against her pussy. "I should be telling you to go back to bed. In fact, I like that. Get back in bed. Naked," I told her, rocking my hips against her.

"I will go back to bed. Naked," she agreed, hands drifting around my hips. "But only if you go back with me. And stay there," she clarified. "For two days."

"I can't go to bed for two days, babe," I told her, my hand sliding up under her shirt, closing over her breast, rolling her nipple between my thumb and forefinger. "I can spare an hour or so, though," I said, my fingers pinching her nipple hard, watching as her head fell back, her lips parting on a silent moan.

"Morning, roomies!" Emilio said from behind us, making my hand slide out from under Gigi's shirt as she let out a quiet whimper.

Yeah.

Emilio was going to be one hell of a cockblock.

I wanted a chance to fuck Giana on every surface of this house. It wasn't going to be easy to do that with Milo constantly popping into rooms randomly.

That said, I said he could crash for a while. I couldn't take that back. Besides, even if I did, he wouldn't listen. He was going to stay close until things were more stable. Or, at least, until I was fully on my feet again.

"You have shit timing," I informed him as Gigi shot me wide eyes, embarrassed at the insinuation.

"I am all for some kitchen fucking, but have the common courtesy to hold off until everyone in the household gets a cup of coffee," he told us, giving Giana a sly smile as he moved beside her to get a cup. "Were you about to cook?" he asked.

"I, ah, yeah. I was going to make some pastries for you guys. And all the men in and out all day."

"Did you hear that?" Emilio asked, looking over at me. "She is going to bake for us."

"She wants to bake for me. You just happen to be here," I corrected.

"I'll still take it," he said, shrugging. "Well, Giana, sweetheart, we will get out of your hair, so you can get right to that. What?" he asked when I glared at him. "Oh, keep it in your pants. When was the last time you had a woman bake for you? Exactly," he said when I had no answer to that. "Besides, we have some things to talk about. You can get some afternoon delight with her," he added, leading me out into the hallway.

I glanced back over my shoulder, finding Giana's cheeks pink with embarrassment, her eyes still hungry.

Yeah.

I could get used to seeing that woman in my kitchen every morning.

What's more, I was looking forward to it.

Giana - 1 Week

"What is all this?" I asked, sitting at the kitchen table, looking at the massive stack of magazines, fabric samples, and paint swatches that Celeste had dropped down in front of me.

Celeste had jumped back into life with both feet.

She'd been to the DMV to get her IDs renewed, had been to the family attorney to get access to all the accounts again, had gotten her nails done, went shopping for a whole new wardrobe, hit the doctor, started at a gym, spent time with both her sons. She'd even gone to the salon to fix the patchy job I'd done with the box dye back in the prison house when she'd insisted that she couldn't go back to New York without her hair done, some makeup to play with, and a nice dress and heels to wear. Luckily for her, she was incredibly charming, and Christopher and Anthony had agreed without even thinking twice.

I knew she was trying to make up for lost time, but I felt so lazy compared to her. I'd ducked into the bakery once, flanked by guards, telling the workers about my father's disappearance, hiring one of the part-time workers as full-time now that the business was no longer indebted to the Costa family. I'd filed the missing person's report with Lorenzo at my side. And I had managed to go to the grocery store, stocking the house for all the hungry men in and out.

I thought it was a lot.

Until I heard what Celeste had been up to.

She'd also, apparently, been to the home improvement store.

"The house is being renovated, darling," she told me, dropping down into the chair across from me, giving me a smile. Her new long layers did wonders to frame her face, made her eyes look brighter, her features sharper.

"I, ah, yeah. Are you decorating?"

"Me?" she asked, brows scrunching. "Why would I ever redecorate the brownstone?"

"Because, technically, it is your house," I reminded her.

"Oh, that," she said, waving a hand in the air. "That is a formality. This house belongs to the family, Gigi. I won't stand in the way of that. Besides, I don't have great memories here. I am happier in Lorenzo's penthouse. It is nice to be up above the world after being below it for so long. Lorenzo and I decided to swap. But the brownstone will stay in my name. At least until he marries you. Then it will go in your name. The houses are better off in the woman's name," she clarified. "That way, if something happens and the war gets bad and the men don't make it, they still have some stability for themselves. For their kids."

"You know a lot about the families," I said, shaking my head. "Arturo didn't seem like the kind of man who shared that information."

"He wasn't. But his father was. And his mother. And my uncle. That was how we met. Through my uncle's connection to the Costa family. I was a Lombardi," she said, lowering her voice like the name was a sin, and I was starting to understand the power dynamic of the families after a couple long talks in bed late at night with Lorenzo.

The Costas were the upper echelon. Their closest allies were the Morellis and the D'Onofrios. The other two families, the Lombardis and the Espositios outwardly played by the rules, but did a lot of things behind the backs of the other families, were always hungry for more money and more power, maybe even the seat at the top.

"That has never been an issue? Loyalty-wise?"

"I had a very loose relation to the family back then. I was fascinated by the whole thing, don't get me wrong, but my parents were never directly involved, so it wasn't like anyone was worried about the alliance. If you can call it that. All Arturo and I did was wage war in private. But, thankfully, that is all over now. Because of you. So, you and Lorenzo, you are keeping the house. Which means you need to decorate it."

"I think that is more Lorenzo's place."

"Darling," she said, leaning forward, placing a fine-boned hand on my forearm. "These powerful men, they really don't care about the drapes and the backsplash in the kitchen. But since you will be the one in the kitchen, you do care. I hear you bake for the men all the time," she added, eyes warm. Dare I think it—approving.

"I am a much better baker than I am a cook," I admitted, shrugging.

"No worries, Gigi, we will work on that together. I know. I don't look like someone who knows a spatula from a frying pan, but I practically lived in the kitchen when the boys were young. They had hollow legs, I swear, always needing more and more food to fill up. But I loved that. Do you want children?"

"I do," I told her, smiling a little at the idea of a bunch of little green-eyed children running up and down the halls.

"You don't worry about bringing them into this?"

"Did you?"

"Of course. But that being said, the world as a whole is an ugly place to bring children. War and homelessness and people dying of preventable diseases, climate change, kids being shot in school—sorry, I have been binging the highlights of the news since I have been away. It's all a little overwhelming. My point is, no one can actually guarantee their kids safety. At least with this family, the kids have armed guards around all the time looking out for them. Do you want just a couple?"

"I used to tell my mom that I wanted a football team of kids. Now, I am thinking maybe a few less than that."

"I always wanted a bunch as well. I probably would have kept going. If it was another man. But, as you can imagine, Art was not a good father. He was harsh and overbearing and I cringed at the idea of bringing more children into this environment. I would love it if you made me a grandma of a football team."

"Well, I mean, it is a little soon to be talking about that, but I like the idea of it. So, what do you think about this one?" I asked, holding up a gray swatch.

"With those new wood floors?" Celeste asked, brows pinching, giving me a "you know better" look.

We spent the afternoon poring over the magazines, hemming and hawing swatches and paint colors and wallpaper.

It was the closest thing to having a mother I had known in a really long time.

"Hey, what's the matter?" Lorenzo said, coming into the kitchen after having said goodbye to Celeste at the door.

It wasn't until then that I realized I was blinking back some rogue tears.

"I just really love your mom," I admitted, giving him a watery smile. "It's nice to sort of... be a part of a family again."

"There's no 'sort of' about it," he told me, pulling me up onto my feet, dragging me against his chest. "You are a part of this family. And I'm glad you love my mom."

"She insisted I decorate the house. But, of course, I am going to run it all by you. It's your house."

"Nope. I don't need to see it. You cover the decorating shit. I cover the making the money and keeping us safe shit."

"What if I picked a pastel pink for the master bedroom?"

"Well, we can fuck with the lights off," he decided, giving me a smile before pulling me up for a quick kiss.

"What did the doctor say?" I asked, having been more worried about his head than he had been. Because, apparently, big, powerful mafia dons didn't worry about pesky things like bullet holes and brain surgery and medically-induced comas.

"He said the same shit the doctor at the hospital did. I might still get some headaches. He said there was always a chance of issues with attention span or seizures. Don't see any of that shit happening, though. I feel fine. Ready to get back to working out. But he wants me to give it another couple weeks. You know what, though?"

"What?"

"He said no running. He didn't say shit about dragging my woman upstairs and fucking her until she can't see straight."

"Well, then he must think it is perfectly safe to do so," I told him, smiling, mostly because we had already been spending more time with our clothes off than on some days, and he was no worse for the wear.

"That's what I'm thinking," Lorenzo agreed, swooping low, tossing me over his shoulder, and taking me upstairs.

Lorenzo - 1 Month

You'd think it would get old.

Having a woman in your space all the time.

But it seemed like with each passing day, I was enjoying seeing her there more and more.

She usually snuck out of bed right before sunrise—a lifetime of habit from working at the bakery—and went downstairs, turned on the coffee, got something sweet started in the oven. By the time I noticed her familiar weight wasn't on my chest anymore, the house was already filling with scents of warm vanilla, oatmeal, chocolate, apples and cinnamon, whatever combination she was playing around with that day.

It was chocolate that day, I realized as I stepped down onto the main floor.

The work was already underway, a small group of men painting the walls in the dining room with Brio perched on the sideboard, legs kicking, cleaning under his nails with an unnecessarily large knife, being as intimidating as he could be without outwardly threatening any average civilians.

He gave me a head nod as I passed. "That woman, she's got it all, man. You gotta lock that shit down," he told me, shaking his head like it was absurd I hadn't put a ring on Giana's finger a month after officially starting to date.

What can you say? Brio was a character.

I made my way into the kitchen, finding Giana poring over a recipe book, her arms perched on the counter, her ass sticking outward in a pair of barely-there silk pajama shorts.

I didn't even pause to think about it, just walked up behind her, dragging her shorts and panties down, exposing her ass, my hand slipping between her thighs.

"What are you doing?" she hissed, body tensing. "We can't."

"This is our house. Sure we can," I told her, fingers plunging into her pussy, making her hips buck.

"There is a crew of men and Brio in the next room," she told me, trying to sound forceful, but her hips were already rocking against me, begging for more.

"Then I guess you are going to have to try to be quiet then," I told her, my free hand pulling out my cock as my fingers left her drenched pussy, slipping up to work her clit.

"Lorenzo we can't," she insisted as my cock slid up her cleft, pressing against her pussy for a short second before plunging inside.

"And yet we are," I told her, lazily thrusting into her, knowing that if I got too hard or too rough, she would have no control over her reaction. And as much as I was liking the idea of claiming my woman with my men only a couple rooms away, I didn't want anyone hearing what she sounded like when she was begging for my cock. That was just for me to hear. And I did. Frequently. So while I wasn't typically someone for sweet sex, that was what I was giving her this morning, pumping into her tight pussy slowly, taking every inch of her, then rolling my hips at the deepest point, feeling her walls tighten at the sensation, then withdrawing before doing it all over again.

I thought it would take her longer, but her legs were already starting to shake, her breathing was quick, ragged, her hands were curled into fists on the counter.

"Lorenzo, I can't..." she started, voice getting louder.

My hand clamped over her mouth as my hips thrust inward, jerking up, making the orgasm crash through her system, her walls spasming around my cock, milking my orgasm from me as well, leaving me half-folded over her, panting, trying to bring some reason back into my system.

We hadn't been great about the protection thing, I realized as I slowly pulled out of her, tucking myself away, reaching to pull her panties and shorts back into place, the smell of sex mingling with the chocolate in the room. It wasn't normal for me to not use a condom. In fact, I'd only ever fucked without one once before, when I'd been too young and too stupid to think about consequences. When Santi knocked up his high school girlfriend, though, I smartened up. Never fucked without one. I didn't want to settle down. And that was exactly what I would have to do if I got someone pregnant.

That said, if Giana happened to skip a cycle, if she came to me with a stick and uncertain eyes? Yeah, I would be good with that.

It was soon, sure.

But when you knew, you knew.

She was the one.

She was going to take my ring, take my name, take my future.

I was going to give her safety, give her stability, give her a home and a family and half a dozen babies with her sass and my eyes.

So it didn't matter if we weren't careful.

You could be a little reckless when you knew you found the one.

"If you made me burn the eclairs, I am going to kill you," Giana declared, eyes going wide, rushing toward the stove, grabbing oven mitts as she went.

"Yeah, boss man," Brio said, casually walking into the room. "I will kill you too. I've been waiting for those for almost an hour now."

"Hey, do I smell chocolate?" Emilio asked, materializing behind Brio, still disheveled from bed.

Giana placed the pans on the top of the stove, turning over her shoulder to give me a smile.

I'd been itching to get the house to ourselves.

But Giana had told me she liked it like it was, busy, chaotic, full.

And I guessed I could deal with that.

Until I could get the house filled with babies, at least.

Giana - 1 Year

"I'm going to slice it off in your sleep," I told him, grabbing his hand so hard he winced.

"Hey, now, you like my cock just as much as I do," he reminded me, reaching to wipe my brow with a damp washcloth.

"Nope. Never again. I hate it. It did this to me. And now you will have to pay for it," I told him, feeling the contraction finally start to ebb.

"Hey, how's it going?" Celeste asked, breezing back into the room, looking like she was going to a runway in her emerald green sundress, instead of helping us welcome her second grandbaby into the world. "Uh oh," she said, grimacing when we both shot her looks. Mine, frustrated. His, worried. "Is she at the point where she is threatening you?" she asked, looking at her son.

"Yeah."

"Well, knowing her track record, maybe you should go take a lap. I will sit with her," she said, moving to take Lorenzo's seat as he shot me an uncertain look.

"More ice," I suggested, knowing he didn't want to leave, didn't want to be useless during all this. It was interesting, I had to admit, to watch such a powerful man look so powerless, knowing he had no control over what was happening to me.

To that, he nodded, glad for a mission, disappearing out into the hall.

"It's always funny to see a strong man look so terrified of childbirth, don't you think? Art turned green, passed out, came to, and ran out of the room when I was having Lorenzo. It's not the prettiest affair, I'll admit, but the end result is nothing like you have ever experienced before. Your little boy is going to be worth all of this, I promise," she told me, grabbing my hand, giving it a maternal squeeze.

"He better be. Because he is going to be the only one. I already told Lorenzo he is getting castrated," I told her, watching as she let out a laugh.

"You are going to be so in love with him. Nothing else will matter. Not all this pain. Not the recovery from it. Not the sleepless nights coming your way. You are going to be such a good mom, Giana."

I wished I could have my own mother here with us, saying these things as well, but my heart swelled, and the pain became suddenly more tolerable having Celeste there, knowing she loved me like her own daughter, that it was her who had taken Lorenzo ring shopping the week we found out I was pregnant. Which, admittedly, was very soon after we started dating. She was the one to help me decorate the nursery. She was the one who sat up with me late at night, quelling my fears about childbirth.

I think I had all but forgotten how important family was until they welcomed me into theirs with open arms.

"You're right," I agreed, giving her a weak smile. It felt like I had been in labor for years. And, last I asked Lorenzo, it had been fifteen hours since my water broke.

"Just coming in to check," the nurse declared, giving us a warm smile as she moved in near my legs. "You know what, Mama? I think we are about ready to push. Where did Daddy go?"

"I'll get him," Celeste said, giving my hand a reassuring squeeze before rushing off to find Lorenzo.

"He is pacing the halls looking very scared," the nurse told me, eyes dancing, likely seeing men like him all the time. "There you are," she said when he rushed in, coming over to the side of the bed, slipping an arm under my back, grabbing my hand. "Are you two kids ready to meet your little boy?" she asked.

And, God, yes, we were.

The next part was somehow the hardest and easiest at the same time. The pain was something I could never describe to someone who hadn't experienced it, but our son was making his way into the world.

All eight pounds and six ounces of him, coming out screaming bloody murder as I collapsed back onto the bed.

He was placed on my chest just a couple moments later, wrapped in a blanket, all squishy and new.

Lorenzo scooted onto the side of the bed, wrapping an arm around both of us, protecting us like I knew he would never stop doing.

Milo Alexander Costa.

Named after his uncle Emilio.

His uncle Brio had dibs on the next one.

Yes, there were going to be more.

Celeste was right.

Everything was all but forgotten except this little human being we had created.

"Lorenzo?"

"Yeah?" he asked, looking at Milo for another moment, eyes filled with wonder. When he glanced up at me, though, the look was still there.

"I didn't mean it."

"Didn't mean what?"

"I won't cut it off. Because I want a dozen of these," I told him, beaming.

"Well, I think we can arrange that," he said, reaching up to brush some sweaty hair off my forehead. "I love you, hellcat," he told me, eyes warm.

I loved him back.

More than I ever could have anticipated.

More than I even knew I was capable of.

"I love you too. Even if you are a sauce hog," I told him, smiling.

Sure, it wouldn't be all smiles and declarations.

Wars were starting on the streets.
Between the families.
Life would never be easy.
But it didn't need to be.
Because we knew we could handle it together.

Also by Jessica Gadziala

If you liked this book, check out these other series and titles in the NAVESINK BANK UNIVERSE:

The Henchmen MC
Reign
Cash
Wolf
Repo
Duke
Renny
Lazarus
Pagan
Cyrus
Edison
Reeve
Sugar
The Fall of V
Adler
Roderick
Virgin
Roan
Camden
West

The Savages
Monster
Killer
Savior

Mallick Brothers
For A Good Time, Call
Shane
Ryan
Mark
Eli
Charlie & Helen: Back to the Beginning

Investigators
367 Days
14 Weeks
4 Months

Dark
Dark Mysteries
Dark Secrets
Dark Horse

Professionals
The Fixer
The Ghost
The Messenger
The General
The Babysitter
The Middle Man

The Negotiator
The Client

Rivers Brothers
Lift You Up
Lock You Down

STANDALONES WITHIN NAVESINK BANK:
Vigilante
Grudge Match

NAVESINK BANK LEGACY SERIES:
The Rise of Ferryn

<u>OTHER SERIES AND STANDALONES:</u>

Stars Landing
What The Heart Needs
What The Heart Wants
What The Heart Finds
What The Heart Knows
The Stars Landing Deviant
What The Heart Learns

Surrogate
The Sex Surrogate
Dr. Chase Hudson

The Green Series
Into the Green
Escape from the Green

DEBT
Dissent
Stuffed: A Thanksgiving Romance
Unwrapped
Peace, Love, & Macarons
A Navesink Bank Christmas
Don't Come
Fix It Up
N.Y.E.
faire l'amour
Revenge
There Better Be Pie

About the Author

Jessica Gadziala is a full-time writer, parrot enthusiast, and coffee drinker who has an unhealthy obsession with acquiring houseplants. She enjoys short rides to the book store, sad songs, and cold weather. She lives in New Jersey with her parrots, dogs, and a whole flock of chickens.

She is very active on Goodreads, Facebook, as well as her personal groups on those sites. Join in. She's friendly.

Playlist

Playlist

"Bad Moon Rising" - Mourning Ritual
God's Gonna Cut You Down - Marilyn Manson
"Every Breath You Take" - Chase Holfelder
"One Way Or Another" - Until The Ribbon Breaks
"Bury Me Face Down" - grandson
"Everybody Wants To Rule The World" - Lorde
"Your Heart Is As Black As Night" - Melody Gardot
"The Devil Within" - Digital Daggers
"Love Is A Bitch"- Two Feet
"Horns" - Bryce Fox
"Devil Eyes" - Hippie Savage
"Hungry Like The Wolf" - Hidden Citizens
"Wicked Ones" - Dorothy
"Gun In My Hand" - Dorothy
"Crazy" - 2WEI
"Love Is A Battlefield" - Wrongchilde
"In The End" (Mellen Gi Remix) - Tommee Profitt
"NFWMB" - Hozier

Stalk Her!

Connect with Jessica:

Facebook: https://www.facebook.com/JessicaGadziala/
Facebook Group:
https://www.facebook.com/groups/314540025563403/

Goodreads:
https://www.goodreads.com/author/show/13800950.Jessica_Ga
dziala
Goodreads Group:
https://www.goodreads.com/group/show/177944-jessica-
gadziala-books-and-bullsh

Twitter: @JessicaGadziala

JessicaGadziala.com

<3/ Jessica

<<<<>>>>